# fall/ng
### into
# green

# falling into green

*An eco-mystery by*
*Cher Fischer*

www.AshlandCreekPress.com

Falling Into Green
*A novel by Cher Fischer*

Published by Ashland Creek Press
www.ashlandcreekpress.com

ISBN 978-1-61822-007-3
Library of Congress Control Number: 2011937839

This is a work of fiction. All characters and scenarios appearing in this work are fictitious. Any resemblance to real persons, living or dead, is purely coincidental.

Printed in the United States of America on acid-free paper.
All paper products used to create this book are Sustainable Forestry Initiative (SFI) Certified Sourcing.

Cover and book design by John Yunker.

*To my son, Jack: the light of my inspiration.*

I watch as the corpse is hoisted up over the side of the steep precipice in a black wire cage attached to a hook on a crane.

I haven't felt my consciousness this fragmented by dread since my best friend leapt to her death from this very same cliff. Charlene Pryce was her name, but I called her Charlie. She nicknamed me Emerald.

Now, almost twenty years later, I remember her last words to me: "I've got to take my chances."

Did this dead girl take her chances, too?

*Ay, Dios mío*, suicide.

It keeps happening here, again and again.

My horse, Sam, snorts and hoofs the dirt beneath us. He wants to gallop. It's a perfect night for a ride, with the hint of pungent California sagebrush between the molecules of warm, balmy air. This ride was to be a sensate voyage on my trusty steed, but it's become a sojourn to hell: bright white forensic lights, rigor already setting in.

How old is she?

Sixteen? Seventeen?

Like Charlie.

My eyes sting.

My friend's death still hurts, even after all these years.

I blink, try to re-focus, adapt myself to the present, but the morbid crush and curl of this girl is nearly overwhelming. It's obvious that the one-hundred-foot drop to the boulders and frothy surf below broke her limbs, and even though she's been meticulously placed by the Los Angeles CSI into a fetal position to fit the cage, one long, slender leg still bends at a disturbing angle. I squint through the glare of lights and see that beneath the mass of wet, gold-streaked hair covering her face, the vertebrae in her neck must be pulverized: A tiny portion of her chin peeks out from the tangled locks, revealing a jaw that's hanging all the way down to her breasts. But what's most garish—yet what I guiltily find mesmerizing—is the girl's skin. Exposed by a torn, black, stretchy top, it's as smooth as satin. Not even a tiny scratch mars its pale surface. There's also something dark and twisty wrapped around her thin, bare waist.

I can't make out what it is.

I look away.

I want to cry, release the tension. The kind of stress that comes with being immersed, at times, in this ancient ritual of manifested psychic pain. I've treated a few patients with suicidal ideation. These days, however, self-destruction seems a growing consequence of attempting to survive the onslaught of twenty-first century confusion—and, sure, I'm talking about people. But also animals, birds, even insects.

Sound bizarre? Yep, it does.

But true.

Case in point: the wild bees. In the past month, I must have seen hundreds pitching down onto the street, the sidewalk, any kind of pavement.

Why?

Or what about the dolphins, four days ago, in the Santa Monica

Bay? It was a large pod—eleven of them, to be exact—young and old, like diligent soldiers following one another up onto shore, lying there, gregarious smiles withering in the sun.

Why?

There are also the countless stories of sparrows, starlings, blackbirds, even seagulls, falling from the sky, a hailstorm of winged life, landing dead on the ground.

*Why?*

I'm a psychologist with a specialty in ecopsychology—in other words, a green shrink—I should have some insight about these horrible things.

But I don't. Not really. Not now.

I turn back to the Los Angeles CSI, working with our small-town PD, and the LA news media as they run to the dead girl in the black cage that the man behind the yellow crane sets with a jangled bump onto the parched grass, and they swarm her—like bees.

There they are, in my mind again.

Bees. Dolphins. Birds. Suicide.

Charlie.

Bloody, bloody Charlie.

Why was poor Charlie's sad, broken body so bloody? And this girl's is not?

I shake my head.

I don't want to know.

I don't want to be immersed in this one. I need to think about something else. What I really need is a frivolous thought before I start obsessing on the past.

Sure …

How about I narrow my mind down to a fraction of its value and think about my current situation with … *men.*

Or, to be specific, a *muy guapo,* very good-looking man. But I refuse to give him more credit than that, even if he's Latin, like me. Or like a part of me. I'm Latin and Irish. A fabulous mix, I say. My dad, on the Irish side, would have said the same thing. So would my second-generation Latina mom. As for my Salvadoran *abuelo*, or grandfather—I'm not sure what he'd call me. But there've been plenty of others to describe me with cutesy clichés, such as: passionate talker, volatile communicator, hot-blooded MacMama.

*Stop.*

I realize I'm mentally fleeing the suicide—but for my own sanity, sometimes I must.

I glance at the dead girl, wince, and once more turn away.

Okay.

What about the man?

He's played me, again.

Probably just moments after this girl with the pale, smooth skin plunged to her death.

My twelve-year-old palomino and I were taking our usual twilight ride on the upper bluffs of Majorca Point, an enormous, sweeping girth of peninsula that extends into the Pacific Ocean between Long Beach Harbor and Hermosa Beach. I was breathing in the warm glow of sunset, scarlet tendrils of the day's last light fanning above a shimmering turquoise sea, and I allowed myself to go into a trance because, very simply, I can. Ever since I was a child, I've been able to understand what I need and want, and what I don't need (but sometimes desire), by "fusing" with the earth's life force.

Maybe I receive messages from the Goddess Gaia?

I like to think so. Anything's possible.

But tonight, the reality of it is I had nary an ecological thought in mind but to clear my psyche of its own toxicity: *the man.* Mr. Gabriel Hugo García, local TV news superstar for the Latino global news organization KLAT. I only rode Sam down the hill because I was practically assaulted by a KLAT news chopper that turned out to be headed to this tragic cliff-side location. Its whirling blades caused such a frenetic commotion over me that I almost went flying off my horse and had to grab the horn of the saddle as if I were on a bucking bronco—which Sam is definitely not—to withstand the churning onslaught of wind, dirt, and dry chaparral.

I coughed, spit out the dust.

Angry, I wondered, "Is García on that chopper? I'm gonna give him some attitude. His transport could have *killed* me."

Now, amazing, or not so amazing: There he is.

I know it seems coincidental.

But out here in the natural-born ether of Majorca Point, even though we're only thirty minutes from downtown LA, we've strived to retain our wilderness so that, among other things, a preternatural symbiosis can occur. That's my ecopsychological take on it: When nature's integrated into the human experience, things get intense. They get *meaningful*.

Hmmm. Right on cue.

García. Scrumptious as ever.

Even at a suicide.

He flicks a wave at me with casual panache—that's his signature, probably contrived.

I nod and give Sam a pat on his neck, feeling better.

The worries about our species, other species, killing themselves, throwing it all away, have gone, and I can focus on something *doable*.

Like moving on.

Then I feel disgusted with myself.

Selfish.

And that's when I see it.

A large, glossy picture of ... *Charlie*.

The photo has been encased in tempered glass and affixed to the orange double railing made of thick metal tubing that's supposed to keep the jumpers away from this highest peak on the Majorca Point peninsula. It was installed by the MP city council after Charlie died. But the deterrent's never worked. Sadly, on average, we see about a half-dozen suicides a year. Majorca Point has even been referred to as an LA version of the Golden Gate Bridge.

I shake my head and continue to stare at Charlie's headshot.

Again, it's nearly twenty years ago—she's sixteen, smiling with the vivacious energy of a beauty, her symmetrical face surrounded by a weathered pine frame that's covered in fluffy, pasted-on, hot-pink silk roses. If I squint, I can see chicken wire wrapped tightly around the large picture to hold it in place.

This is *impossible*.

Tears pulse down my cheeks.

No ... no.

Sam whinnies a warning.

I've been with him since the day he was born—which could be why he always senses my distress.

I wipe fast at my face.

García's walking over, ducking under the yellow-and-black crime-scene tape to where Sam and I stand in the shadows, near a picnic table, at the edge of the small, adjacent park. García's every move is a testament to smooth. He extends his palm, a round, unwrapped peppermint in his hand, as if he's planned this rendezvous—the pale-skinned suicide victim merely a prop for his flirtations.

Sam takes back his warning.

He's been bribed.

He eagerly takes the candy.

Sam loves candy. And Gabriel Hugo García.

"*Hola*, Dr. Esmeralda Green."

"Hi, Hugo." I take one more wipe at my face, trying to give the impression that my thick, shoulder-length, strawberry blonde hair was whipped across my eyes by a nonexistent breeze, then rub the tears on my jeans.

He looks up at me, his black-as-onyx hair curling around his wide, furrowed-to-perfection forehead. His tan eyes are flecked with yellow, like a feral cat's hunting orbs, and they glimmer in the high beams of the vast array of lights as he chides, "Will you ever call me Gabriel?"

"I won't," I answer with an uncomfortable huff.

This has become one of our opening conversations over the past year I've known him. There are others, but this might be the most profound because I refuse to associate him with a celestial being, and, even though I'm not Catholic—my religion born more in the wild ambiguity of the soul of the wind and the sea than a church—I do know, for certain, that Gabriel Hugo García is no angel.

He asks, "What are you doing here?"

I emit nonchalance. "I'm just out for a ride. What's going on?"

He responds, "Do you know something about this?"

As usual, he's answered my question with one of his own. It's a professional gambit, a TV journalist's strategy. But two can play that game ...

I ask, "Who's the girl?"

His cat-eyes twitch in annoyance. He can't go much further without disclosing ... something.

He answers, "Her name's Abigail Pryce. She took a fall off this cliff. I don't have a timeline yet."

I stifle a gasp.

Hugo's tone turns ominous. "Do you know this girl?"

My voice is calm. "I don't."

It's true. I can honestly say I've never met her before.

But I have met her voice ...

I heard it this morning.

It was *her* wistful voice on my phone.
Just like Charlie's.

## 2

I'm back at The Falling Majorca Point Stables, named in half-jest after our falling, slipping land.

You see, The Point, as we often call it, is a geological anomaly. What that means is that this breathtaking sweep of peninsula used to be a wide, craggy island off the Pacific coast, millions of years ago, until it merged with the geologically turbulent mainland after a huge, primal temblor literally hurled the two entities together.

Now, everyone who lives here is a little tippy.

I'm not talking about drunk—or dysfunctional, for that matter— but slightly on edge, ever since those two ancient landmasses started to rise up against each other in small but growing seismic fits at their forcible bondage. That's how I perceive it.

Not that we haven't always had earthquakes—we have.

But lately they've become almost nonstop, all over California but especially here, on The Point, as the island and the so-called mainland (how those of us who live in Majorca Point usually refer to the rest of Los Angeles) duke it out.

And it's affecting us, whether anyone will admit it or not.

For one, the suicides off the cliffs have increased.

That poor girl tonight.

So like Charlie.

Except for the blood.

Not even the foaming surf could wash the blood from Charlie's body.

I take Sam's bridle off and, with purpose, move my mind away from the unhappiness I still feel that Charlie's gone. I'm amazed that I still grieve for her so intensely. I went through the grief process and worked to accept her passing a long time ago.

I want to believe that Hugo's wrong.

There couldn't possibly have been another suicide in the Pryce family.

Could there?

I wince.

But why did Abigail Pryce contact me? She left me a message on my landline voice mail, explaining who she was, asking if we could meet. I listened, hand shaking, stunned. She sounded so much like Charlie—that same wistful tone—I nearly fainted.

And I'm not one to faint.

But, at that moment, I was sure I was listening to a ghost.

After a few deep breaths, I returned her call and left a message. Abigail hadn't told me why she wanted to meet with me. I'd assumed it was about Charlie, maybe some kind of ancestral research. I probably sounded hesitant. I wasn't looking forward to confronting my best friend's death. Not again. But, still, I'd consented, arranging to meet her at a café near the beach. I gave her my cell phone number. We played phone tag. She called me back on my cell and left a message saying she'd see me at the café in the morning.

I sigh, frustrated.

If only we'd arranged to meet today, instead of tomorrow.

Today, before she ...

Jumped?

I shake my head.

I need more time to digest this, to process it. My remaining emotions over losing Charlie are all mixed up after Abigail's … demise.

I attempt a different tack and think of Hugo.

I could have ended our relationship tonight. But that might confirm that we actually have a relationship, and I'm just not sure I want to take that path.

Hmmm.

No good thinking about him right now either.

I try to stay busy.

Still, my mind travels back to Charlie as I realize, once again, that she was integral in shaping who I am today.

And, ultimately, I should be thankful

I remember she always told me I'd do something green with my Green surname. It was a bit of a running joke between us because it was ironic, even weird, that I had a name that corresponded so closely with my passion for ecology. She thought I'd end up inventing something, like the electric car.

I wish …

The primary reason I even knew about ecopsychology was thanks to Charlie. She'd been the one, in our junior year of high school, to point out that a new psychological theory allowed for the earth to have a role in the human mind. She gave me a magazine she'd found at a local bookstore—but I didn't get a chance to read the article until after she died. Then, I read the first line over and over: *Ecopsychology acknowledges the environment as an important part of the human psyche.*

This seemed, to me, like an obvious concept, though Dr. Sigmund Freud apparently didn't think so. The article went on to explain that for Freud, the father of psychology, only an individual's identity could be formed in the mind: the ego, superego, and id. There was very little room for a mountain, ocean, or even a blade of grass.

Well, things have changed, and these days I genuinely relish saying: "This is *not* your daddy's psychology."

Back then, I needed a buoy to cling to in the gale-force storm that was Charlie's death.

And I found it in ecopsychology.

I sigh, set Sam's bridle down on a wood bench, put his harness on, and give him a pat on the neck.

He nuzzles my shoulder.

Anyway …

After Charlie's suicide, I wanted to find out why she'd killed herself—and it had occurred to me that the shaking beneath our feet, here on The Point and, heck, sometimes the entire Pacific Rim, might have something to do with it. With a determination born in sadness, I set out to prove it. I researched it as an undergrad: geological volatility and emotional instability. Is there a connection?

I think there is, though I've got no solid documentation.

Still, perhaps one day I will.

I get a sense of it before it happens.

An almost imperceptible lurch in my gut.

Sam and I are still standing inside The Falling MP Stables. Two rows of well-lit, impeccable stalls line a long, wide cement corridor that, for the moment, is empty. I clip Sam's harness to the crossties. I pick up the bridle from the bench and carry it, along with the heavy saddle, back to the tack room and plop them both down on my oversize tack trunk.

The earth beneath me abruptly jolts.

And sways.

I track my feelings, leaning against a stall.

Initially, I feel headachy.

Then, dizzy.

I wobble back to Sam.

For an instant, he appears surreal—stretched out and melting, like a Salvador Dalí painting.

But when I get to Sam, he's calm.

Probably still has his mind on peppermints.

I smile wryly, but my heartbeat's rapid, and I'd be willing to bet that this shaker was a bit larger than most, maybe a four or so on the Richter Magnitude Scale.

The shaking stops in seconds—counted in eternity.

I take a deep breath.

Nothing's fallen down. Nothing's broken.

I soothe myself by petting my horse, scratching behind his ears, cooing at him. "What a good boy you are, Sammy. Good boy."

My heart rate slows.

Sam's got such a sweet, steady disposition, I can't help but be mellow in his presence—which is also why Sam and I have been giving equine-assisted therapy to patients for years.

I take another gulp of air.

And move on—what else can I do?

I unclip Sam from the crossties, clip the lead rope onto his harness, and walk him outside, his horseshoes making hollow-sounding echoes on the cement. We stand together under a crescent moon so he can have his bedtime snack.

He munches the sparse tufts of grass.

I barely hear him.

Instead, I hear Charlie's voice.

Or the memory of it; her tone always held a hint of wistfulness, which, after she'd leapt to her death, I realized was more like sadness, even melancholy—and, after grad school, I surmised, clinical depression.

I grimace.

Still wishing after all these years I'd recognized she was in such deep emotional turmoil, thinking I might have been able to help her.

But when you're a teenager, so much of life is egocentric, and back then I'd genuinely appreciated the wistfulness in her voice, even been a little envious of it, because it seemed romantic, and I'd heard the boys thought it was sexy.

I can hear her, both of us sixteen, on the phone, speaking in our code.

"Hi, Emerald."

"Hi, Charlie."

"Do you want to go study sharks for Mr. Dorfman's class at the library down by the blue cove tonight?"

That meant: Do you want to go to the baseball game down by Majorca Cove to watch the hottest team that ever lived, the Point Sharks, play the other hottest team that ever lived, the Majorca Dolphins? But we liked the Sharks better.

How typical, when it came to guys, that we both preferred the bad boys.

The predators.

"Sounds good," I said.

I was caught up on my homework anyway.

"I'll see you there," she replied, a little trail of diminishing hope at the end of her sentence; I can discern that now. But back then it had sounded like a wisp of fairy dust, promising a magical night.

Incredible, really, how much perceptions can change.

Sam yanks on the rope in my hand.

He's finished with the grass.

There's not much left by October—especially in these last few years of more drought than rain.

Rain ...

I realize my thoughts are wistful for rain, trailing off, like Charlie's, into a diminishing hope—a last fluttering flight. I wonder, suddenly, if Charlie's longing tone was initiated by something similar, at least in an ecopsychological metaphor: a lack of life-quenching sustenance.

But her family had always seemed to have enough—more than enough: fancy meals every night, expensive clothes, big house, exotic vacations.

What, then? Love? Parental attention?

Is that what she'd lacked?

No, her family appeared very loving, happy.

Still, to be wistful, one had to have had something, then lost it—like rainstorms, before they became harbingers of mudslides and not much else.

Had Charlie's family lost something?

Both in the past, and now, too?

What did Abigail lack?

I'm speculating, confused and reaching.

I'll have to think about it later.

Sam is nearly dragging me to his stall.

My horse knows when he's tired.

I do, too, when I'm not worrying about suicidal bees, dead best friends, and a girl's last words on a voice mail.

# 3

I'm home, getting ready for bed, washing my face, which is still salty from tears and the night sea air.

I actually walked, taking the shortcut—a dirt path that angles across the chaparral and brush-strewn hill that we all cling to and lets me off at the door of the yellow clapboard ranch house that my *abuelo*, my grandfather on my mom's side, built in the sixties. Like everything else on The Point, it's shaking and will eventually slide all the way down to the Pacific Ocean. Yet as inevitable as that seems to be, I still adapt the house, at least once every two or three years, to the slipping land.

This year, I'm moving the second bedroom down the slope of my backyard, but in all honesty, the view I'll have will offset any physical discomfort—I hope. I have plans for a cute little window seat that will have an uninterrupted vista of wildflowers in spring; windswept, rolling bluffs; and an expansive, ever-changing sea: turquoise blue one minute, gray, green, lavender-hued the next.

Ahhh. I can almost feel the tingling release of it—sitting there, meditating on the transformative powers of nature.

But I'll have to muse on that later.

I've got five minutes before Hugo's broadcast on KLAT.
I need to know about Abigail Pryce.

—∞—

I lean up to the mirror and scan my face for blemishes. My Latin heritage (Mexican and Salvadoran), gives my skin a light-brown tone, but I also have a scattering of Irish-red freckles that runs across my nose and cheeks, and I get quizzical looks every once in a while from people who probably wonder whether I'm biracial or just cultivating a really good, precancerous tan.

Nope. No blemishes.

No wrinkles either—at least not yet.

That thought spurs me to check my blonde-red hair for gray. Not that I don't feel good about being in my thirties. I do. I feel confident, about me. About being able to handle, and adapt to, whatever comes up—or down. Like my house. But the aging thing?

Nope.

You see, about certain things ...

I'm happy to let my mind deceive me. In fact, I can completely convince myself that I'll never get gray, never get old, never need a hip replacement, or have a walker, or have drool coming out the side of my mouth.

About other things, like the degradation of the environment—then I don't do denial so well.

Radiation, pollution, carbon free-for-alls, oil in the ocean, famine, extreme weather, drought.

I can't deny any of it.

Which moves my mind to ...

Will we have enough water to drink if we don't get any rain?

I'd actually *like* to deny my present circumstances when it comes

17

to water because I'm still not sure how I'm going to come up with the big (by my standards) money to pay for the new plumbing lines that almost everyone in Majorca Point is mandated to get. The PWE, the giant utility company that supports the main line, has recently determined that the land on The Point has slid more than they'd estimated it would, and soon they're going to have to move everything about a half a mile down the hill from the small cluster of houses and town. What that means is we've got to add on pipe to reach their new water lines, enormous, round things that are above ground and must remain visible and accessible, since they've had to be moved three times before. You can see the pipes running adjacent to Majorca Point Road—they break open sometimes, in the rain.

Rain. Water. Rain.

There it is—that wistful feeling again.

This time, it gives me an idea: the stock market.

Okay …

Don't get me wrong—Wall Street can be treacherous—but I've made some extra money investing in stocks using my own ecopsychological strategy. I also only trade green stocks, usually solar or wind power.

Maybe it's time I check out green stocks again, see if anyone's come up with cutting-edge water technology.

I recall a few names of new companies: Buenaventura in Colorado, Grandview in Oregon, a few in California, too.

They're into water. I think …

I'll have to research it.

But …

Who knows?

I might even find a symbiotic, ecopsychological connection between the lack of rain, the PWE's monetary demands, and the stock market. Thankfully and, I believe, accurately, ecopsychology allows for the integration of *everything.*

I swipe my toothbrush under the faucet. Turn it off to conserve water.

I stand in front of the sink, brushing my teeth.

My mind has moved on again ...

I'm remembering Charlie and her family.

They seemed happy.

Except for ... Anthony.

He always appeared morose.

Charlie would say, "He's got zits and can't get a date."

Which, I realize, is a callous explanation for a sibling's moodiness—but normal for a teen.

Oops.

Almost time for the news.

I take my toothbrush out of the bathroom and over to a laptop computer on the small, built-in desk in my bedroom, and with one hand still brushing my teeth, the other hand touches the keys to access the Spanish-language broadcast on KLAT. I still know a little Spanish, but I understand it better than I speak it. My grandmother, or *abuela*, who was originally from Cancún, México, tried her best to make sure I kept up with her native language, but her husband, my *abuelo*, who was from El Salvador, was against it.

They would argue about it.

My *abuelo* was convinced that speaking Spanish in *El Norte* would only bring us trouble. My dad, a tall, freckled, red-haired Irishman, would also argue about my *abuela*, my mom, or me speaking Spanish in their home. My dad thought the Spanish language was beautiful, and by his passionate account, he'd worked hard to learn it so he could woo my mom. My *abuelo* would listen to my dad's soliloquies for a few minutes, nod his head, then mutter something under his breath about gringos and walk away.

But he would mutter it in Spanish.

Go figure.

After a few minutes, Hugo's square-jawed, sexy face appears, and what I hear and see is upsetting.

I return the toothbrush to the bathroom and nearly run back to sit in the swivel chair in front of the screen.

Hugo's standing in front of the garish lights. I can see the large pine picture frame with the pink silk roses and Charlie's gorgeous, smiling face—or is it Abigail's face?—hanging from the rail in the background.

It's shocking that I can't tell them apart.

Then, I *can* ...

The camera abruptly cuts to Abigail's body, zooming in on her bare arms, so close that the tiny blonde hairs on her skin are visible. The black basket wire creases into the still-pliant dermis of her shoulder, and it's so smooth, so strangely unharmed, that for an instant I'm absolutely certain she can't be dead.

But, of course, she is.

I cover my mouth, feeling queasy.

Yet I keep watching.

Sucked in.

Her shirt, a stretchy black material with a pink lace pattern in front, is pulled up around her slim waist, her left breast bulging from a sheer, nude-colored bra. And it's as if I can almost reach out and touch the twisted swath of shell-encrusted seaweed that's wrapped around her naked stomach.

The camera pulls in even tighter.

*Mierda*, Hugo.

Pardon my Spanish.

But this is total exploitation.

*Awful*.

I realize it's not his fault.

Hugo's tan eyes look concerned, and I know him well enough to differentiate fake from real, at least most of the time. But the camera lingers right on top of Abigail's exposed torso, as if it's about to mount her. Hugo reports, "This is a story with a very tragic history. The young woman, Abigail Pryce, who was found dead tonight at the bottom of the highest cliff at Majorca Point, is the nineteen-year-old niece, or would have been the niece, of the long-ago suicide victim Charlene Pryce, who was only sixteen when she leapt to her death at this very same location ..."

I shriek out loud, my palm pulsing with heat and moisture.

My own sad, sickened breath.

I mute the broadcast.

I stand from the swivel chair.

I go to the kitchen, flick on the solar-run lights, take in the contrast of the new, pristine, champagne-colored, eco-friendly countertops made from recycled glass running alongside the ancient, cracked ranch cupboards. What can I say—I ran out of money.

I search the stained, splintered drawers.

*Where did I put my old address book?*

I find stacks of organic cotton underwear in a drawer that's supposed to hold a mishmash of things I don't often use, like pens and pencils, Post-its and paperclips, but in the last few days I've had to move my belongings out of the second bedroom—which used to be my grandparents' bedroom, then my parents'—into the kitchen because that room is now completely gone.

It's blocked off by a floor-to-ceiling tarp.

I look over at the tarp for a minute, dark green and firmly held down by rope and blocks of cement.

I grimace, knowing what kind of a mess is behind it.

I turn back to search for the antiquated address book. These days, I enter the contact info for my friends, family, and patients into my smartphone.

Where did I put it? It had a floral design …

Did I finally recycle it, along with all of my other old paperwork?

I look in the drawer again.

Nope.

I raise my head and notice that I accidentally blocked the hall closet when I hauled out the second-bedroom mattress.

I take a big, supposed-to-be-soothing breath and flick off the lights.

I walk back to my bedroom.

Okay, forget the address book; I'll just Google him.

Anthony Pryce.

I must express my condolences.

## 4

I wake to the sound of peacocks weeping; their loud, eerie cries echo up the hill, as most mornings they can be found standing on top of the Majorca Point Beach Club's rust-colored tile roof. For what reason they congregate there, no one's sure, and although the owners of the club have petitioned our town several times to have them removed from the peninsula (peacocks seem to have quite the penchant for pooping on every and any available surface), it's never come to pass.

They're an institution.

The large, beautiful, precocious birds were brought to shore hundreds of years ago, as the legend goes, after a pirate ship ran aground off the coast, and so their ancestors thrive, and stay, no matter how obnoxious.

Me—I like them.

I find their calls to one another comforting, and, as haunting as their wailing can be, they help me to easily conjure precious childhood memories.

Besides, bird poop is a part of life.

But then, I'm not a member of the club.

A snooty club, and just about all that's left of our snooty past, because Majorca Point, before it started to practically heave itself into the ocean, was where many of central California's rich agriculturalists built their second homes. So did the heads of some movie studios and a few film and TV stars, too.

Now, we're forgotten here.

Most of those mansions have already been lost to the waves since they were also those that were built closest to the water, usually on outcroppings of rock that were later found to be unstable. The owners, I'm sure, were initially thrilled to get that stunning view.

My *abuelo* and *abuela*, like the rest of the common folk in Majorca Point, weren't so unlucky, as it turned out, to have been relegated to building in the back bluffs. My *abuelo* was just a truck driver for a company that served the Long Beach Port, yet his home is still intact. It's one of life's insatiable ironies that the common folks' small, wood ranch homes are standing, while there are remnants of literally dozens of wealthy homes littering the coves.

I used to scour the beaches looking for pirate treasure. According to Majorca Point legend, a pirate ship capsized during a storm off our shores one long-ago night, and its booty of gold and jewels sank with it. I never found any gold, but I did find pieces of a crystal chandelier (I was sure they were diamonds at first, but I was only eleven years old). I've also come across Louis Vuitton luggage; a corroded, broken silver pocket watch that I gave to the Lost and Found at the MP Community Center; and a big, plastic Nordstrom bag full of Jimmy Choo shoes—waterlogged, with lots of tiny barnacles attached to them, but it was an exciting find.

Some of the larger remnants have become landmarks.

If you hike about a quarter mile north up the coast, there's a huge, white marble staircase leading to the sky.

My father used to say, "Now, there's Led Zeppelin's 'Stairway to Heaven.'"

It's hard to believe that the house that bore that staircase slid down the hill more than a dozen years ago and the owners still haven't cleaned it up—or a lot of other old mansion stuff, like a rusting Audi, for one thing. But if the land here wouldn't hold those enormous homes, then neither did the economy—and, now, a lot of those people don't have the money to clean up their messes.

Or so they say.

And my dad's gone—he climbed the stairway to heaven.

The peacocks continue to wail.

I roll over, away from the window suffused with hazy, yellow morning light, and I cozy up to memories of my dad.

And mom.

Then other memories filter in …

I look at the clock.

It's only 6:00 a.m.

But I'm remembering last night.

Charlie and … Abigail.

Then, I'm awake.

My landline rings.

Apparently Hugo is, too.

I have caller ID—I can see it's him.

My landline stops ringing. Then my cell phone rings. Then my landline, then my cell.

He's the big-deal reporter on the beat—a hot story.

He can tell I know something.

Well, he's right.

But …

I finally pick up the landline.

"So you *do* know her," he says.

"Nice of you to call," I reply, wishing I sounded sleepier.

"Ez …" His voice trails, but not in a wistful way, more like a scolding way.

Here's a man who should actually *work* on wistful.

"You're not very polite," I tell him.

"You're not very forthcoming with information that could be relevant to a police investigation that Detec—"

"Ah, yes," I say, cutting him off, knowing where he's going. "That your good friend, Majorca Point PD Detective Suzy Whitney, is heading up—right?"

"Right."

"Say no more. I'm going back to sleep."

I hang up the phone.

The psychologist in me feels a little embarrassed—not only because I've always been bothered by Hugo's closeness with that detective but because we're usually perceived as such a cooperative bunch. The ecopsychologist in me, however, feels just perfect, if you please, because the natural world is not so cooperative.

This I know, maybe better than most, having grown up with not only the wails of peacocks but also the howls of coyotes; the roars of mountain lions; the rock slides, the mud slides; the rising, tumultuous ocean; water shortages, raging wildfires; the rearing and tumbling of horses in the dark of night when the orange flames burst into the sky; the shaking, quaking of the living Mother Earth; and the falling stores, homes, and best friends, falling—and my mom and dad, caught up in extreme weather, in a commercial jet that should have been able to withstand a wind shear, slamming down, falling down.

That's how ecology has shaped me.

I demand some respect for it—because I have respect.

For human beings. For animals.

For nature.

A healthy, *survivable* respect.

Nature is beautiful, but it can also be dangerous, and I've spent much of my life surviving between those two aspects of reality: beauty and danger.

And falling …

And getting back up.

Falling—getting back up.

It's all symbiotic. It's all integrated.

Sometimes I perceive it this way: I'm a good horsewoman.

I have respect for my horse; he's a wonderful horse, but if he rears, I could be killed, and I understand that, so nothing's taken for granted. Not the slightest nuance; he might be unwell, or alarmed, or just having a moody day.

Nothing.

If I fall, I get back up in the saddle—and learn to ride him better, Learn to be more *attuned* to him.

Again and again.

I do that for my horse, and, subsequently, I'm happier.

Safer.

And so is he.

I do that for my patients.

My friends. My loved ones.

I help them get back up.

I wish I could have done it for Charlie.

But that doesn't mean I'm giving Gabriel Hugo García a leg up on his career—not this morning.

He calls back.

Landline. Cell. Landline.

I pick up the cell.

"Listen, Ez …"

"Hmmm."

"Can I take you to breakfast?"

I'm silent, thinking.

Finally, I say, "If you want, Hugo."

"I want."

"Okay, how about this? I'll make that scramble you like. With the chilies."

"You will? At your house?"

I can almost hear his stomach growling.

I can also feel my own tummy flutter. I've only made breakfast for him once, and I swore it was going to be the last time.

We're both silent for a moment, remembering.

He's probably also sensing a catch.

Still, it's a *respectful* catch.

I reply, "Yep. I will. At my house. But then, after breakfast, maybe you could help me with something? Carry some lumber?"

He groans. "Ez ..."

"*Buena*," I say. "Thanks."

## 5

He's flashing his famous, quirky grin.

I flash my own grin back at him—I can't help it.

He's really so good-looking, especially out here working: His round, hard muscles pop out of his white T-shirt; his brown skin raises a sheen in the mid-morning sun as he carries the planks of wood over his wide, square shoulders. I've made sure the wood carries the Forest Stewardship Council label, or FSC, which stands for a non-profit organization that works to assure the responsible management of the world's forests. The FSC wood is also VOC Free, or free of Volatile Organic Compounds, those very nasty invisible things that are emitted by various building materials and contribute to smog, soil, and water contamination, as well as cancer. And even though they've put some stringent restrictions on the use of VOCs in California, I'm still vigilant in making certain I'm not sold the old stuff off of somebody's back shelf.

The ground has already been leveled, much of it by a contractor, but I assisted, getting down on my hands and knees, pulling up roots and scraggly bushes, rocks and stones, doing my best to make sure the jacaranda that my mom planted when I turned five can remain standing. Although the new bedroom will be smaller for having saved the tree, retaining the images of my mom and the light-purple blossoms that she adored, as well as rewarding the tree's remarkable tenacity at hanging on to the side of this itinerant slope, is worth it.

I also participated in pouring the concrete, and eventually I'll do the dry polish, which is more environmentally friendly than wet polish, and then I'll seal it with a silicate sealer that, again, has virtually no VOCs.

But first, the bedroom frame has to be built.

Hugo sets the wood down on the concrete with a grunt. "Don't you need a permit for this?"

I set my armload of wood down next to his, realize my peach-colored tank top is wet with sweat and getting a bit transparent, and I start to feel self-conscious, but, I have to say, in a somewhat titillating way, as I shrug. "I've got a contractor, you know. But he's actually not as strict as me, especially on the environmental regulations—I've got very high standards."

I look him up and down. I'm thinking about …

*What?*

No. This is not a man I should be involved with—ever.

He looks me up and down, lingering.

I almost gasp.

We stare, for a moment.

Sex in the air, the blue sky almost blaring potential, and the smell of the fresh soil, and the wood, and the sage, and the ocean, and the stuff that is earth and lusty and good begins to work on my body like a seductive vortex, and, for an instant, I'm sure we're both going to topple to the dirt and start rolling around like animals.

But …

There's also a jagged saw, a couple of hammers, and nails on the ground, and I don't believe I will lie down on nails.

I say his name: "Hugo."

"Gabriel?" he urges hopefully.

A part of me knows that I should probably let myself … fall … with him.

For all of my insight into why I've been shaped to get up from the slipping land, and the sensation of falling, there are also times when it could be a good thing for me to just let myself, my *determination*, go.

But right now?

I can't.

I repeat, "Hugo."

My tone is serious.

We stand, facing each other, hands on hips, squinting in the October sun.

We've had our breakfast: organic coffee, organic fresh-squeezed orange juice, organic wheat tortillas, and a scramble made with tomato, onions, avocado, green chilies, and just a sprinkling of diced jalapeno, all of it organic.

I don't eat meat, poultry, or fish.

No dairy either. And I don't use eggs; I scramble tofu instead.

When Hugo asked me why, that first time he had breakfast in my home, I didn't eat "normal" food, I told him what I tell everybody: "It's a personal choice— but it works for me. You see, many cows, pigs, and chickens, even when they're so-called 'Animal Care Certified,' sometimes—heck, more than sometimes—aren't treated humanely. Besides that, the meat's loaded with antibiotics. That scares me. As for seafood, the ocean has been so overfished it barely has enough left in it for the sea creatures that live there. And the eggs?"

He'd waved me off. "No, no, don't tell me." He'd put on a face of horror, making choking noises, staggering a bit, and blanching as if he might be sick.

He definitely can exhibit the drama of our culture when it suits him.
Still, he did come back for more, didn't he?

Yep. Because my vegan dishes are *delicious*.

I smile to myself.

Anyway …

He's helped me move the wood.

The deal is done.

We know it.

His tan eyes glint gold in the sun. "So tell me about her, your friend. Charlene Pryce."

Ecopsychologists and psychologists often have very different opinions on what psychotherapy means. For instance, I might take a walk with a patient by the beach, or explore some equine-assisted therapy, in my belief that the synergistic relationship between human beings and nature can be as beneficial to their situation, whatever it may be, as a traditional office setting, if not more. Most psychoanalysts, on the other hand, still adhere to the couch.

But wherever we might differ, ecopsychologists and psychologists may as well be joined at the hip when it comes to one intrinsic tenet of all psychotherapy: We both answer questions with questions.

But so do journalists.

Yep. Two can definitely play this game.

I ask, "How do you know I know her?"

He retorts, "How *do* you know her?"

I'm silent.

He shrugs. "Come on, Ez. You spoke at Charlene's funeral. I just downloaded archives."

I remain quiet.

He starts again. "Did you know Abigail, too?"

"What makes you think I know Abigail?"

"But you know the family, right?"

I shrug and ask, "Can you know a family if you haven't spoken to them in decades?"

"Ez ... "

We're at an impasse.

He's stone-faced. So am I.

Finally, he says, "Your friend's brother married Penelope De Vos."

I nod, feeling satisfied that he gave up information first.

I tell you, I'm only this competitive with him.

I wonder, for a moment, what that says about me?

Oh, who am I kidding? I know *exactly* what it says. I'm very attracted to him, yet I don't trust him, so we're stuck in this perpetual loop: attraction, the need to diminish the attraction, competition, victory, attraction ...

Okay ... on to something else.

I didn't know anything about Abigail's mother—until now. But I've been very concerned about the Pryce family: Charlie's mom and dad; her brother, Anthony, and his wife, Abigail's mom; any siblings. I must send flowers, a card, *something*, before I disclose to Hugo, or anyone, what I know about Abigail's final days. When I was asked to give a statement about Charlie, so long ago, I was actually grilled—at least it felt that way—by the Majorca Point PD, and it was hurtful for the family, especially when the media got hold of the info.

Thankfully, this morning, I recalled the name of the street in Palm Springs where Charlie's parents had moved: Desert Shadow Avenue. They'd refused to live in Majorca Point after they lost their beloved daughter. By all accounts, they didn't keep in touch with anyone here. Not even me. I remember sending letters, just to let them know I was thinking of them. But after a few years of getting no response, I stopped. The connection I'd had with Charlie drifted away and finally vanished, like a paper boat on the water.

A child's dream.

I shake my head, slightly.

Hugo doesn't notice. I can tell by his stance that his mind is intent on my next words—whatever they may be.

I'm still *thinking*.

I was relieved that Mr. and Mrs. Pryce were easy to find; their address in Palm Springs was the same.

Finding Anthony was a different story.

Considering Charlie used to berate him much of the time, as siblings will do, I never paid much attention to her brother, except to agree with her that, usually, he *was* annoying.

I guess, unconsciously, I still perceive him as a kid.

But I discovered that now, he's a big executive with a multinational corporation called De Vos Industries, or DVI. And now, thanks to Hugo, I know what the name means—that Anthony married into the business. They've got offices and buildings scattered around Los Angeles and all over the world. But Anthony's office is listed in the nearby harbor city of San Pedro, down by the waterfront, where high-rise office space, luxury condos, and trendy lofts overlooking the Long Beach Port are actually starting to go up in price and are sometimes inciting bidding wars, even in these challenging economic times.

Google yielded absolutely no info about Anthony's personal residence, or residences, though.

Nothing on his personal life, either.

*Nada.*

I ask, "Do you know where Abigail's parents live?"

But Hugo's quickly back on his game, demanding, "Do you know why Charlene killed herself?"

I ask, "Do you know why Abigail killed herself?"

He's immediately all over that. "Why do you think she killed herself?"

I take a literal, and figurative, step back. "I don't."

Damn—I answered.

But I also realize why he must think this—Detective Suzy Whitney—and *she* doesn't like me very much. One, because she likes *him* too much, him being Gabriel Hugo García. Two, she can be an ecological tyrant, and she's proud of it. We've even had a few recent run-ins at Majorca Point town hall meetings—she wants to allow ATVs on our bluffs. Can you imagine: all-terrain vehicles speeding around on the unstable land, crushing the flora and fauna, one of them eventually falling into a crevice? Needless to say, I don't support the plan. So if she thinks I'm aware of something, anything, regarding Abigail's death, she'll have me in her office in a millisecond.

Hugo comes in for the kill.

He even steps toward me, feral, like his cat-eyes: glowing, hungry.

I gulp.

I ask, "Why were you at the cliffs last night? This is a little removed from your area—isn't it?" I toy with the words, letting a hint of sardonic innocence creep into my voice. "I mean, aren't you the big shot now? Aren't you supposed to be anchoring?"

I've caught him off guard.

I knew I would.

I follow the verbal jab with, "Hmmm. Could it be you wanted to come over to this neighborhood to see *me?*"

I've got him.

He doesn't blush or fumble; he's too adroit for that.

But he blusters a bit. "I'm turning down the desk job. I'm not old enough. Got too much energy for that."

Then he gets me.

His voice as innocently sardonic as my own, he says, "There's too many fish in the sea to be tied down to just … one … desk."

It's cliché, I suppose.

But it hurts.

It does.

I just nod.

The sun is nearly on top of our heads; sweat beads down both our faces.

Finally, I say, "Thanks for the help, Hugo."

He reaches to the ground, picks up his light-blue button-down shirt, and wipes it under his T-shirt, and when I catch a peek of his hard abs my heart flutters, so much so that I've got to feign looking down at my dirty, uneven fingernails as he brushes the moisture off his biceps, his neck, his chiseled face, then tosses the material over his shoulder.

"Anytime, Ez ..." He turns away.

I know ...

I could just let him go, but I want to see what he's driving these days.

I follow him up the hill, make a left turn around the front of the house, and stand in the driveway.

There it is ...

His same old, same old.

The Hummer.

It's a vintage car, hasn't been manufactured in several years. But it lives on as the universal symbol of gas-guzzling atrocities.

I can almost hear him inwardly groan. He knows what's coming. He tries to deflect it by glancing over at my little Ford and saying, "Nice hybrid."

I tilt my head over toward the Hummer.

"Nice gigantic carbon footprint-maker," I respond.

"Don't judge a car by its cover."

"I'm not judging the car," I say. "It's you, Hugo. When are you going to get the environmentally friendly car that you're always telling me you're going to get?"

He gives me a look, at once vulnerable and fierce.
"I'll have Suze call you," he says.
Ouch. Now, that *really* hurt.
*Suze.*

**6**

I watch him drive away in a cloud of dust.

I practically choke.

Suze.

Hah.

Have her call me—fine.

My eyes, my *senses*, search for a place of quiescence: I need to clean the image of that man from my mind.

I walk back down the slope, around my house, to the backyard.

I look at the nails, the wood, the cement, and, finally, the jacaranda tree.

That's where I need to be.

I allow myself to fuse with it.

*Become it.*

This is how, in my head and my heart, I can best communicate with nature. It's definitely Zen-like because I feel in a deep, meditative yet active way that I'm tapping into the life around me. Even before Charlie died, the environment seemed to give me little glimmers of insight about how to perceive certain situations—or, sometimes, even a precognitive sense of what might be coming next.

My mom always said I had a special connection to the earth and that it must be the Mayan in me. My dad would smile softly and say it was the Irish Gaelic. But I truly believe it evolved from our family relationship; nature not only gave my mom and dad a way to feel close to me but to each other. My parents were from such different cultures and family backgrounds that they tried to bridge those gaps with me, their only child, and the most apparent bridge, I guess, was the love we all felt for ecology.

We shared it, you see. Relishing the ocean, the bluffs; swimming with dolphins; wading in tide pools off the many coves that dazzle the Majorca Point coast. Nature was a part of our family, too.

So when, years later, I told them I wanted to go to college and spend their hard-earned money studying this barely known theory called ecopsychology, they were very supportive, and it was in college that I learned that my seeming affinity with nature wasn't unusual, just buried within me, like a recessive gene. As some of my professors so aptly put it: Before the guiding signals of human reality became a technological barrage of computers, cell phones, TV, sonic booms, and traffic lights, the signs we'd rely on to inform us of necessity, or pleasure, had been the curve of the sky, the transition of seasons, the calls of animals, the whisper of trees.

But, through time, we lost our curiosity about these things.

Well, I want my curiosity. Don't get me wrong—I rely on technology as much as the next person. I just try to turn it off every once in a while. And even though there are those in the traditional psychological profession that call me, or people like me, odd, clinically subversive, or even crazy, I do believe I'm able to hear a voice from nature.

Maybe not all the time, but today … ?

It's in the jacaranda, somehow.

Why did Charlie kill herself?

My mind slips in and out of this moment to another, the ecopsychological metaphor coming through …

It was June.
Late in the spring.
The sun was direct.
The shadows were short.
Charlie couldn't find shade.
She was hot.
Most living creatures ...
In those days before summer...
Feel the fire.
It's the season.
Of ... hormones.
But she could find no coolness.
No respite.
My inner voice asks ...
Why did Abigail commit suicide?
The jacaranda whispers in the breeze.
She didn't.
It's late October.
The sun is indirect.
The shadows are longer.
Cooler.
Even cold.
She was pushed from the cliff.
Cold-heartedly.
*She was pushed.*

I've been in a trance.

I come out of it.

The answer was in the tree. Perhaps.

My methods are in no way infallible.

But then again—in this blend of psychology, ecology, spirituality, and science, too, there seems to be a hint of something genuine because the scintillating, sensory delight of spring has, throughout time, sparked the world's creatures into a fiery, reproductive dance.

And the shadows *are* longer in the fall.

But I'm also not discounting the power of my own unconscious because, you see, I know certain things about Charlie's last days that no one else knows. One particular thing that I didn't disclose to the police, mostly because they didn't ask me—and it didn't seem relevant at the time—Charlie was in love.

Or ... lust.

I remember her telling me, "He's awesome, Emerald. I mean it. I'm going to ... have sex with him. Lose it to him. I decided."

She looked at me with her large, jade-colored eyes, as if for confirmation.

I replied, "Are you sure you want to do that?"

She nodded, her blonde-streaked hair—surfer hair, as we called it—bouncing in long curls down her back.

I hadn't had sex yet, either.

But I said what I thought was probably most important at the time because the info about AIDS had been everywhere: "Make sure you use a condom."

"I will." She giggled, wistfully.

Then we talked about other things.

I never said a word, to anyone, about the boy she loved. It seemed like the only part of her I could protect.

And, like I said, they didn't ask for that information.

But the tree knows. Or it's my unconscious. Or, in ecopsychological terms, it could be a melding of the two, as if my willingness to try to intuit Charlie's and Abigail's dark, psychic travails was working in concert with nature's healing, clarifying light to form a union of truth.

It strikes me again.

I must locate Anthony Pryce.

I'll start with DVI.

Hmmm.

What exactly does a high-level executive of a multinational corporation do?

This is a new one for me. Or who knows? Maybe it's not.

All things are integrated—I believe.

You just have to be … receptive to it.

—m—

I grab my smartphone off my counter—so smart now, maybe it could transport me to where I want to go.

Gee, I wish I could invent *that*.

I could teleport myself to any situation—even a crime scene.

That's how I met Hugo—helping to solve a crime.

I'd been called in because I knew the suspect. She was a seemingly altruistic woman who'd started a shelter for homeless women in North Hollywood. But in the large garage in the back of the house that she'd refurbished with clean, dorm-style bedrooms was a fight ring. Apparently, she'd started an illegal fight club, and one of the homeless women had been injured in a fight, a broken arm. The North Hollywood PD had immediately closed down the club and started doing background checks on a few of the younger-looking women fighters, making sure they weren't minors. I was asked to help because the so-called ringleader had once been a patient of mine. I remembered there might have been a reason for her criminal behavior: Three years earlier she'd been walking her seven-year-old pet collie, Rex, when a homeless teenage girl had snatched the leash out of her hands, stolen the dog, and sold him to a dog-fighting ring.

I was able to contact the woman, and, without breaching confidentiality, I'd urged her to plead guilty to a lesser charge and get out of the fight club business before she ended up in jail for a long time.

But it was very sad: the fate of the collie, Rex, who'd been killed; the pit bulls who'd been forced into the brutal sport; and the dog-napping girl, who'd eventually been arrested. Later, it was discovered that the dog-napping girl was a runaway and had needed money to escape a home where she'd been forced to watch her mother get beaten every night by her stepfather.

This is also the symbiosis of ecopsychology and psychology. The runaway who'd stolen the collie had only done what had been accepted in her home as truth: Abuse the weak.

Then suffer at the hands of the strong.

My patient had expanded on that theme: a dementia born of tragedy.

I believe the cycle of abuse permeates the psyche of our species and all the other species that share the earth with us. And breaking that cycle of abuse goes deeper than just our species: It is a cycle of human against human, human against animal, and, finally, human against nature.

One night, after meeting with the North Hollywood PD, Hugo asked me to go for coffee, and I accepted, curious about the charming, handsome rising star of a very popular Latino news channel. We talked for hours, and I was surprised when he agreed with me that the human cycle of abuse was ultimately destroying the planet. In fact, he'd been adamant. Yet when I asked him to explain his passion, he became quiet and told me nothing more.

Hugo. In many ways, he remains a mystery.

Even about his choice of cars.

If he really has such a passionate concern about the planet, why doesn't he drive a hybrid?

Hmmm.

I enter the address for Anthony Pryce's office at DVI into my phone and slip it into the right front pocket of my recycled, low-on-the-hip jeans. The loose-fitting jeans are great for riding Sam, and they come in handy for my cell phone, keys, and small wallet made of hemp, too.

I hate to carry a purse.

I take a look around the house—windows are open—it's going to be a hot one.

Especially for autumn.

Even if the shadows are long.

I think about Charlie again, and how much she *wanted* that guy—what was his name? He was from Majorca Point High School, like us, but in all honesty, she hadn't known him more than a few months. But that's what happens with lust, isn't it? Maybe I should get to know Hugo better, and then the heat I feel for him would dissipate.

I grab my keys off the counter.

Justin Fellowes. That was his name.

I wonder what became of him.

I step out the front door.

I realize with a lurching in my stomach that I'm actually hoping Hugo's still here, in his car, waiting for me.

I'm in lust, all right.

But *nothing* more.

# 7

Thought processes, like roads, can take some unexpected, unpredictable turns.

I'm driving along the Pacific Coast Highway, the part where it leaves the beach, cutting through Torrance and Lomita, both of them large, busy middle-class suburbs, and suddenly I must steer into the right lane to get out of the way of a monster SUV that I see proudly touts a hybrid emblem on the rear.

I almost guffaw.

It's an enormous vehicle—what can it get? Really? A whopping twelve miles per gallon instead of a mere seven?

What a sham.

My little hybrid gets upward of fifty miles per gallon and keeps going, even when the gas is gone. Actually, I really want to switch to total electric, but the money thing just keeps coming up. Imagine that. Thankfully, I've got two patients this afternoon.

And, in an addendum to all that, I wish I could be riding Sam—but that's impossible.

Anyway, back to the hybrid issue.

Well, not so much the hybrid issue but my feelings about Hugo and the hybrid issue. Apparently, I've been assessing him, at least somewhat, based on the kind of car he drives.

I've never, in my life, *defined a man by his car*.

Or the size of his you-know-what—but that's something else, isn't it?

Hmmm … maybe.

Maybe … not.

Still, I've always thought it was the height of gauche to do that.

I've had a few girlfriends who've bragged literally for hours about how great a guy was—and what a fantastic lover—when it was as plain as the sparkle in their eyes that what they'd really been admiring was his fancy, the-more-expensive-the-sexier car. They'd be going on and on about the smooth, lush feel of hand-tooled leather seats, while I'd be thinking: "Stop! Don't you get it? If we didn't have cars, we wouldn't be in this climate-change mess!"

But this morning, there I was *doing the exact same thing*.

At least … sort of.

Still, would it really make a difference if Hugo bought a hybrid car? If he did, would it prove that he's capable of being a caring, compassionate mate?

That he's trustworthy?

Or maybe I'm expecting too much.

Can a gas guzzler actually come between a man and a woman?

It certainly isn't doing much for Hugo …

Not for his sex life.

Or mine, for that matter.

I shake my head.

Well, there's no way on this green … gray … sweet … polluted earth that I'm going to determine my choice of mate *by what kind of car he drives*.

Even if they come up with a vehicle that gets 250 miles per gallon in the city.

Wait—I think they already have …
*¡Ay, Dios mío!*
Why don't we have more high-speed rail?
*Can human beings ever get away from the automobile?*

—⁓—

I run through these thoughts as I ride the road.

I try not to get too stuck on any single theme, which is another skill I picked up trying to adapt in one way or another to the slipping land, and although some traditional psychologists would say I'm running away, most likely from the things I can't control (which could be true), if I blend that perspective with ecology, it's also a matter of flow.

Keep on moving that mind, Esmeralda.

Keep on shifting those neurons.

Nothing in nature, after all, can exist very long without change.

And nature confirms my point—it always does.

That's the … nature … of things.

Like driving.

Whoa!

I almost have to slam on my brakes as I make a right onto Western, but I'm able to yank the wheel to the left, just missing a U-Haul pulled up illegally against the curb.

How's that for adaptive prowess?

I enter the sprawling port city of San Pedro, with its eclectic mix of fast-food drive-thrus, coffee shops, mom-and-pop liquor stores, tattoo parlors, hair stylists, dry cleaners, do-it-yourself doggie groomers, block-long supermarkets, low-slung digital billboards, and way too much traffic.

After a few truly aggravating waits at red lights, at which I wonder how many cigarettes I'm inhaling per minute by way of car exhaust in my face—I enter the fresh-mown air of a vast expanse of hilly, brilliant green cemetery.

I breathe deeply.

It's bizarre, really, that cemeteries can provide so much clean air amid the twenty-first century re-shuffle of carbon—as if death tempts with sensorial visages of a glorious future in eco-heaven.

You just have to die first.

I sigh.

Charlie's buried there.

If I turn my head to the right, within the next thirty seconds I'll see her gravestone on the green, rolling hill where she was laid to rest so long ago.

I clasp my hands tighter to the wheel.

This time, I have to force my mind to keep moving.

I finally pass the large cemetery and start veering left to take a turn on Seventh Street, heading down a slight hill to the water.

I find myself on the bustling port-side street of South Harbor and look for the DVI address. I see Fisherman's Wharf, but it appears different, cleaned up, no longer the clapboard venue of fish sales, funky seafood restaurants, and a diverse crowd of families alongside bikers and gangbangers. It emanates gentrification. I'm not sure how I feel about it. I was never a big fan of the garbage, rats, and gangland warfare down by the docks—but at the same time, it felt real—a tangible entity amid the mirrors and lights of greater Los Angeles.

Yet all things change.

They must …

My mind's flowing again.

And …

There it is: I turn into a thin strip of driveway that leads to a small, discreet parking lot with a valet at the back door.

The building is three stories of glass and concrete, each floor smaller than the first, with solar panels on the sides and a small windmill on top.

I'm impressed.

A green building at the docks.

Who would have ever guessed that could happen?

If this is an indication of what DVI does, I'll buy what they're selling.

What *are* they selling?

I pull up to the valet, a small man in a simple white uniform, and ask, "How much is the parking?" If it's more than five dollars, I'll go somewhere else. Truly. No one should charge more than five dollars for parking ... cars ... of all things. The man, solemn in his white suit, with a thin, dark mustache and light-brown eyes and skin, replies, "No charge." He nods courteously and gently motions his hand toward a narrow space on the right.

"Thanks," I say, and pull in.

I get out of the car, lock it, and take in the sustainable adaptations made by the architects of this eco-building: the concrete, the recycled glass.

Maybe the sealers are even VOC-free and the paint's non-toxic?

This could be the building of my dreams.

I watch for a moment as a small stream of water cascades down a concrete outer wall, and, like a piece of art, it pools in ever smaller levels before trickling back into a rectangular hole at the bottom of the building. I'll bet the water is gray water from the building's bathroom sinks, kitchen sinks, dishwashers, or showers if they have them—as opposed to black water, which is from toilets—and that it's being recycled throughout the building. I could be wrong about the sustainability of all of these design factors, but since these are also things I want for my own home, I have an eye for them. I just don't have the money.

There's that cash flow problem ... again.

Oh, well.

Adaptability means I'm ready for anything, right?

How about an infusion of money for a gray water system for my slipping, sliding, will-it-be-there-in-ten-years house?

Yep.

I'm ready for that, too.

I move to the back door, which turns out to be the front door, and as I briefly run my fingers over it, it feels like a mix of recycled wood, fiberglass, and aluminum. It's painted a bright indigo blue. It has no doorknob or handle of any kind, and I push it. The door's well-insulated and makes a tiny *whoomp* as it opens.

I walk in, suddenly feeling nervous.

Maybe this is a mistake.

I want to offer comfort to Anthony.

I don't want to bother him.

## 8

If the outside of DVI looks like an eco-friendly building, the inside is a veritable rainforest.

Trees are everywhere.

Ficus at all corners of the entry—small palms, too. I also spot a lemon tree, a bonsai, and a Boston fern. At the very least, it looks like a nursery, except for the white concrete-and-bamboo front desk and the gleaming white concrete floor.

It all flashes through my senses in seconds.

It looks like eco-*paradise*.

The trees, however, sound like they're weeping.

They might be—but so is a dark-haired woman sitting behind the immaculate white reception desk. Her hands are in front of her face, and she sobs, "Oh, no … no … "

I take one step forward and clear my throat.

I don't want to startle her, but she doesn't seem to hear me.

I take another step and say, "Hello … "

She looks up. Her eyes are puffy and red, and her mouth trembles when she sees me. She whimpers, "Are you here for … for … "

Abruptly, she hiccups and begins to hyperventilate.

I try to make soothing noises. "Okay. No hurry. It's nothing urgent. Take your time."

Then I do what I always do first with every patient, or friend, who's having a hard time: I breathe.

Still looking her in the eyes, I breathe deeply, visibly, and after she watches a couple of my own deep breaths, she begins to take deeper, longer breaths, too.

Finally, I ask, "Are you all right, Ms. … ?"

She breathes out. "Yes … no … "

She brings herself to a stand.

"I'm Christi Shah."

She's tiny, about 5'3, 115 pounds, in her early twenties, and probably a blend of Indian and Asian. I'm pretty good at spotting a biracial mix because I'm a mix, and ever since I was a girl, I've felt an unspoken sense of shared experience with others like me. It can, sometimes, be comforting. I can tell she feels it, too: Her shoulders begin to relax, and her hands slowly drop to her sides.

She takes another long, deep breath and explains, "The police are coming to talk to my boss, Mr. Pryce … "

This time, it's me who needs to … breathe.

Release it.

"Is he here? Anthony Pryce?"

She shakes her head. "No." Her mouth quivers. "He's usually here from early in the morning until late at night. This building's almost brand-new. He helped design it for his wife's family. He wants them to build more like it. But … he's had … had … "

I say gently, "I know. There's been a death in his family."

She nods; her eyes well up with tears again, and she cries, "I heard the news last night. I really like her … Abigail. She comes in a lot. With her dad. I—"

I hear the thick, recycled door abruptly open.

I turn and see that it's painted white on the inside.

I also see: The cops are here. Two big, bruiser-looking men. Neither is familiar to me—they must be San Pedro PD.

But then, as if parting a testosterone sea, a tall, blue-eyed, blonde, buxom, and—I have to admit—gorgeous woman in a tailored powder-blue suit and shiny black pumps struts into the room. She uncurls full, red lips; exposes perfect white teeth; extends a thin, long-fingered hand; and in a deep, sultry voice says, "Ms. Green. Excuse me … *Dr.* Green."

"Hello, Detective."

That's right.

Here she is.

Detective Suzy Whitney.

## 9

Detective *Suze* is quick to escort me outside, where she asks me to wait, in a tone that's more like an order, in her black-and-white police car.

She makes me wait a long time.

I should have known.

I'm out here in the small DVI parking lot, sitting in the rear seat of what seems to be the only Majorca Point PD vehicle at the building. The right rear door is open, and my gold-hued cowboy boots, made out of the finest silky recycled leather, are stretched out and crossed on the pavement, so I'm not incarcerated. But it seems a bit like I am, especially since I overheard the detective whisper, and not too softly, to the officer sitting in the driver's seat, "Lieutenant Brady, I want to talk to this woman. If she gets restless, buy her a soda, or if all else fails, something to eat."

She then turned on her shiny pumps to go back inside, presumably to talk to Christi Shah, the weeping receptionist.

Here we sit.

With nothing better to do, I muse, for a while, on the detective's outfit. Why does she dress like a model on a photo shoot? Well, why not? She's an attractive, and very tall, woman. Then why the heels? Why not designer loafers? It's got to be tough to chase a criminal in heels. Right? Or is her fashionista persona ultimately about something more? Like … is she hoping to get her own reality show? This is the land of Hollywood, after all.

I can't help a wry smile at that.

Even the hard-boiled from homicide can get obsessed with glamour.

As if to affirm my conjecture, Lieutenant Brady sits in the front seat, hunched over, intent on reading a *People*-type magazine.

After half an hour, I give a fairly loud sigh, peer over his shoulder through the wire cage, and ask, "How long does the detective want me to wait?"

He doesn't bother to raise his head from the article he's immersed in, and I can see it's about a pop superstar who recently took her clothes off at a trendy downtown Los Angeles club. He ogles the picture of her body—private parts barely covered by square black inserts.

He says, "I don't know, ma'am." Then he asks, "Do you wanna soda?"

I reply, "Nope, I don't drink soda. Thanks, though."

He grunts. "You wanna burger? Some fries?"

I hold back a wince. "Nope. I'm fine. Thanks."

He shrugs, goes back to "reading."

I sigh again.

Look up at the sky. A few clouds have wafted in.

Abruptly, so do the media choppers. They seem to swoop in without a sound, then hover, loudly. I put my face down fast. I don't want to see if one is KLAT.

I definitely don't want to see Hugo.

I turn my attention to my smartphone.

I decide to distract myself from being stuck in a police car by accessing the Yahoo! Finance page and typing the words "alternative energy" into the "get quotes" display. I scroll down a list, recognize a few names, and I'm about to go visit a website when I notice I'm running out of time.

Confirming the digital clock on my screen with the digital on the black-and-white's dashboard, I'm surprised and appalled to see it's almost 1:30 p.m. I wonder if I should call my patients to let them know I won't be able to make their appointments. The first one, Bethany Hawkings, a ten-year cancer survivor scheduled for 2:30 p.m., is doing so well she'll probably be fine with postponing our session until next week. But I worry about the second one, a nine-year-old boy, Jonah Brown, who suffers from PTSD (the acronym for Post Traumatic Stress Disorder), and I feel he needs to visit with me and Sam. Jonah's one of my equine-assisted therapy patients.

I really don't want to miss my appointment with Jonah.

I could leave, I suppose.

I don't feel any loyalty to Detective Whitney.

But I do feel a loyalty to Charlie.

Abigail would have been her niece.

And Abigail wanted to see me—but, so far, no one knows this but me.

I make a workable compromise: I'll cancel with my first patient, Bethany. I scroll for her number, and that's when I hear Detective Whitney say in a throaty, almost satirical way, "Making a call to your lawyer?"

I look up at her, startled, a flush rising in my face.

My perpetually tan-looking skin has gone red.

Like my hair.

I probably look like I'm on fire.

I *hate* that.

A boy in fifth grade used to call me "Match Head."

I'm humiliated.

Then angry.

But …

For the Pryce family—the memory of Charlie—I've got to be nice.

Sort of.

I slide the phone back into my pocket and say, "Oh, yes. That's funny, Detective Whitney. Glad to see in your line of work you've kept your sense of humor."

Her smile vanishes.

I decide to ask a few questions—I'm good at that. I start with the obvious. "What do you want to talk to me about?"

But she's good at questioning, too, and in a perfectly red-lipped kind of way, she asks, "What are you here for, Dr. Green?" She smiles down at me, patronizingly. "Are you feeling nostalgic?"

Oh, so she knows I knew Charlie.

What else does she know?

Did Hugo tell her?

Momentarily, I'm insecure.

Then, consciously, forcefully, I shake off the self-doubt and stand from the black-and-white.

Detective Whitney, however, quickly extends a red-nailed index finger and tells me, firmly, "We'll talk in the car. The helicopters are much too noisy."

Brady's still looking at the magazine, but I can tell by the little quiver in the back of his jaw, next to his right ear, that he's suddenly paying close attention.

*¿Qué pasa?* What's going on?

I get back in, moving over to the other side to allow the detective to sit, and I watch her smooth the light-blue silk of her skirt over her knees. She's so tall that she has to crunch and fidget, just a bit, but it gives me time to conjure a response. I'm trying to get a fix on this woman.

In a way, I breathe her in: her scent, her aura.

Her *nature*.

I sense diligence, and high intelligence, too, but also great frustration, along with a massive ego, as if internally she's so caught up with herself that she's wrapped tightly—no, make that *coiled*—around her mind's reflection, like a snake. *That's* what she reminds me of: a Southern Pacific rattlesnake. They live all over southern California: in the hills, the canyons, even at the beach. I see them occasionally when I'm riding Sam.

My horse and I will back up slowly.

Both of us ...

*Keeping our cool.*

It may sound like a cliché, but that's the way to deal with them because rattlers are actually heat sensitive; it's how they detect their prey, and the hotter or more fearful their prey becomes, the more information on the species and its size, location, and level of vulnerability the snake is able to discern. Basically, their reptilian brains receive heat images like optic nerve impulses.

So that's what I've got to do in this instance—keep my cool.

Back up from any attitude I may have had, tell the truth, and get outta here.

"I was just looking for Anthony Pryce. I Googled his business address," I say, in a purposely non-threatening tone. I slowly motion my hand in the direction of the towering DVI structure and continue, "But he's not there."

I gaze, placidly, into her baby-blue eyes, and my voice exudes calm. "I just wanted to give my condolences because, as you might have heard"—I do my best to remain the epitome of relaxed—"perhaps from your good friend at KLAT ..."

She's quick to confirm his name. "You mean Gabriel?"

I surmise, at this point, both intuitively and clinically, that she must get a feeling of control, maybe even ownership, by saying his name. She rolls it over her tongue again: "Gabriel."

Inwardly, I feel a little queasy, but outwardly I continue, slow, cool, making sure not to mention his name, not even his middle name, as if letting her know I certainly have no control of him, no ownership, and absolutely no interest. "That's right, *him*. I happened to run into him last night. It was awful. Poor Abigail Pryce. But then, he probably told you, I knew her father, Anthony Pryce, a long time ago. And Charlene ... " My voice trails. I sense Charlie's wistfulness in my own voice.

Strange.

My spine tingles in the closed, stuffy car.

I turn red again, confused.

Detective Whitney picks up on it, leans toward me, and says, with a subtle yet phlegmy rattle in her throat, "Yes, Gabe told me."

Now it's *Gabe?*

Ugh.

It's as if he betrayed me.

With her.

As if they're conspiring—but why would they do that?

I'm feeling self-doubt again. Feeling like prey—frantic yet inquisitive. Like one of the squirrels that run up and down the bluffs—a tasty morsel for rattlers—but, oddly enough, they usually escape.

I know Detective Whitney senses it: the heat of my fear, my vulnerability.

I think of the squirrels.

What do *they* do when confronted with a rattlesnake?

How do they defend themselves?

It comes to me.

Squirrels are able to discern how much danger a rattlesnake

represents—how big, how fast, how close—by kicking sand to provoke the snake into rattling out more and more information about itself.

I do a little sand-kicking myself.

I say, "You must be so knowledgeable about forensics, Detective. I wish I could say the same for myself. For instance, Charlie's body was very bloody after she fell from the cliff. It's interesting, don't you think, that Abigail's wasn't?"

In such a way, I hope to stroke her ego, just enough so she'll feel overly confident, or more so than she already does, and feed me some info.

Because …

I don't understand things like forensics, do I?

No …

But I do understand intuition, and I've learned to listen to it. The way I feel that Abigail didn't jump, as Charlie did. That she was pushed.

Detective Whitney says, "You noticed that, did you? That your friend Charlie was bloodier than Abigail?"

"I did notice. But I don't understand it."

She replies, "Well, lest we forget, your friend Charlene *jumped.*" She tells me this in a biting, cruel way, as if trying to hurt me with the details. "I read the reports. It's obvious. She had absolutely no trajectory and bounced off almost every rock, all the way down."

I shake my head, envisioning it, trying not to. Failing. Detective Whitney knows it, and when I look at her, her eyes are even brighter as she continues. "Any fool could put that together."

I nod, mumbling, "Any fool."

Whitney continues, "But Abigail's death was different. We've heard from a source, a hiker, that there may have been someone with her on The Point last night. Someone—"

I almost shriek and cover my mouth in reflex. "So she *was* pushed."

She turns to look at me full on, eyes glinting. "What did you say?"

Uh-oh.

I'm silent: a furry little rabbit.

Whitney is coming in for the strike.

She's going to swallow me whole.

Eat my head.

What should I do? Kick up more dirt? Finally, I simply deny the last moment ever happened and ask, "Someone was with her?"

The detective practically spits. "Yes. Didn't you hear me?"

"I thought I did," I reply softly. "I thought that's what you said."

She glares at me, pink tongue darting out over red lips.

I do my best to appear … foolish.

I shrug.

The rabbit and the snake.

Prey and predator—utterly perplexed by each other.

Good.

My face is on fire again.

But that's fine, too, because Detective Whitney has disclosed quite a bit.

I know it seems bizarre.

But the jacaranda could be right.

If someone was with Abigail …

Maybe *this person* pushed her.

Which means she was …

Murdered.

The detective's voice rattles deep in her throat. "We'll see what the coroner has to say. I may have more questions for you, since you're so close to the family. You'll be in town?"

"Umm," I reply, not sure how to answer.

I can't be a suspect, right?

Just then a KLAT news van enters the parking lot, pulling up alongside the other news vans.

She sees it, too.

"Can I go now?" I blurt.

Hugo may not even be in there.

Oops.

Thought too soon.

There he is, hopping out of the sliding door with his usual panache.

Palpable excitement fills the detective's eyes, and when she looks back at me it's with irritation. She turns, opens her door, and with a deft smoothing of her skirt and a dismissive flick of her hand, she says, "Yes, go."

"Okay," I reply.

But she's already extending her long legs out of the car.

I open my own door and slide out.

"Bye," I say to Brady.

He grunts.

I creep around the cruiser, head down, not wanting to be seen by you-know-who, but as I give a backward glance, Hugo waves.

The thing is: Detective Suze and I are both still so close to the black-and-white, I can't tell if it's a wave for me …

Or for her.

I let it go.

Hugo.

Detective Suzy Whitney.

Charlie. Abigail. Anthony Pryce. Christi Shah.

I let it all slip away.

Sure, it's another slipping-land metaphor, but really, whether it's a traditional psychology session or an ecopsychological walk on the beach, a therapist must learn to leave her own stuff at the proverbial door: relationship, murder, a bad hair day—you've got to let it fall ...

Away.

For a while.

My session with Bethany Hawkings is a pleasure. She finds so much joy in life because she never expected to survive breast cancer for this long, and as we stroll by one of the many coves that line Majorca Point—this one a small, dew-drop-shaped inlet—I say, "You did it, Bethany. You did it by *doing*."

Bethany throws back her pert, dimpled chin and gives a long, ebullient laugh. "By picking up trash, you mean?"

"That, too," I reply, smiling.

We both carry trash bags, small shovels, and picks.

This is what we came up with ten years ago, when Bethany was first diagnosed. She'd been referred to me by a colleague because she'd wanted to consult with a therapist who would understand her desire not only to survive cancer but also do it as "greenly" as possible. We took our first walk by this very cove, talking about her various treatment options, and we began to notice many bright colors poking out from between the rocks in the tide pools exposed by the waning tide.

When we looked closer, stepping out onto the long, flat, sea-worn stones that form the deep pools where sea urchins, sea cucumbers, and sea stars make their homes, we were shocked to find that all those pretty colors came from plastic of some kind. More than the oversize pieces of fallen mansions that litter the Majorca Point coastline, these were hundreds of tiny shreds of plastic from streamers, shopping bags, toys, balloons, you name it, stuck in the wave-pummeled rock, and because they were so colorful, they had likely been mistaken for food and eaten by fish, and probably by birds, too.

We were both silent, on our haunches, looking down at a broken piece of vivid red plastic spoon that was lodged in a crack between two large rocks—a spoon that would outlive us both, cancer or not.

Bethany finally said, "That's it. I want to clean up this cove. I want to come here every week and clean the trash out of the pools. I adore tide pools. I always have."

And that's what we've been doing for ten years.

Walking and talking with our trash bags, picking out the plastic.

There were studies done, years ago, on altruism: giving, sharing, and the health benefits associated with it. There's also the healing benefit of exercise and the release of endorphins. And, of course, the healing of talk therapy—just being with someone else and letting it out.

Bethany is living testament to all that.

"It was you," I say again. "Your idea. I just followed."

We stand still for a moment, looking out at the ocean. The October afternoon sun casts a shimmering glow on the water, like liquid light, and the tide's on its way back to shore, one wave breaching the next. We step backward in tandem, a natural rhythm. Then we both giggle like girls as a large swell overtakes our feet. I hold Bethany's bag of trash as she races into the frothy sea to rescue a purple flip-flop. I squish down in my reef walkers, and the water feels warm. Too warm for October, I know.

Still, we have a glorious time, and Bethany Hawkings—forty-eight years young, with two grown children; just married again to the same man and going on their second honeymoon to Australia in three weeks to snorkel at the Great Barrier Reef   has never looked better.

Well, *that* session was a breeze.

—⁓—

My session with Jonah Brown isn't so easy—for him or me.

He's nine years old, with hair that's redder than mine and a scowl that almost always turns down his wide mouth, and there are lines of anger and consternation developing between his eyebrows.

Jonah's waiting for me in his grandmother's sedan when I arrive, right on time, with only still-damp reef walkers to betray my hurried pace up the hill. I pull into the dirt lot of The Falling MP Stables and stop the car.

I quickly change into socks and cowboy boots and give a smile and wave to Grandma Brown, who nods. Jonah gets out of the passenger side and slouches over to me, wiping his hands on his gray T-shirt, smudged with ketchup and ice cream and dirty fingerprints.

I ask, "Burger King?"

He grins a little, and, knowing Jonah, I'm betting it's because I've guessed wrong, which he confirms: "McDonald's."

I nod. "Okay."

I make a note in my mind to ask his grandma if he's gotten any DHA lately—preferably from a plant-based source, like flaxseed oil. DHA, or docosahexaenoic acid, has been found to be invaluable to healthy brain development and the prevention of all sorts of psychological and neurological ailments such as depression, myriad stress disorders, and even ADHD and ADD.

Jonah shuffles past me into the stables, kicking dirt up with his boots.

I notice he's got brand-new cowboy boots on, and my first inclination is to tell him, "Awesome boots," or words to that effect. But the great irony is, even though Jonah's been coming to see me for over a month, he doesn't like talking to me. In fact, the less I have to say is usually better because the core of equine-assisted therapy is the patient's relationship with the horse, and Jonah loves—and I mean truly loves—Sam.

I walk behind him. His pace speeds up as he gets closer to Sam's stall, and he's murmuring, "Sammy. Hi, Sammy ..." Sam snorts in greeting.

Before I can even get to the lead rope, Jonah's got Sam out of the stall and standing at the crossties that he eagerly clips to Sam's harness so that he can begin grooming. My big blue grooming pail is full of the usual accoutrements, and Jonah knows them all well. First, he takes out the shoe pick, and, bending over, he gently, even tenderly, lifts up Sam's front left hoof and, while resting it on his right knee, starts to clean out the caked dirt.

Last night, I purposely did a very light cleaning of Sam's hooves so Jonah could do just that.

*Last night ...*

After Abigail Pryce's body was discovered.

I shake my head.

Wrong thought.

Not here. Not now.

Jonah, like many people, especially children suffering from PTSD as well as the depression that often accompanies it, can sense my mood, anyone's mood, anyone's level of inherent danger, or potential for betrayal, or just plain absentmindedness, because from their perspectives, even another person's momentary lapse of attention feels like a gaping hole, leaving them defenseless and vulnerable to attack.

Jonah has experienced severe trauma and loss. His parents' divorce, by all Department of Child and Family Services reports, was devastating, as they apparently waged a near war on each other, including domestic abuse that was perpetrated by both They'd promised in court to attend anger management classes in order to retain custody of Jonah, but eventually, sadly, they'd abandoned him. Jonah's father had left for parts unknown. Soon after, his mother left for another man on the opposite side of the country. Grandma Brown has recently been given full custody. Then, last session, Jonah was very excited, telling me his mother had finally written him a letter. But Grandma Brown called me just two days ago to let me know her daughter still has made no effort to communicate with Jonah. To be honest, Grandma's not much for communication either, her affect as flat, tired, and disenchanted as some of the incarcerated women I used to treat when I had an internship at a maximum-security prison. But what's most concerning to me is that Jonah obviously felt compelled to fabricate a story about his mother—an intricate story—because the letter his mother supposedly wrote to him was very sweet and promised she'd be "home" by Christmas.

Now, I worry that if his grandmother is correct, and his mom truly hasn't contacted him: *What will happen to Jonah at Christmas?*

I'm not sure what to do.

I don't know whether to bring it up, or not.

Jonah needs hope, and love, so he's created it in his mind. He's given himself something to look forward to.

That's not something I want to take away.

I smile at him, making sure I appear benign, because he's watching me closely as he cleans Sam's hooves, his gray eyes filtering my every nuance with suspicion and doubt.

He speaks defiantly. "It's time for me to ride Sam."

I nod. "Yep, it is."

He carefully puts a white-and-gold riding blanket on Sam's back and retrieves the saddle from the tack room. He climbs onto a stool to put the saddle on while I release the crossties, remove Sam's harness, and slip on his bridle.

I give the reins to Jonah, and he leads Sam out of the stables. From there, they walk the fifty or so feet to the outside riding ring.

There are no other riders. I scheduled it this way. Jonah is one of three equine-assisted therapy patients, and the trainers at The Falling MP are my friends, so we work out a schedule that's good for all of us.

Jonah gets up on Sam, I adjust the stirrups to his legs, and they begin to slowly amble around the white-fenced ring.

The sun begins to set, and it glows a deep scarlet, like last night.

I suddenly feel …

*Miserable.*

The last twenty-four hours have taken their toll, and Jonah senses it.

I see him looking at me as he and Sam walk by, and I do my best to keep a smile on my face, even though I want to weep.

*Ay, Dios mío.*

I'm having a *muy* hard time.

Images of Charlie hitting every stone …

And then, that inexplicable horse magic happens.

Maybe because of my own vulnerability—my own PTSD

symptoms brought on by Abigail's death—Sam gently cuts across the ring, to my side.

And, maybe, Jonah realizes Sam is loyal to me, and I might not be such a bad person after all.

Whatever it is …

Jonah starts to cry.

"My mom didn't ever write me … *She doesn't care.*"

I look up at him, tears in my own eyes.

Jonah leans over and throws his arms around Sam's neck, sobbing.

I lean against Sam.

Throughout history, horses have carried us to new lands, helped us to overcome snow and rain and starvation, stoically assisted us in building cities, even empires, but mostly, they've just

Been there.

Ever dependable.

Non-judgmental.

True.

The three of us stay like that for a while.

When Grandma Brown comes for Jonah, he looks me in the eye, for the first time, and whispers, "Thanks."

"Thanks to you, too," I reply softly.

We both found safety in Sam.

It's the beginning of a bond.

At last.

—∿—

After Grandma Brown steers the sedan down the winding road, I go back to the outdoor ring where Sam's tied to a white gatepost, waiting patiently, as he always does, knowing as well as I do that it's time for our twilight ride.

I adjust the stirrups back to my own longer length and give Sam a loving scratch behind each of his ears.

I grab onto the horn and hoist myself up into the saddle, and we stroll over the smooth, rolling bluffs and down the hill. I breathe in the sage and the sea, roll my head and shoulders, and start to relax. Sam picks his way, ever adroit, along the thin, twisting dirt paths that lead to the water, and I don't stop him, don't rein him in or turn him around, even though I'm pretty sure of where he's going.

Does he somehow have the idea that Hugo might still be there—with an offering of peppermint candy?

Hmmm.

Sam would walk a thousand miles for that.

But Hugo's not here.

No …

It's not Hugo but another man who stands alone at the thick orange metal tubing that blocks off Charlie's cliff.

The man seems to watch as the sun slides into the ocean, the fireball's last descent until tomorrow.

But Abigail will have no tomorrow.

My heart lurches.

I haven't seen him in almost twenty years.

But I know …

It's Anthony Pryce.

nthony?"

My voice is low as I slowly get down from Sam and gently let the reins drop to the ground. I'm careful to step over the yellow crime-scene tape that's fallen to the withered grass, and I almost tiptoe because if he doesn't respond, I'll leave.

I don't want to disturb his reverie.

I can only see the back of his head: the wavy hair, streaked with sun, that curls at his shoulders—surfer hair, very much like Charlie's. I'm reminded that we used to surf right below this cliff, too, a long time ago, taking a steep, winding path down to the ocean.

That memory cuts through me—the way, at times, we lived the teenage equivalent of the California dream.

I turn back to Sam, realizing I'm still sad—for Charlie, for Abigail, and for losing a way of life that seems irretrievable: when plastic didn't line the coves, when wild bees and birds didn't inexplicably drop from the skies. I certainly don't want to burden Anthony with my own feelings of loss. Then I hear, "Emerald?"

I can't help but gasp.

I haven't heard anyone call me that name since Charlie last spoke it.

I turn around, facing the night, a single red tendril of flame shooting across the nearly black horizon behind him. His light-colored eyes appear to glow an impossible jade-green in that last shard of light, and I repeat in a whisper, "Anthony?"

In a moment, he's by my side, holding me.

Charlie's funeral sweeps my mind.

Anthony held me just so then.

His body shaking in the same way, wracked with the horrible pain of bereavement and the repression of tears that won't come.

It was like that for me, too.

With Charlie …

And my mom and dad.

I couldn't cry until I'd fully accepted they were gone because to cry before that final stage of the grief cycle would have been too frightening. I think a part of me was keeping them alive, in my mind, by withholding my tears. As if, somehow, I could forever hold them close by trapping my sorrow, like water in a dam.

Well, that sure shows my controlling side, doesn't it?

I wonder: Does Anthony have that same need to control?

I whisper, "I'm sorry, Anthony. Very sorry."

He's much taller than I am, but his face is buried in my neck, and my arms circle his large, quivering shoulders. Then, as quickly as he reached for me, he lets me go and looks at me, his mouth tight.

"I … I can't talk about it right now."

I can barely see him—there are no lights at this park, and the marine layer has started to roll in, thick fog blocking out the moon and stars.

"I understand," I say with a little hush. "I'm so sorry. If you need anything, please, let me know."

I hear him more than see him as he extends a hand to my face, touches my cheek, and replies, "I'll call you."

I nod. "Any time."
I turn and walk to Sam.
I'm certain: I'll never see him again.

—⚬—

The next morning, he calls me.
"Emerald," he says. "I need your help."
So—for Charlie, Abigail, and Anthony, and with the hard-earned insight that withholding my own grief has, at times, left my life as bereft of comfort and attachment as a drought-stricken plain—I go.

# 12

nthony rushed me his home address over the phone, and I wrote it down without really looking at the significance of this location. But after driving for more than an hour, I get past the traffic-from-hell on the North 405 and West 10 freeways to exit into the upscale beach city of Santa Monica. I take the Fourth Street exit, make a right on Ocean, go past Santa Monica Boulevard, Wilshire, and Montana, then make another right on Rosarita.

Only then does it begin to seep into my consciousness just how well off Anthony Pryce really is.

I turn into a driveway that's discreetly hidden by the branches of several thriving hundred-year-old eucalyptus trees. I stop at the white iron gates where a man in a white booth, dressed in a white uniform, with a salt-and-pepper mustache, takes my name, makes a call, nods, and solemnly lets me through. I wind around a large, circular white marble fountain that holds two white marble angels cavorting in water that's being spouted out from another white marble angel's trumpet. By the time I look up, craning my neck way up to see the three-story, white Georgian Tudor mansion in its vine-dripping glory, I'm realizing he's not only well off: He's *hugely* wealthy.

I pull my little red Ford hybrid behind a white Jaguar and a white stretch limo, and I swing my cowboy boots onto the ornately designed red brick driveway. I'm wearing my standard hip-rider loose-fit jeans and a silky, black, short-sleeved bamboo shirt. I hear a parrot squawking from deep inside the enormous house. It sounds as if it's crying, "Abby! Abby!"

I sigh and begin to climb the white marble stairs.

I can't help but wonder how much it cost to transport all this marble, and what method of shipment was used, and how many carbon footprints that left on the planet, because stone like this is far, far away from being local.

I'm musing on the fact that the house, for all its glory, appears to be the antithesis of the DVI office building in San Pedro with its concrete and gray water and obvious attention to green materials and sustainable practices.

Really—this place is like a shrine to ecological devastation.

¿Qué pasa?

And then Anthony opens the door.

He's wearing a black T-shirt, khaki trousers, and leather sandals, all of it worn-looking, but the inner sanctum of the mansion behind him looks positively bejeweled. An enormous round chandelier with diamond-shaped crystals (even bigger than the ones I'd found on the beach in Majorca Point) hangs from a domed ceiling, and it appears heavy enough to bring the whole house crashing down if we got a sizeable shaker.

Hmmm.

Don't want to be here during the Big One.

I also spot three large, lush indigo-blue-and-red tapestries lining a massive wall to the left, a red-carpeted mahogany staircase with gold banisters, and, to the right of the steps, a towering suit of silver and gold armor.

Anthony reaches out his hand and clasps my own warmly.

I get a chance to look at him in the sunlight, seeing the dark circles under his light-green eyes, his mouth still tight.

I also get the chance to realize …

He's gorgeous.

"Well, no zits now, Charlie," I silently report to my long-dead friend.

What else can you do when your deceased childhood friend's predictions for her older brother's ugly future don't quite jibe with present-day reality?

I walk next to him through the immense foyer, and we enter the very definition of a "great room." It's vast and elegant, and the theme is, again, white—which, as I recall, was also a theme at the DVI building—white concrete-and-bamboo desk, white concrete floors. But these white floors are, once more, made of marble from some faraway location, and there's also a huge white marble fireplace. The white furnishings are mostly leather, and I'm willing to bet that it's not recycled leather.

I feel confused by the incongruity with the DVI building—and disappointed. My eyes reflexively dart for other eco-inconsistencies, but Anthony has already taken my arm and is leading me down three wide, highly polished stairs.

Ugh. More marble.

I'll think about the hypocrisy later.

Now, I must focus on the faces in front of me.

There's a gathering, and I search for Anthony's mom and dad. I think they're the sad-looking older couple dressed in matching white tennis outfits, sitting very close together on a white loveseat. I notice that although they both have gray hair, they're remarkably fit, with deep, bronze tans.

Anthony says, "Mom, Dad, you remember Esmeralda Green."

The two tan people nod morosely.

"Hello, dear Esmeralda," murmurs Mrs. Pryce.

I make my way over to the white loveseat but am abruptly approached by a wispy cloud of a woman with smooth white hair cut so close to her scalp that I can see the pink skin and blue veins underneath. Her skin is extremely pale, and her tiny, sharp-yet-classical features are heavily powdered, like a geisha's. Her eyes are big, dark, watery smudges. She's wearing a skintight, low-cut, floor-length black leather dress. Her breath is a subtle combination of lavender and pepper. She offers me a delicate, very pale hand, and says breathlessly, "Hello, there. I'm Penelope De Vos. I'm Abigail's mother. Anthony's wife."

I clasp her moving hand and offer my condolences.

She wisps away.

I wonder if Penelope's the reason Anthony lives in this oversized monstrosity? But is she also the reason he's got a cutting-edge green office building in San Pedro? Or am I blaming her for the bad and giving him credit for the good? Why? Because I know him? I don't want to be biased. Besides, it can be difficult, sometimes, to find the individuals within couples who've been married for a long time. Still, given the contradictions I'm seeing—her dressed up, for instance, him dressed down—I'm guessing these two are as different as night and day.

Anthony has my arm again and swiftly glides me over to his mom and dad. In a low, soft voice, he says, "Esmeralda's a psychologist now, Mom."

I flick him a glance.

How did he know that?

He nods and adds, "Er ... an ... ecopsychologist."

Must have Googled me.

Then he kneels in front of his mom, pulling me down, too.

I'm a bit flustered—what is he doing?

But when Mrs. Pryce starts to talk, I'm made fully aware of why

77

I've been invited here. She begins to ramble, "If you talk to me it will kill me, if you look at me it will kill me, if I have to sit here for one more minute it will kill me, because I'm dying, yes, I'm dying, and can't you see that you're killing me, Anthony, Penelope, Esmeralda, Abigail … Where is Abigail? Does she know she's destroying me by being late? She's always late, always, and it's killing me, killing me …"

Then she puts her head on her husband's shoulder, eyes glassy.

He gives her a sorrowful, devoted smile and remains silent.

Anthony, still holding my arm, pulls me up to my feet.

He whispers, "Can you help her? She started … saying these things … last night. But we've got funeral arrangements to make, and we're busy trying to keep the media out of all this."

I instinctively listen for the whirring of a KLAT chopper.

Not a sound.

Besides, I kind of think the De Vos family can silence the news media.

Anthony continues, "I've also got to see some detective, Suzy Whitney, about Abigail. I was supposed to meet her yesterday at my—"

I probably say it too quickly: "The sustainable building. It's marvelous."

Now it's his turn to give me the questioning glance.

I explain. "I was trying to find you to give my condolences …"

A piercing scream interrupts me.

It echoes through the house.

13

A nthony keeps his tone as calm as possible. "Mom, Dad, please don't move."

The scream continues unabated.

Mrs. Pryce says matter-of-factly, "If you tell me to stay here it will kill me." Her head still rests on her husband's shoulder; her eyes appear nearly catatonic.

Anthony barks, "Joseph."

A white-clad butler is immediately next to him. He hands the older Mr. Pryce a glass of water with no ice in a crystal tumbler, with an exquisitely shaped lemon rind perched upon the sparkling edge and a long white straw. Anthony's dad urges his wife to sip through the straw. She does, dribbling a little, but at least she's taking sustenance.

The scream becomes a howl.

Anthony turns and starts to run—so do I.

We race through the main entrance, past the suit of armor, then veer left and under the stairs, down a white marble hallway to the back of the vast house into a room on the right.

It turns out to be a recreation room, scattered with twelve plush, white leather recliners, six huge flat-panel TVs mounted on three white walls, a massive pool table—and a picture of Abigail hanging on the fourth wall. A full-length photograph, it captures not only her beautiful, almost perfectly symmetrical face but also her body, slim and graceful. She's dressed in a white graduation gown, and the white cap with the gold tassel is in her right hand. It must be her high school graduation, taken just a year ago.

Penelope has collapsed onto the white carpet directly beneath it, and she's sobbing. "Oh, my baby. My sweet baby. Please, come back to me. *Please.*"

Anthony goes to her and lifts her by her thin arms.

She lashes out. "Don't touch me! Don't ever touch me again! If you hadn't allowed her to get involved with that documentary ... that environmental documentary ... she wouldn't be dead right now. I know it! Daddy always said that we De Voses needed to fly under the radar. That's what he said! We needed to be out of the public eye if we were going to survive our ... our ... success!"

I hear Anthony mutter under his breath, "Some of us need our own success. Our own identities."

I stand there, watching them. Anthony appears sad. Penelope glares at him with hard, cold hatred.

Her voice is vicious. "You should have offered her a job yourself. You should have kept her close to the family. You ... you ..."

Anthony says with a sigh, "She had her own conscience, Pen. Her own way of thinking."

She sneers. "You weakling."

Then Penelope puts her two hands atop her ghostly, pale, bald head and runs from the room.

Anthony grimaces.

"I'm sorry you had to see that, Emerald," he says. "Penelope's very upset."

"I understand," I reply with heartfelt empathy.

I can't imagine anything worse than losing a child.

Anthony looks ready to cry.

I wonder if I should reach out to him again, but I just stand quietly, breathing, in my way. Here to offer support.

The vast recreation room almost feels peaceful after a few minutes.

Anthony's staring lovingly up at the picture of his daughter.

We both take a moment of respite.

Just then, Joseph bursts into the room, replete with apologies. "I'm sorry, sir, I tried to stop her—"

For a moment, I don't know what he's talking about. Then, who struts into the room but Detective Suzy Whitney. She moves with speed, stealth, and supreme confidence—until she sees me.

I can tell she's surprised, to the point where she nearly trips as she transitions on her shiny black heels from the ultra-polished white marble hallway to the white carpet.

I bite my tongue, breathe, and wait for her to recover.

The last thing I want, or need, is for her to blame me for a broken ankle.

I'm standing near the pool table, in front of Abigail's graduation picture. Detective Whitney quickly regains her composure and pointedly makes her way over to me in a truly fabulous, tailored, lilac-colored silk suit. She stops and takes a long, full-on view of Abigail. Then she angles her baby blues at me and chides, "We've got to stop meeting like this, Dr. Green. If you keep butting into my investigation, I might have to arrest you."

"For what?"

"For hindering an investigation, for starters."

I try to put my words together without slapping her across the face, but Anthony walks over to the detective, his right hand extended, and says, "Esmeralda's a friend, and she's been kind enough to come help me today."

"Really?" replies Whitney. "With friends like this …"

"Yes?" Anthony says, obviously defending me.

Whitney, wisely, lets it go.

"Nothing," she says. "I assume you are Anthony Pryce?"

"I am," he answers.

"Is there somewhere we can talk?" She looks over at me, then back at him. "Privately?"

"Sure," he says.

Whitney turns to me. "I have a few more questions for you, too. Since you're here, I'd like to see you in about an hour. Is there somewhere you could wait?"

Like yesterday at the DVI building, it sounds like an order.

I want to ask, "Where's Lieutenant Brady with a soda?"

Anthony faces me and attempts a smile. "Why don't you relax in the garden, Emerald? It's just down the hall, to the right. I'll have Joseph bring you something."

I nod.

He takes my hand for a moment. "Maybe you could meet with my mom after you talk with the detective?"

"Fine," I say.

He tries to give me a look of encouragement, but his eyes are drooping, and his mouth is now crushed.

It's all too much.

The detective sweeps him off to parts of the house unknown.

—⁂—

On my way to the garden, I realize I'm thirsty, so I find my way to the kitchen, taking only a couple of wrong turns. The kitchen—if you can call it a kitchen; it looks more like a hangar at LAX to me—is, to my surprise, empty, and I open six cupboards before finding a small, ordinary water glass.

I'm holding the glass under the faucet when I hear a voice from across the room.

"What are you doing?"

I jump. It's Joseph, standing in the doorway, giving me an oddly panicked look. "I'm just getting a glass of water. Is that okay?"

He's at my side in an instant, and he reaches for the water glass. "Please, allow me to get you a glass of spring water."

I shake my head and reply, "No, thanks. I'm fine with the tap water." All those plastic bottles. All that waste, when studies show that the vast majority of municipal water is actually safer than bottled.

But he already has his hand wrapped around my glass, and he wrests it away. "Or how about some iced tea?"

I give up. "If you have something herbal, that would be nice."

"I'll bring it to you," he says. "In the garden."

"Okay."

I make my way outside.

# 14

I walk through the wide, white French doors onto an enormous white veranda and sit down on a white, plush-cushioned iron chair under an umbrella-topped white iron table, feeling like a zombie in a movie.

I'm experiencing my own PTSD symptoms—an unconscious, lingering sense of doom, which arose in me so long ago, after Charlie's death, and then when my mom and dad were killed in that terrible plane crash. Stress can trigger PTSD; it can lie dormant in anyone who's experienced it before. With me, since I know exactly where it comes from, I can usually allay the symptoms before they escalate into something more serious.

Still, for a moment, I can't help but feel that danger may be hiding around any corner, even in this pristine, impeccably tended garden under the brilliant blue sky of a too-warm October morning.

I breathe in the fragrance of autumn blossoms.

My eyes almost hungrily scan for any source of vegetation I can fuse with in my eco-Zen way. I take in a bushy abundance of gorgeous, multi-hued roses and a vast expanse of carpet-like green grass.

I get up.

*Is* it carpet?

What do they call it?

Astroturf?

Didn't a big environmental group want to ban it? I think it's made from a type of plastic that could leech into the soil and groundwater, contaminating it. But didn't another big environmental group come out in favor of it? I remember them citing that if you've just *got* to have grass, the fake stuff serves a very important water conservation purpose. And this year, California, particularly the county of Los Angeles, has implemented very tight restrictions on water usage, especially for lawns.

So, during drought years, seeing plastic grass in southern California isn't all that uncommon.

What a tough conundrum we're in, though.

In our attempt to save our water supply, we end up polluting what we have left.

Some things never seem to change.

I wonder why the Pryce family—or the De Vos family—doesn't make this backyard into a showplace for drought-resistant vegetation?

It's not as if they don't have the money.

Thinking of money …

Or other people's money …

I flip out my phone and Google De Vos. Again.

I come up with …

A Midwest dynasty.

It began in the late 1800s, in Iowa, with agriculture: corn, wheat, and alfalfa. Charles De Vos—a Belgian-born, hardworking, soft-spoken man—managed to turn a little over fifty thousand dollars of inherited capital into an empire estimated today to be worth tens of billions. In fact, DVI has become one of the largest corporations in the world and now owns massive amounts of land, farms, salt mines, coal mines, slaughterhouses, and various factories all over the U.S., Russia, Central and South America, and Africa, where they produce oil, coal, and natural gas, as well as grain, beef, pork, poultry, coffee, salt, and a sugar substitute.

I put the phone back in my pocket.

Anthony Pryce is married to a lot of money—more money than I can fathom.

And, despite his green office building, he's married to a company that does a lot of ecological damage.

So, what does that make him? A hypocrite? A charlatan?

I look around.

This kind of wealth has, historically, been made by the rampant plunder of natural resources, and no matter how *mucho* dazzling it looks—it's just one more exquisitely constructed façade for eco-destruction.

And yet I can … almost … understand the seduction.

I take in the Olympic-sized pool at the end of the enormous yard in one of the priciest real estate markets in the country, if not the world: The vivid green running alongside the wide white swath of immaculate tile that surrounds the turquoise-blue water is conjuring up images of an island paradise, and I begin walking, utterly compelled to dip my hand into the glistening water.

On the way, I bend down to touch the grass beneath my boots, and I am shocked that it's real.

What kind of fines do they pay the utility company for the gallons of water it must take per day to keep this much grass this amazingly green?

Or do they pay the fines to Santa Monica?

Or do they bribe somebody?

I hate to be so cynical, but, really, is this what happens when you're super rich?

You become used to getting your own way, no matter what. You get used to believing you're above it all—above even water restrictions put in place to assure that the rest of us have enough to combat fires and keep trees, plants, animals, and food sources alive, while ultimately not dying of thirst—because you can pay for it.

I do a little ecopsychological speculation.

Is that where all this ... white ... comes from?

Clean, white, clean.

The house.

Clean, white, clean.

The furniture.

Clean, white, clean.

The marble floors.

Clean, white, clean.

The thin layer of hair on Penelope's head?

Clean, white, clean.

Has it permeated their psyches?

Don't mind the graft, the oil spills, the contamination, desertification, complete devastation of land.

We're clean.

I'm walking on the green, very green grass, to the edge of the blue, very blue pool, and I ...

*Fuse* with something.

It comes to me.

Slow.

Soft.

With the fluidity of water.

I sense ...

A darkness at the bottom of the pool. Something vile. Something hidden. Something very ... dirty.

Then I hear it ...

A slithering through the grass. A voice: It's Charlie, whispering, "Follow it, Emerald. You're on track. It's vile. It's *obscene*."

My eyes are saucers, staring at the long rectangle. The pool is still filled with pretty blue water but now, it has a face.

A drowning face.

Howling.

## 15

My phone's happy little bells begin to chime.

My hands are shaking, my eyes fixated on the water.

But there's nothing in the pool.

Nothing at all.

I answer, not bothering to check who is calling—I don't care—I just want to talk to a real person about real things.

"Ez," says Hugo, "are you there?"

"Where?" I breathe anxiously, feeling the sun hot on my skin again, my senses returning, because I was lost in some kind of eco-psychic vortex. I sit down hard on a white marble bench near the pool, kick off my boots, and yank off my socks. I need to feel the ground, but it's just more white stone, so I get back up, walk fast to the grass, and nudge my toes into the tickly blades.

I sigh, relieved.

"Ez." Hugo's tone verges on urgent. "Are you all right?"

Hugo …

"Yes," I snap, realizing, right then, that I'm still annoyed with him. "I'm fine."

"Why do you sound so frightened?"

Oh, no, I can't play the question game—not right now.

"I'm not frightened."

He's silent. We know each other in this way. He's debating whether to question me, or to go ahead and show his emotions.

"I was worried about you," he says, his voice muffled.

I nearly melt.

I scrunch my toes farther into the grass, unconsciously digging for the sweet, fecund earth underneath. The fear of a few moments ago is gone; the pool twinkles like a benevolent cove in the ocean, a breeze wafts the sultry, deep scent of hundreds of roses to surround me, and I almost feel wrapped in his arms.

Then Hugo lets me have it.

"What were you doing at DVI yesterday?"

Here we go with the questions.

"What do you mean, 'What was I doing?'"

"What were you doing?"

"Is that really your business?"

"Are you being rational?"

"What is *that* supposed to mean?"

"Ez, I don't—I don't want you to get hurt. There's something going on with your friend Charlene's brother, Anthony Pryce. His daughter is dead, and whether it's by foul play or not doesn't matter at this point. Suzy's eyeing him as a suspect. He's already bailed on one meeting with her. Is this *muy rico* person playing games? Or is he hiding something? I know you probably feel a sense of duty toward him, but …"

But …?

I've already got my boots and socks in my other hand, and I start walking up the stairs to the veranda and the house.

"I've got to go, Hugo," I say into the phone.

"Ez, where are you?"

"I'm helping an old friend."

"Oh … *Ez.*"

I can tell by his exasperated tone that he knows exactly where I am.

"Bye."

"Dammit," he says.

I hang up.

—m—

I stride onto the white polished marble hallway, take a few steps, and almost careen into Anthony, who's being led out the front door.

He's in handcuffs.

I work quickly to process my feelings because Hugo could be right. Anthony, a member of the De Vos family, albeit by marriage, could be just another rich guy playing games with the system. But then, unlike the rest of the De Vos family, he seems to have a conscience about certain important things. Okay, they're things I can relate to and admire. Like the wonderful green choices at the DVI office building that his receptionist, Christi Shah, said he designed. And he also defended his daughter and her environmental documentary, which I thought was valiant of him.

But if Anthony can so easily compartmentalize his life—having a green building as a way to offset guilt about his eco-disaster of a house and his planet-destroying company—what else can he justify?

Heck. I don't know.

Ultimately, I wonder whether Anthony may be a rebel within these white walls … a black sheep.

I have a soft spot for rebels.

My dad was one, too.

Besides, Anthony asked me to come to his house to help his mother, and I want to make sure she's all right.

I *do* feel I owe it to her.

And to Charlie.

Anthony stops and turns, the two men on either side of him stopping, too, as if the overt wealth of this place has some kind of subliminal, controlling influence, even on the thick-skinned officers of the LAPD. Anthony's eyes are forlorn, his mouth still crushed, as he tells me in a voice that remains polite, "Emerald, thank you so much for coming."

I reply, with empathy, "I'll stay with your mom and dad for a while, okay?"

"That would be wonderful. Thank you again."

I nod. "You're welcome."

The door opens, and who do I see?

Oh … no.

He's standing on the front steps with a smattering of press: the lucky ones, I guess. The ones on Detective Whitney's good list. It's Hugo, front and center, mic in hand. He sees me, and his usual sexy, devil-may-care grin is wiped away in a rush of frustration and anger.

I give him a little wave.

The door closes.

—⁂—

The white-clad butler, Joseph, appears at my side with barely a sound, a silver tray in his hand, a crystal tumbler of iced tea with the same kind of exquisite lemon rind that graced Anthony's mom's water delicately perched on the edge, but without the straw.

Interesting.

Did he surmise I don't use straws?

Or did Anthony?

Because I don't—they just create more litter.

Regardless, I offer a solemn, "Thank you."
He tells me, "Detective Whitney will see you now, Dr. Green."
"Oh?" I reply, my heart speeding up.
Like a rabbit's, I suppose.

# 16

I follow the butler down another long white marble hallway, this one to the left of the massive gold banisters of the staircase, one hand still holding my boots and socks, one clasping my tumbler of iced tea.

We enter that enormous kitchen, and this time I notice that all the white is accented with black: black granite countertops, black cupboards, black-and-white tile floor.

Interesting choice.

If my ecopsych speculations are right about the De Vos family's unconscious display of: "Our hands are clean, white, clean in the midst of our various corruptions …"

What does the black signify?

For an instant, hopeful words run through my mind: harmony, equality, unification, justice.

Then Joseph gives a subtle bow and leaves me in the vast room.

I can't help but internally cringe. There she sits: Detective Whitney, impeccably coiffed and tightly coiled atop a high black stool.

I want to say, "I don't mind cooperating—I just don't want to be eaten."

For a moment I think I might have spoken my thoughts out loud because it appears as if her tongue is protruding and she's getting ready to strike.

I walk toward her, slowly, wondering what my game plan is *this* time.

I don't think I have it in me right now to be the metaphorical prey—especially in a kitchen with such huge pots hanging from the rafters.

I set my tumbler on the massive black granite island countertop, directly across from her, and pull up a stool. It's an awkward situation made more awkward by my trying to put my socks and cowboy boots back on while perched on a high, rather wobbly chair—but I manage.

She waits, like the patient snake.

Finally, I sit upright and give her a grin.

"Well, Detective, always a pleasure."

"Let's cut the bull, Green." She glares at me. "As you can see, your dear old friend is headed to jail."

"You think he killed his own daughter?"

"I get paid to think many things, Dr. Green. Like, why are you here? And why was Abigail fighting with her father just two nights before she died?"

She leans forward, her white camisole slipping under the lilac-colored jacket. The shiny black granite reflects her deeply defined cleavage, and she seems to hiss, "When did you know that Abigail Pryce was working on a documentary film before she died, one that was going to expose the very, very illegal practices of her father's company?"

I'm flabbergasted.

I take a quick swig of iced tea and nearly regurgitate it.

Finally, I'm able to take a breath.

I look her in the eye and say, as truthful as can be, "I have no idea what you're talking about."

She leans even farther over the counter, and I can feel myself reflexively lean back on the stool.

"Abigail Pryce was earning her bachelor's degree in Energy and Sustainability Policy at the University of California at Santa Barbara," Whitney says, with obvious disdain for anything regarding eco-friendly sustainable practices. But, of course, she's also the one who wants to allow ATVs to race and careen over the Majorca Point bluffs.

I feign casual interest. "Really?"

But I can't help but feel proud of Abigail, and I know how proud Charlie would be. Charlie, who encouraged me to read about ecopsychology. Charlie, who happened to mention to me, a mere week or two before her death, that she wanted to study marine biology.

Charlie: such a waste.

Now, Abigail: a terrible loss.

I say, "About an hour ago, I found out Abigail was making a documentary about the environment. I don't know anything else about it."

"You really don't know?"

I can feel it, suddenly: I've reached my limit with this woman.

No more animals of prey to her predator—finally, it's my turn to lean in—albeit sans the cleavage.

"Listen, Detective," I practically growl, "I haven't seen these people for a long time. What do you want from me? Some kind of easy fix? Well, guess what? I don't have it for you. So don't try and intimidate me. I don't like it."

She sits back, startled.

I continue, my teeth bared, "And, by the way, if you are all that your press releases say you are, why aren't you trying to cooperate with me instead of competing with me?"

Her eyes get fidgety.

She sputters, "C—competing with you? For what?"

My eyes are steady.

I don't respond—because I know she knows.

Hugo.

As if in confirmation, she looks down at the shiny black granite, and I can see her eyes momentarily close, then open; she notices the overt reflection of her cleavage and deftly pulls the camisole up in a faint move of discretion.

I get the distinct sense, for just an instant, in this round we are like alpha female dogs, and she just backed down.

Submitted.

I take the opportunity to say, "For instance, I bet you'd like to know that Abigail contacted me right before she died. She left a message. She sounded just like Charlie. It spooked me. But I called her back and left *her* a message. I agreed to meet her. But we never actually spoke. And we never had the chance to meet."

I've regained my strength.

The stool no longer wobbles.

I'm tall in the saddle, and secure.

I follow up with, "I also have no idea why you arrested Anthony Pryce. He loves his daughter and supported her work on that film."

I pause. I gotta ask.

"Are you even sure a crime was committed?"

The detective sighs.

She puts her palms faceup on the granite, those long red nails pointing down, as if signaling a truce, and when she speaks, it's with a hint of warmth and—dare I think it—respect. "Were you able to save the message?" she asks.

I nod. "It's still on my cell."

I'd deleted the orginal message, which Abigail had left on my landline answering machine before I'd given her my cell number. She'd said something like: "I know we've never met before, but you knew my dad's sister, and … well, I really need to talk to you. I'm wondering if we can meet?"

There'd been no reason to save it. I expected to be seeing her in a couple of days.

I reach into my jeans pocket, retrieve the phone, and put it on speaker.

Abigail's whispered voice is chilling in its similarity to Charlie's. "Thank you for calling me back. I know I'm not making sense, but it's important. I'll explain everything when I see you tomorrow."

Click.

Whitney asks, "Can I hear it one more time, please?"

I repeat it.

"… I know I'm not making sense, but it's important …"

I listen, sensing more urgency in Abigail's voice this time around.

Whitney asks, "What did she want to talk about?"

I look at her, seeing her face set in determination.

I reply, "I don't know. I'm more lost listening to it now than I was when I first heard it."

We both sit gazing at the thin phone on the black granite for a few minutes.

She says, "I need to confiscate that, you know. I need to bring it to the lab. It's evidence."

It's my turn to sigh.

"Okay."

I push the small black-and-silver phone toward her.

She tells me, "When the investigation's complete—"

I pick up: "Then I can get it back."

She says, "It could be a while."

I nod. "Yep. It could."

For some reason, we're both sounding … wistful.

As if the feeling of loss—whether it's loss of life, loss of hope, loss of power, loss of respect, or loss of a phone—is contagious.

And, again, I'm wondering ...

What did Charlie lose so long ago that was embedded in her very cadence of articulated thought?

And what could a beautiful, over-the-top wealthy young woman like Abigail Pryce have lost?

Before she lost her life.

*What?*

17

The detective lets me go.

For a few minutes there, it almost felt as if she were going to take me to jail—just for the spite of it.

But I'm sure she wouldn't want to appear as if she's competing for Hugo's affections by locking me up?

Right.

She'd be handing me the martyr card.

Not a wise thing to do—especially when you're intent on winning the heart of a Latino man. I know from my mom, and my grandmother and grandfather, that almost any good Latin-born Catholic will take the side of the martyr. It's just the way of it. And for my mom, that always translated to the earth, the animals, and that jacaranda tree.

I think of its whisper …

*Abigail was pushed.*

After Detective Whitney lets me go, I follow Joseph up the towering red-carpeted staircase in the Pryce mansion to a bedroom where, apparently, Mr. and Mrs. Pryce stay when they're visiting from Palm Springs. Joseph and I walk without speaking down a long red-carpeted hallway. The walls, devoid of any artwork or family photos, arc painted a stark white, as are the many doors. When Joseph gives a light tap on a door on the left, Mr. Pryce opens it, and I see that the room—including bed, curtains, dresser, and armoire—is all white.

Big surprise.

Mr. Pryce is still in his tennis shorts and shirt. Mrs. Pryce is in a high-necked white nightgown under a white silk duvet, her small head resting on a plump white silk pillow. She snores softly, her darkly tan face a stark contrast to the pale around her, but she appears almost serene.

Mr. Pryce motions me over to a small room off the bedroom, and I sit on a comfortable white chair facing a large window that looks out over the brilliant green backyard and glistening turquoise pool. I look away, not wanting to be reminded of the dark, howling vision I saw there only an hour ago. I keep my eyes on Mr. Pryce as he sits down opposite me in a matching chair and in a husky whisper says, "Gracie took a sedative, a Xanax. She's had a prescription for anxiety for a long time. But when this terrible … thing … happened to Abigail." His voice breaks. I reach over and take his hand. Despite all the time I'd spent with Charlie, I hardly remember him, except for the occasional dinner at Charlie's house. He'd usually arrive home late, having worked extra hours at the Long Beach Port. Almost everyone in Majorca Point—or, I should say, almost every *commoner*—seemed to work there back then. I forget what he did. Something on the docks.

He struggles to continue. "The doctor said she could take up to three pills a day. She usually only takes them when she's … nervous." His voice breaks again.

I'm still holding his hand, big and tan and calloused by years of heavy labor.

It seems to calm him a bit to talk about his wife's anxiety. "Gracie has been having anxiety attacks ever since Charlene … left us. She'll get real nervous, and get the panicky breathing. Things like that. Oh, about once a week. Then she'll take a pill and feel better. But ever since we heard about … Abigail … the pills don't work. I keep the bottle on me, so I know how many she's taking. Not more than three—but they could be … what's it called? Placebo. 'Cause there's no relief for her. And she can't stop saying that everything is killing her—and she doesn't remember Abigail's … gone."

I can only keep hold of his big hand.

I'm not here to diagnose; I haven't seen Mrs. Pryce for any length of time. Sudden and traumatic loss can initiate a wide array of symptoms—a psychic break, temporary amnesia, or, once more, PTSD. For a moment I wonder how many of us are suffering from PTSD, going through each day more traumatized than the last by the constant barrage of crime, economic instability, and war, followed by the increasing surge of natural disaster after natural disaster—what an ever-growing number of people are calling "human-made" disasters, since so much of what has been happening these days seems to be intrinsically connected to climate change.

That feeling of being volleyed back and forth between so-called "normal" human challenges and the escalating consequences of abnormal, or toxic, human production could be taking its toll on the collective human psyche.

Hmmm.

It's not enough that our own weapons are turned against us, but the earth's defense mechanisms are, too, since it's been posited by many environmental scientists that climate change might be a kind of defense strategy—the way a fever is the human immune system's response to combat the flu—the planet is trying to fend off a virus, or a dangerous intruder, such as our own species, with heat.

There are also some people, and scientists (though fewer all the time), who think that's crazy.

Me?

I've always had the sense that the earth is a whole living being in itself, a Gaia, and I have no problem envisioning her having an immune response to disease; everything else that lives does.

Why shouldn't the biggest of us all?

But, then again, there are some people who like to think *I'm* crazy—talking to trees.

Oh, well.

I hold Mr. Pryce's hand.

He bows his head and weeps.

Tears roll down his tanned face.

I'm relieved he's able to do that—let it out.

His son can't; nor could I, for a while.

We sit, hands clasped, for a few minutes.

When he looks up at me, it's with a flash of genuine recognition.

"Esmeralda Green," he murmurs. "You and Charlie were quite the pair. Always giggling about something. My daughter ... I miss her."

"So do I, Mr. Pryce," I say, tears stinging my own eyes. "So do I."

## 18

I drive home.

Mrs. Pryce was still sleeping when I left, and I gave Mr. Pryce the name of a colleague who practices in Santa Monica because the trip north on the 405 freeway, even on a remarkable day with less traffic than usual, is very long for me, and she needs access to help right away. Thankfully, Hugo and the rest of the media were gone by the time I got into my car, and I was able to make a quick exit from the mansion and all of that white, white, white.

Now, as the sun sets, I enter the four-digit code onto the barely lit keypad that's embedded in a nondescript wood post at the unguarded gate to my street, Del Mar Avenue; the ever-deepening shadows on the narrow, winding dirt road are a relief compared to that bleached-looking house. The house reminded me of a documentary I recently watched on coral reefs that are being killed by fertilizer runoff and acidification in the world's oceans—they turn as white as the Pryce home, like the brittle bones of a skeleton.

The thought makes me shudder.

Too much death.

I slow down to enter my dirt driveway, and the hybrid switches to battery as it decelerates, the engine making barely a sound at this speed. I cut my headlights out and come to a full stop, turning the car off. I sit for a moment, gazing at my small, yellow house in the semi-moonlight. The marine layer isn't as thick as it was last night, and I can just make out the foundation, which looks slanted.

Even though I already knew it was tilted—the contractor helping me with the second bedroom having been quick to alert me—it makes my stomach feel queasy.

Not only are the houses in Majorca Point being seismically shaken off their foundations, but the foundations themselves are sliding as well. It's a geological phenomenon known as "block glide," in which large areas of overlying rock and soil sometimes glide along the sub-surface layers, and there are a few—heck, more than a few layers of land under our feet here, like slippery Bentonite or volcanic ash that's turned to clay.

And, one day, we'll just start to glide—down.

It's happened before, albeit a hundred years ago.

It will, more than likely, happen again.

At the very least, my bedroom will have to be moved—maybe even destroyed, as it sits at a most vulnerable spot.

Which pains me, greatly.

Not so much for the expense, or the work, though both of those will hurt, a lot. But what will nearly break my heart will be the destruction of the built-in shelves that house my computer. My dad surprised me with those one August morning when I was twelve and a half years old. I'd been away for a week at a local summer camp, and while I was gone he'd made them. My dad was hardly a professional carpenter, but he'd crafted them with so much love that they look, to me, like pieces of art. And now they'll probably have to be torn out.

I sit in my car remembering my dad leading me around the house by my hand with my eyes shut, telling me not to peek, and my mom tiptoeing, holding my other hand, and when we finally got to my bedroom, he said, "Oh, no, Esmeralda, your ... *bed* ... is sliding down the hill!" This wasn't too hard to believe, even then, because Majorca Point had been slipping, in one way or another, for as long as we'd lived there. So I opened my eyes and cried, "Noooo!" But, instead of a falling bed, I was staring at the sturdy, built-in wooden shelves in a corner of my room, next to the window, so I could feel a breeze while I did my homework.

We all laughed and laughed.

I must have thanked my dad a thousand times; those shelves were awesome, solid, my own piece of the house.

It's a wonderful memory, and I smile.

That's when I see a shadow, darker than the rest, creep around the other side of my house, next to the two compost bins that are near enough to my kitchen to make it an easy distance to walk and throw some scraps inside—and then the shadowy, slinking figure moves to the front door.

I make sure my car doors are locked, then turn the Ford on and flare the headlights.

The beady eyes flare back at me.

A coyote, its mouth open, panting. I watch its ribcage rise and fall, really skinny, obviously hungry and thirsty.

We stare at each other.

Then it disappears, remarkably silent, into the shadows.

I turn my car off again.

Unlock the doors.

I debate whether to put water out. I know some of my neighbors would have a fit if they found out I was giving water to a coyote— but these poor wild animals, all of them that try to survive this latest southern California drought, are dying of thirst.

I get out of the car, boots crunching on the dirt and gravel. I find my way to the wooden storage bin that's next to the front door, squinting, feeling, looking for a bowl or bucket under the pale light of the moon, when something brushes my hand.

I swivel on my heels.

Is it the coyote? Is it hungry enough to attack me?

They're usually so shy ...

But then I hear, "Ez?"

"Hugo?"

Right—I gave him the Del Mar gate's entry code the morning after Abigail Pryce died.

He grabs me to him and kisses me.

I smell leather, and soap, and the pure male scent of desire, and I kiss him back, hard.

Why not?

It's been a tough day.

Until now.

## 19

This morning, when I hear Hugo's voice in my ear, along with the peacocks' voices, I'm not as annoyed as I was a couple of days ago with his incessant back-to-back calls on my landline and cell phone. I turn to him under the window's hazy yellow light.

We kiss with slow, burning abandon, and make love.

The dark, heavy feeling of the last few days seems to lift.

Even my thoughts of Charlie are fond, without fear or ghostly chiding.

It's obvious that neither of us wants to lose these sweet, delicious sensations, and although it's not the first night we've spent together (it's the second), our way with each other—the smooth, eager yield of my flesh against his; our breathing in deep, passionate synchronicity— seems to have reached a different, higher level. There's an acceptance of each other. A melding of respect and ebullience. So even when the clock reads nine, and we know this is Thursday, a workday, we both procrastinate, pulling our heads under the covers, facing each other, smiling, almost conspiratorially.

Maybe we can hide … here.

And, we do, for another thirty minutes.

Finally, we get up and shower, together.

This time, Hugo doesn't put on so many sickly faces when I scramble the tofu in front of him. I can tell he's working hard to tolerate it. But when I take the soy bacon and lay it flat in the oven, he turns away.

I smile.

I guess good sex only goes so far.

Still, when I put a heaping plate of breakfast before him, he eats it with zest.

We're sitting at a small wicker table on my salt-and-sea-worn porch that faces the wild grasses of the sloping backyard. We look beyond the ongoing second-bedroom construction, out to the seemingly endless expanse of Pacific Ocean. This is one of those rare mornings when the water is as smooth as glass, and when we've finished our meal, we're both silent, immersing ourselves in the beauty of this shimmering aqua-and-silver tableau.

Nature's gift.

We grin at each other, not talking, no questions, no need for sexually frustrated banter; life feels good.

Full, peaceful.

Stable.

At least internally.

But life, being what it is, particularly in the twenty-first century, is an exercise in adaptive skill, even prowess ...

And there comes a knock on my door.

We hear it through the wide sliders that lead to the living room and the front hallway.

Hugo's eyes hold mine, and we both unconsciously reach for each other's hands, our fingers intertwined and lingering, as if the phalanges have minds of their own, in this tiny, cherished moment.

The knock is loud. Insistent.

Then, a voice: I recognize the intermittent grunts.

It's the cop from the DVI office building, in the black-and-white cruiser: Lieutenant Brady.

Hugo grabs my hand tighter.

I stand to answer the door.

Hugo's still got my fingers.

He's not releasing me.

Brady knocks on the door—louder.

Hugo's palm turns wet against my own. He's working to say something, but my heart feels as if it's thumping in my head, keeping time with Brady's fist at the door, and I realize, in an instinctive, trapped-animal kind of way, that Hugo may have had an ulterior motive in coming up this hill last night.

A motive beyond the sex. Even if it was good, was great, was hot as hell, it may have been just a perk—because there could be a story in this.

*A news story.*

"*Mierda*, Hugo!" I almost spit. "Let me go."

"It's not what you think, Ez," he says, standing, still gripping my hand. "Don't worry, *mi amor*. It's just a few questions—"

"You mean an interrogation?" I shriek, incredulous. "What in this polluted shambles of a world would I need to be interrogated about?"

Hugo draws me to him, holding me tight.

I break free and stomp on his foot.

Not too hard, but enough for him to know he's no longer welcome near me, or in my home, or …

"Esmeralda Green?" Lieutenant Brady shouts.

"Just a minute," I finally shout back.

Hugo pleads, "Let me drive you, Ez. It's no big deal."

I turn away from him, go to the kitchen, grab my keys off the recycled counter, and my small hemp wallet that fits in my jeans pocket. I reach for my smartphone but remember that the detective took it.

Is that what this is about?

I open the door, shooing Hugo out of my house. He skulks to the driveway like the coyote of the night before, except I've got no sympathy for *this* dog.

Brady offers to drive, and I let him.

Not because I want to ride with him but because Hugo's car is blocking mine, and I don't want to ask him to move it. It's also at this moment that I make a silent vow never to speak to him again.

In no small part because he's still driving that same old … *Hummer.*

I ride in the backseat of Brady's black-and-white and look out the back window as Hugo follows right behind, motioning with his hands to me in a gesture of prayer, which I suppose from his corrupted perspective also passes for apology.

I turn to face forward, and Brady mumbles, "Thanks for comin' in. Detective Whitney wants to talk to you is all …"

Hmmm.

Talk to me about what?

Abigail's phone call?

Did she learn something more about it?

And why?

*Why did Abigail call me?*

20

She keeps me waiting.

Again.

This time, I'm waiting in the lobby of the San Pedro Abalone Cove Police Station. It's a small, nondescript building, and I guess Detective Whitney wanted to meet me here because the Majorca Point Police Station is even smaller and is most often used as a storeroom for an overflow of salvageable old-mansion beach garbage.

I smile at the police officer behind the desk. She's got a beehive's worth of gray-blonde hair on top of her head, and I get a sense that she used to be a surfer.

She grins back at me; everyone's been friendly so far.

I wonder why Detective Whitney made me come here? After all, she already questioned me last night.

Is this another attempt at intimidation?

But what does she gain from it?

I take a deep breath and smell the port—but it's not as pungent as it might be if the Abalone Cove Police Station were closer to the onslaught of cargo containers that line up offshore from all over the world. They wait out there in the water for hours, sometimes days, to pass customs inspection. I've got to give the new San Pedro mayor credit for trying to wage a vigorous cleanup campaign for the LA Harbor as well as the Long Beach Port, but the air in both harbors can still be hazardous.

And even though nobody talks about it, most of us know that while those monolithic containers sit there, they've just got to be off-loading their sewage.

Right?

Anyway …

The Abalone Cove station is located near an isolated beach, which is why it's also so small.

But …

I'm digressing because I don't want to face the obvious.

Detective Whitney probably has an idea, if not direct knowledge from Hugo, that he spent the night. Now, I can't help but speculate: How will this knowledge affect this interrogation, and will she even realize it, consciously? Or will it remain hidden in her unconscious somewhere?

And …

Just what could she want to ask me that's so important that she's got to bring me down here and mess up my day—and, maybe, hers?

After all, I'm not too happy about this—and I won't mind telling her.

I find out soon enough.

I follow the nice officer with the beehive as she leads me down a hall, past five or so neatly framed pictures of San Pedro's finest posing with various groups of at risk kids on the beach at Abalone Cove as they help return rehabilitated seals to the ocean.

When in this kind of unpleasant situation—being interrogated about an incident I really know nothing about—I have a tendency to forget that both the Majorca Point and San Pedro police forces do many good works, especially for children *and* injured marine life.

We walk silently down another short hallway, where Officer Beehive opens a thick metal door and gently nudges me into a room.

My jaw nearly drops.

It's a tiny, stuffy room that's got the quintessential cigarette-burned wood table, with two straight-backed chairs on either end. A bright, one-bulb light hangs low from the ceiling—otherwise, the room is dark.

I feel as though I've just entered the TV studio set of a cop show.

On cue, Detective Whitney appears out of nowhere, this time wearing an exquisite, tailored shark-gray suit—the skirt very short, her legs extremely long—and I look for the dreaded dorsal fin as she begins to circle around me, most likely sensing self-doubt, even fear, especially when she motions with a crimson fingernail that I should sit down in the uncomfortable-looking chair on the left.

I do.

Searching my mind for aquatic behaviors.

What do marine mammals do in these circumstances?

With a shark?

How do they ... *live?*

The detective slides into the opposite chair and says, "Save your shrink-talk for somebody else."

I'm perplexed.

She nods, and under the harsh light I can see a dark smudge under her right eye where a daub of makeup got smeared. It's then, with a lurch in my gut, that I think I know what she's talking about, and she knows that I know, and now she makes it obvious that she doesn't care *who* knows, when she says, "Don't even try it. Nobody treats me that way. Nobody."

She's talking about Hugo.

The bastard—he must have slept with both of us. I don't know how many times he's been with her, but if he was just a *poquito* bit smarter perhaps he could have figured out that if he's going to be a player, he probably shouldn't play with a woman of some judicial power and repute because she might get ... upset ... and actually have the capacity to *do* something legal—or illegal in a legal-looking way—about it.

Apparently his brain is in his ...

*Hummer.*

I tell her, "I need to see my lawyer."

"Who's your lawyer?"

I stumble on that. I don't actually have a lawyer. Now what do I do? Ask to see a phone book? Or my cell phone? Can't I have it back for just a minute while I Google the best, and most affordable, criminal attorney in Los Angeles?

The shark gets up and starts circling again, cruising the murky waters of the interrogation room.

She says, "I've got some pictures ..."

"P—pictures?"

I can't believe I stuttered, but does she have photos of Hugo and me, in bed, *my* bed, and was she somehow lurking around my house? How ...?

She throws the pics on the table.

I gasp.

There, under the harsh light, are pictures of Abigail's body, taken the night she died. Once again, I'm looking at her broken body, disjointed in the black-wire cage, her skin remaining smooth as silk, her beauty unmarred by the hundred-foot fall.

I look away.

Detective Whitney's voice is terse. "Don't think I didn't catch on that you knew Abigail was pushed. Well, guess what? I've got the coroner's report to confirm it. There's evidence of a struggle.

A bruise on the inside of her right wrist that's consistent with a thumb and index finger. A deep scratch on the palm of her hand, like she was cut with something. That scratch is not consistent with the injuries she sustained when she went over that cliff. When she was *pushed*."

I stare up at her: the shark in all her informed glory.

She asks fiercely, "How did you know?"

I keep staring, mulling over my answer.

Adapting it … because I could say my mother's jacaranda tree told me, but I don't think that would go over very well.

Whitney says, seething, "Like I told you, your friend Charlie's body was so bloody because she had no trajectory and bounced off every rock on her way down."

I'm still staring, forcing my eyes to go blank.

Whitney's voice drops a notch lower. "But Abigail suffered not a mark, did she? She hit no rocks. She practically *flew* over the side of that cliff. Far enough out to hit sandy bottom."

I groan audibly, sadly.

Finally, I ask, "Why are you telling me this again?"

She circles again, the hungry shark.

She says, "I want to know how you knew, Dr. Green. I want to know how you knew she did not jump."

She keeps circling.

I keep mulling over an answer. The jacaranda tree … the weather in October … the length of shadows … hormones in the spring …

Nope.

I've got no answer.

I've got to get out of here.

I think of dolphins—they're the only marine mammal that's got a chance of surviving, even running off, an attacking shark.

And dolphins are so playful.

Impossible to incriminate.

Really.

I take a deep breath.

Give it a try.

"A tree told me," I reply.

The shark stops. "What did you say? Are you making a mockery of my investigation?"

I shake my head, adamant. I answer, "I'm telling the truth."

Whitney's voice bites with disgust. "Tree hugger."

I smile. "That's true, too."

Whitney's teeth are actually bared. But what can she do? Insist that trees can't talk? That would be an interesting conversation.

Whitney starts to circle again.

Faster and faster.

She keeps repeating, "Tell me how you knew, Green. Tell me, tell me."

I know that one of us will crack, break, and go insane, clinically speaking.

And guess what?

It's not going to be the shrink. Especially not the eco-shrink who can also be a happy dolphin by giving an entirely truthful non-answer.

There's a knock on the door.

Whitney appears somewhat anxious.

I'm getting to her.

She opens the door with a huff, and Officer Beehive whispers to her.

Whitney turns to me and says, "I see you've lawyered up."

"I have?" I'm confused. "I can't afford a lawyer."

"Your friend Anthony Pryce sure can." Whitney continues, "Yes, Anthony Pryce. A strong man with good lawyers. Strong enough to heave a body off a cliff. With lawyers good enough to keep him out of custody."

She motions with her red-painted nails for me to get up.
"What do you think, Dr. Green? Is he strong enough?"
I sigh and walk out.

# 21

In a different context, the sight I see in front of me would be hard to distinguish from fantasy: Both of these men are gorgeous, successful, and waiting for me.

Waiting … to save me.

Abruptly, I remember being an undergrad in Ecopsych 101, writing one of my first essays: "The White Knight and the Dead Tree." It was an intense piece on how the Roman Empire destroyed the European pagan cultures and their beloved forests, as well as their ancient lore of wood gods, wood nymphs, forest fairies, and magical beings. The pagans were devoted tree worshipers and were careful to treat the surrounding forests with care and respect. But the Romans ridiculed the pagans and called them uneducated country folk, backward heathens who needed to learn the graces and civility of the city dwellers. Most of all, the Roman Empire believed the pagans' souls needed saving. Yet, as it's been documented many times, what the Romans were really after was the wood. The Roman Empire, along with the Catholic Church, knew that cutting down the forests would make them money, and so that's what they did—and any pagan who didn't like it was either burned as a witch or killed in some other gruesome manner. Eventually, the transformed pagans became the European Christians, and they, in turn, did much the same thing to the Native Americans because, as they said, those people were heathens, too, and their souls needed to be saved. It's still going on in Africa, especially in Sudan, where the pagans, or animists, are regularly massacred by Muslims and Christians alike, as they, too, are perceived to need saving.

Or ...

Their land needs saving.

Needs stealing.

Needs exploiting.

The two men—one dark, muscular, Latino; one blond, lanky, Caucasian—turn to face me as I walk through the hallway leading from the interrogation rooms into the lobby. I watch incredulously as both men see me and immediately, albeit probably unconsciously, spread their legs into subtle but strong straddle positions.

They must be mounting their chargers, no doubt, ready to sweep me off my feet. Ready to save me.

But ...

I don't want anybody to save me.

*I do the saving.*

That's my field—my expertise—my *raison d'être.*

Figure it out, boys.

"Ezzie," says Hugo, possessively, as if using my nickname makes him the property owner of my mind, soul, and body.

How like Detective Whitney he can be. Anthony, not to be outdone, calls out softly, "Emerald." My other nickname from so long ago.

It's hard to say which one has the upper hand here.

Because ...

*Neither of them do.*

Officer Beehive is back behind the front desk, and she gives me the smile and roll of the eyes that every woman understands as the universal sigh of exasperation: "Men."

I nod in silent agreement.

She nods back and returns to her paperwork.

I reply first to Anthony because I feel obliged. "Thank you, Anthony. I don't need a lawyer, though. I didn't do anything wrong."

The two of us move toward the exit and stand, for a moment, at the door.

Hugo is behind us.

Anthony moves close and, in a hushed voice, tells me, "I know how you must feel. I didn't do anything wrong either. I think this detective is looking for an easy resolution to Abby's ... death." He's still wearing the same worn-looking clothes. His eyes are puffy, and his mouth visibly trembles as he says, "I want justice for my little girl." His voice rises. "Not some *sham* of an investigation."

I take his arm and open the door with my shoulder, leading him outside.

I can't help but feel his bicep under my hand; it's firm but not overly muscular.

Hugo follows behind us, frowning.

Anthony continues, "Please, Emerald, let me know if you need a lawyer. It's the very least I can do. After all, you wouldn't be here if it weren't for my own troubles."

I let his bicep go.

He really doesn't seem all that strong.

But more than that, he hardly seems capable of killing his daughter.

Detective Whitney's treating him like a criminal—and it may be completely unjustified. My intuition is usually more right than not—and he emanates bereavement and innocence.

I'm actually worried about him.

Hugo, on the other hand?

Hah!

I'll never spend another moment of my precious time worrying about him. Or his penchant for cars the size of … dinosaur genitalia.

Which is then further exemplified as I walk outside into the parking lot, bright sunlight glaring into my eyes, and see the Hummer.

I keep walking.

Hugo and Anthony follow—I don't look, but I can sense both of them vying for my attention as I walk faster.

Anthony's regained his composure and calls after me. "Emerald, can I give you a ride home?"

I turn on my cowboy heels, facing them. They both stop.

I hesitate.

Hugo pounces on the moment, a hint of victory in his voice. "How about with me, Ez?"

I glare at him and decide: "I'm going to take the bus."

Good old public transportation: I'll pollute less and stay out of trouble.

Anthony says, "Okay, but my car's right here …"

He points.

It's an …

*Electric Porsche.*

I mean *totally* electric …

The latest model.

And it's …

Beautiful.

Oh …

Wow.

This is tough.

It's Hugo who makes my decision for me when he says, "Come on, Ez. They cut the budget on the buses down here. You'll be waiting half the day."

I hadn't thought about that.

Anthony says, "Ride with me. We'll carpool."

Hmmm.

To carpool in a Hummer or an electric Porsche?

I say, "Thank you, Anthony. And maybe you could tell me more about the lawyer on the way home?"

Hugo glowers.

I throw him an over-the-shoulder "bye."

And I get into the plug-in iridescent-blue Porsche.

Ready for a fabulous ride.

I deserve it.

# 22

I sit back in the low-to-the-ground passenger seat, expecting the sound of the near–race car to be ferocious, and I prepare my ears for a pounding vibration because I've read it's got mega-horsepower engines—but, since it's electric, it makes barely a whisper.

I guess cutting down on air pollution cuts down on noise pollution, too.

I take a deep breath.

I've got the window open all the way, and I push my face into the rushing wind, the speed of the car seeming to clear the lingering smell of the busy port—a scent that always reminds me of burning hair and oily potato chips.

I squint my eyes against the fast-moving air, then crane my neck back to catch a glimpse of the glimmering turquoise ocean and the massive port's channel behind us as we start to climb into the canyons. In a blur, I can see the huge cargo containers lining up from Asia, Africa, and all parts in between, a sea-bound traffic jam.

Ugh.

But I'm in a plug-in Porsche.

Life is *fantástico!*

At least for this minute.

Anthony's taking the back route to Majorca Point, away from San Pedro, onto Majorca Point Road, the electric race car hugging the jagged twists and bumpy rolls that follow the ever-slipping land, paralleling fragments of other long-past MP roads that have since fallen, literally off a cliff, into the sea.

There's a feeling of closeness in our silence, probably a long-internalized recognition of Majorca Point instability. It's as if we already know how it feels to have the rug pulled out from under our feet, and we've known it since childhood, so we don't need to discuss the inevitable shake-up. Not right now, anyway. Sure, things will most likely get worse. So let's appreciate the spilling curves of land and ocean as they meet in a sensuous, undulating dance—the car speeding around each inlet and precipice of the peninsula like a blue lightning bolt.

Eventually, we arrive at the entrance to Del Mar Avenue.

Anthony deftly shifts into neutral, and I give him the gate code. In a breathtaking transition, he slows and takes my winding dirt road with visible care, on the lookout for kids, or pets, or wildlife. When a small lizard, camouflaged almost the exact color of the brown-and-tan dirt, skirts onto the street, Anthony somehow spots it, and he shifts and brakes in one smooth motion of concern.

I'm truly impressed.

He'd never have been able to see such a tiny creature if he were in a Hummer.

I stop my thoughts short.

Quit thinking about Hugo!

*Quit thinking about cars.*

Anthony pulls the silent Porsche into my driveway, behind my Ford, and he comments, "Your hybrid's a great car."

I can't help it—I feel a little flutter.

Look what Hugo has driven me to—I'm starting to judge people by their cars. Even people I hardly know, like Anthony Pryce.

I glance over at him, seeing that Anthony's tender mouth has the slightest hint of smile, and my heart flutters—again.

A very …

Dangerous sensation.

After all—he's married. And he may have murdered his daughter.

I quickly unbuckle my seat belt and say, almost brusquely, "Thanks for the ride. I've got to go."

But Anthony turns to me, his green eyes abruptly misty with emotion, and in a hushed voice says, "I need to tell you why they arrested me, Emerald."

I shake my head. "No, it's all right."

But I turn to listen.

He continues, "They think I pushed my little girl … off the cliff."

His voice breaks, and my own eyes begin to sting.

At that moment, I know in my soul that he didn't do it.

"I believe you, Anthony," I tell him.

"Thank you, Emerald," he whispers.

—⁓—

I stand at the top of my sloping driveway and watch him wind down the hill, as slowly and carefully as he came up.

His life is a tragic mass of uncertainty, yet I would be pushing the limits of American Psychological Association ethics if I treated him in a professional capacity.

I shrug and pull my shoulders up.

Back in the saddle, Ez.

I'll shower … for the second time today.

Wasting some water, I know, but between the grimy interrogation room, the shark-skirt Detective Whitney, and Hugo's befuddled expression in the Abalone Cove Police Station parking lot, I've got to wash all of it off.

Then …

I'll go see Sam.

## 23

I'm unloading my personal issues on the best horse trainer at The Falling MP Stables: Dove Valencia Tollgood.

She sits in her high-tech wheelchair, like Buddha, smiling at times but growing more solemn as I relay the day's events.

Dove is paraplegic, bucked off a horse in a small desert suburb north of Los Angeles when she was eighteen years old. The way she tells it, the kids from the old ranch neighborhoods and the "traccies" (the new kids that had been named after their own neighborhoods of seemingly endless, freshly built tract homes) had an ongoing animosity (because their parents did), and one spring day the traccies started throwing stones at her (a "ranchie") while she was trail riding a bridle path on the outskirts of town. Dove kept riding, doing her best to ignore them.

Her paint, Callie, was a lot like Sam—a calm horse, rarely bothered by external stimuli. But the stones turned to larger, more lethal objects, and the gentle, multicolored mare finally reared when a piece of broken glass stabbed her left eye. Callie pitched through the air, and Dove was sent flying, landing on the crest of her head by the side of a pocked two-lane highway next to a weathered gas station.

The lone attendant, an eighteen-year-old high school dropout named Shelley Haversford, saved Dove's life, and by doing that probably saved her own, too.

They've been together ever since.

Dove and Shelley.

Saving each other.

These women haven't needed the man on the proverbial white charger for quite some time.

They say that, someday, they might get married.

Or they might not.

Many of us at The Falling MP make bets. Nobody's won—yet.

Anyway …

Shelley's the other best trainer at The Falling MP—she handles the actual riding during the training of young, green horses, and she also rides some of the owners' horses during various out-of-town shows.

They work in smooth tandem during lessons—Dove in her wheelchair in the middle of the ring, giving instructions in a calm yet firm voice, sometimes with the aid of a microphone since her lung capacity isn't as strong as it used to be—while Shelley will ride as a visible example to their students. They teach Western saddle and together have helped produce dozens of medal winners.

They've got a great system, and while a lot of stables closed during the last economic downturn, The Falling MP is still thriving.

"I keep thinking about that poor coyote," I whisper, since we're inside the stables, in the aisle between stalls, near the tack room where one man and three women are getting ready for a group lesson. I hear them chatting idly as they retrieve their saddles and gear, and I softly continue, "I saw it in my car's headlights last night, ribs sticking out, thirsty, searching for food around my house, and I wanted to help. Then Hugo showed up—"

Dove gently chides, "Isn't that what you psychologists call a projection? You projected your feelings for the starving coyote onto Hugo? Then you wanted to help *him?*"

"Come on, Dove." I can't help but feel flustered. "Give me a break."

But I also know she's got a point.

Shelley's standing just behind Dove's wheelchair, a sleek, shiny apparatus with an electric motor, but Dove's devoted mate is usually pushing it, or standing very close, and I watch as she rests her hands on her loved one's upper back and begins to carefully massage her small, round shoulders.

Shelley contemplates out loud: "Some of my classmates would say you were anthropomorphizing."

Dove chuckles. "There she is—our girl, the scholar."

It's true; the former dropout is on her way to graduating as a vet with a specialty in large animals, specifically horses.

It's taken her more than eleven years, mostly because Shelley's so protective of her significant other that Dove practically had to force her to leave the stables to start even a part-time school curriculum. But next summer, Shelley will finally graduate—at age thirty-three, with built-in clients. Dove knew how much Shelley wanted to become a vet, so she paid for Shelley's education with the rest of the money she'd been awarded in her lawsuit against the parents of the traccies. She's always said that she probably wouldn't have sued, even though the kids were convicted of the crime of aggravated assault and she'd been left wheelchair-bound for life—instead, it was her horse, Callie, who'd been the deciding factor because Dove had no insurance to cover the mare's eye surgery. Then, sadly, she'd also needed the money for a specially outfitted stall since the damaged eye became infected and Callie eventually lost her sight in both eyes.

Dove bought The Falling MP for almost nothing when real estate was low. Later, Dove also found she liked running the business aspects of the place, and five years ago she received her MBA from an online college.

Between Dove and Shelley, they could probably keep The Falling MP going forever.

If only the slipping land would ... not ... slip.

And Callie's still here—blind but doing well, though very old.

All in all, these are some of the best people I know.

Smart, caring women, good friends, and they provide a great place to hash out the ambiguities of life, if you don't mind debate.

They just *love* to debate.

Shelley reiterates, "Who's to say that the analytical psychological term, projection, isn't a variant on anthropomorphizing?"

Dove replies, "Just to clarify, by 'anthropomorphizing' you mean that a human being would ascribe human feelings to an animal, like sadness, or happiness, or love, and in psychological terms that would be the same as a human projecting his or her own feelings onto another human?"

"Yes." Shelley nods emphatically, her hands still gently massaging her loved one's shoulders. "But what came first? The idea of anthropomorphism initiated by the scientists who were experimenting on animals for the so-called human good? Or was it the Freudian idea of projection? They're so similar—attributing feelings to someone or something other than oneself. So what if the Freudians actually adapted their theory of projection from the animal scientists, the vivisectionists of their day? Remember, the consensus back then was that animals had no feelings, except for those that the lower-class, illiterate humans gave them."

I interject. "You're saying it was the scientists experimenting on animals who first used the theory of projection by assigning it to, in their perception, the illiterates who thought animals actually had feelings?"

Shelley pauses, then nods. "Maybe not even the animal experi-menters. It could have started much earlier. With the hunter-gatherers.

Or how about the farmers who had to slaughter the chicken or the cattle to eat? Looking at it that way, the idea of projecting feelings onto another living being, and the dubiousness of that, has been around a long time. Probably for as long as humans have eaten meat. So it could have been much later that those scientists who were experimenting on animals, and the Freudians, adapted the idea to suit their own theories."

Dove frowns. "Many animals are still said to have no feelings, especially when they're being used to test cleaning products, and hair color, and—"

Shelley huffs. "I hate that."

Dove seconds, "Me, too."

I agree. "Yep."

For a moment, we're silent, grimacing.

But I've got to try to clarify my behavior last night, and I say, "Let me get this straight. You're saying I projected my feelings that the coyote needed help and care onto Hugo, and that's why I took him into my house?"

Dove gives me a wry smile. "And gave him more than water."

I feel myself blush. "Hmmm."

Now they're both grinning at me.

"Thanks, ladies."

They say in happy unison, "No problem."

Sometimes Dove and Shelley's loving, caring relationship, and their ability to debate, come back together, and still respect each other, makes me wonder why the heck I like men.

But then, I *know*.

# 24

I'm standing with Sam at Charlie's cliff, allowing him to graze, the reins resting lightly in my hand.

It's been a very early twilight ride, the sun only midway down the cloudless horizon. But I was compelled to get down here as soon as I possibly could.

To look for … what?

Abigail's murderer?

A sign of what happened?

Or am I really searching for what killed Charlie?

For what lay embedded in her psyche?

I don't know.

*Something.*

I realize that the Majorca Point PD has probably scoured this area, especially since they've determined that Abigail was pushed or, as Detective Whitney said so cruelly, "She practically *flew* over the side of that cliff."

I shiver under the setting sun.

I focus on Sam, listening to his soothing, methodical crunching of brittle grass, and I let him pull me around the small Majorca Point park, though when he gets too near the bright orange tube fencing, I turn and face the bluffs, away from the ocean.

I look up at my own neighborhood.

I can just make out a glint from The Falling MP's weather vane, a local artist's rendition of the singing cowgirl Dale Evans from long ago: curly hair, cowboy hat, waving happily from atop her rearing horse.

I suddenly feel weak.

Disappointed in myself.

It's as if I've given my identity, my sense of purpose, over to the fates—the slipping land.

I couldn't even put the coyote and Hugo projection together!

How pathetic.

Speaking of pathetic ...

When I called from The Falling MP's phone about an hour ago to retrieve my landline messages, since I still don't have a cell phone (just one more completely unexpected thing I've got to spend money on), I learned that Hugo had left me fourteen messages.

Fourteen!

*That's* pathetic.

Okay, so I'm projecting my own pathetic feelings onto Hugo now, but at least I'm aware of it—this time.

I gasp.

*Mierda*—pardon my rude Spanish again.

But, knowing the way he plays speed-dial switch-off between my two lines, he probably left fourteen messages on my cell phone, too.

I gasp one more time, and Sam snorts.

"It's all right, boy," I soothe.

But where is my phone, really?

Is it in evidence, as Whitney said it was going to be? Or did she keep it? Because if she did keep it, then she's probably seen and heard all those calls from Hugo. Great. Now she'll want me in for questioning every day.

What has my life come to?

*It's out of control.*

No ... no.

I will not slide down this hill of fate.

I am not dirt.

I will not be treated like dirt.

I'm thinking like this, thoughts spinning round and round, down here looking for something to prove ... what?

But I go on with my circular questions, like a shark myself.

Who were the hikers who said they saw Abigail with someone that night?

Aren't they being interrogated?

Hmmm.

I'm standing level with the precipice from which Abigail fell. It extends outward to a point, so from my perspective, I can see the curvature of the cliff and the jagged earth that drops to the sea. I run my eyes down to the surf below, the water beginning to reflect the colors of the setting sun, and that's when I see it. A flash of light, so brief I almost miss it. I squint and catch the glint again. I take a few steps forward, Sam ambling forward with me. I give him a rub behind his ears and tie his reins to the orange tubing. I gently tell him, "Whoa, Sam. Stay here."

My faithful steed drops his head to eat more grass.

I look to see if anyone's around, but the park is empty. I duck down and crawl through the orange bars to the other side of the security fence.

Okay, I know I'm not supposed to do this—but I just want a closer look.

Again, I squint into the sun, to the cliff below, and see the glint of something shiny, maybe plastic, or metal. I'm not sure. But there's definitely something there. The CSI must have missed it the other night. It was dark. They couldn't see it. But ... what if it's a clue? What if it has some significance to Abigail's death?

What if it's, in ecopsychological terms, a gift from nature?

The ever-crumbling earth offering up a revelation?

The signs that nature gives to us inevitably hold truth. That's something we humans forget about nature: It does not lie.

I must get to that object.

But it's impossible.

Right?

The cliff angles down slightly to the edge, then sharply plunges one hundred feet. On the top and the sides of the cliff are long wild grasses, dry and yellow, and large white-and-gray rocks protrude from the rust-colored dirt. The glinting object is about fifteen feet down.

I sigh, looking at Sam, pondering.

I realize I'm actually staring at the answer right in front of me.

I've got a lasso rope on my saddle, just below the horn, a reminder that I used to be in horse shows, a long time ago. Now, I use it for an extra lead rope or to secure objects to the saddle. It comes in handy.

I go back to Sam, uncoil the rope, tie it around the orange rail, then wrap it around my waist, two times, with a couple of sturdy knots, and stoically make my way to the edge of the cliff. I take it one step at a time, slow. I crouch, face the dirt, hold on to one rock, and find a place for my foot on another, feeling the thirty-foot rope tighten, secure. My recycled cowboy boots stay firm on the rocks—well made and strong. I refuse to look at the crushing drop to the ocean. I keep my eyes on the shiny prize, and when I'm next to it, I reach out with my left hand. I have to dig at the dirt; it's stuck in a tuft of weeds. I grab the object in my hand; it feels sharp and smooth at the same time. I open my palm slightly, seeing that it's a broken piece of cassette tape—the kind people used to listen to music on. Who uses cassette tapes anymore?

With that thought, I'm suddenly careening into the air, upside down.

I reflexively shriek, "Whoa! Whoooaaaa!"

Sam starts to whinny.

I feel the rope around my waist slide to my hips.

*¡Mierda!*

My body crashes back into the cliff, and I flail out with my free hand for anything to hold onto. I grab a rock. My nails scrape against the hard surface, and then I fly out again, crash back, fly out, and finally catch an outcropping of grass. I frantically grip the weeds and pull myself back upright, then kick my dangling legs toward a rock. My left foot lodges on a boulder. Red dirt and stones fall in heavy clumps to the waves below. Sweat pours down my face as I yank the rope back around my waist and heave myself up the cliff. I lie on the edge of the precipice breathing hard and fast.

Sam is stomping a front hoof in the dirt.

Snorting. Scolding me.

I groan. "I know ... I'm sorry."

But I still have the piece of cassette in my hand. Most likely it's got nothing to do with Abigail. A piece of antiquated technology thrown off the cliff as litter, exposed by the latest earthquake.

I push myself to a stand and make my way back to the rail. I give Sam a calming pat on the nose, then slip out of the rope and hang it over the saddle horn. I wince. My shoulder hurts from crashing into the cliff. I shake my head and take a glance back at the sun dropping into the ocean—low, red, and ominous-looking.

The water, for a moment, appears black.

Like a hole for a grave.

One I was almost buried in.

I tremble, finally allowing myself to feel the terror of the past few minutes.

Then, Charlie seems to whisper from the recesses of my own consciousness—or could it be the wind racing up from the ocean?

I hear …

"Water …"

My heart lurches, and I mouth, "Water?"

But there's no reply.

# 25

It's night. Sam's cozy in his stall. I'm home.

I carried the piece of cassette up the hill in my pocket, and immediately I put it in a baggie: I have them for emergencies, kept in my pantry. Even though I hate plastic bags of any kind, these are 60 percent recycled. I'm waiting for the company that mass-produces soy-based sealable baggies. You can bet I'll buy stock with them.

I've got a call in to Detective Whitney.

She needs to come get this evidence.

If it is evidence.

I don't know.

My mind immediately leapt to its having something to do with the case.

But that seems farfetched.

Still, the police need to retrieve it.

Now, I want comfort food. Mexican comfort food. My right shoulder still hurts, and I need a soothing break. I pull three tamales out of my refrigerator, pop them in the oven, and have myself a feast. Even if these small packets of corn dough were store-bought, they came wrapped in the traditional corn husks and are, remarkably, vegetarian, filled with a *muy* delicious combination of sweet corn, sugar, and cilantro.

My mom used to make them with *pollo* and *queso*—chicken and cheese.

But never any lard.

She was ahead of her time.

An hour later, Detective Whitney still hasn't called.

I feel full, and a little groggy.

I carry a large bucket of water up my driveway, and I set it just off the turnout, for the coyote.

Thus, I've assured that my do-gooder projections will never find their way onto Hugo's persona again.

Heck, maybe the coyote will bring all his friends.

Fine.

I'll put more water out.

Now, in my bedroom, at the built-in desk that my dad made for me, I'm on my laptop, Googling up a storm, searching for the latest news stories on Abigail Pryce with a finesse not witnessed by anyone in virtual space in decades, or at least since the moment I lost my phone to Detective Whitney and was forced to quiet my obsession.

Is it an obsession? Googling?

Could that be?

I shake my head.

At this moment, I don't care.

Because I've got Charlie on my mind.

Obviously, since she's talking to me. Or I'm talking to me through her because I haven't resolved her death yet. Why? I'm not sure. Maybe because there are so many unanswered questions about it. Like: Why the heck did you jump, Charlie? I still don't know.

*I want to know.*

Out there under the cliffs, I heard the word *water*—but what does it mean?

Googling isn't going to bring me the answers, if this whisper really did come from Charlie. Or from my unconscious.

Then I remember …

It was something Charlie said to me before she died. I struggle to get the words back—words I hardly remember because, at the time, I didn't know they would be among her last.

"Promise me, Emerald," she'd said.

Promise what?

"Stay out of that water."

What water?

I close my eyes and try to bring the moment back, as painful as it is.

"Don't swim in that cove anymore," she said.

Our cove? The one we swam in every summer?

"It's not safe."

Why?

But this is the answer I can't find in the recesses of my memory.

I do remember that I stopped swimming there.

But if I kept my promise, it wasn't because of Charlie's warning. It was because, for too many years, it was too painful even to think of swimming there alone. Without Charlie. And then, the more I learned about the pollution of our oceans, the less I wanted to swim anyway.

What had she been warning me about? Pollution? Sharks?

Thinking of sharks reminds me, again, of her old boyfriend. He played baseball for a team called the Sharks.

Justin Fellowes.

The man she was sure she wanted to spend her life with.

No, I remember suddenly—he wasn't a Shark. He was a Dolphin.

I remember that the first time I met him was late afternoon, and Charlie and I were sitting on white wood bleachers in very early spring at the bright-green baseball field down at Majorca Cove. We were watching a game between the hot Point Sharks, who aptly wore gray-and-white uniforms, and the equally hot Majorca Dolphins, who congruently wore blue and white.

And yes, despite our leanings toward bad boys, Justin was, amazingly, a Dolphin.

He was sexy, smart, and *nice*.

After they'd dated a couple of times, Charlie would giggle in her wistful way. "Can you believe it? I'm attracted to a nice guy? Not a shark. Not a jerk."

I'd giggle, too. "Incredible."

For a while, he'd seemed genuinely *good*.

And, for a while, Charlie's voice even lost that wistfulness. It was as if she'd found a treasure that was real, tangible. She stopped seeming so agitated.

Then, later, maybe five or so months into their relationship, things changed.

She seemed anxious again.

Or maybe that was just hormones.

It's hard to tell—especially almost twenty years away from it.

Justin Fellowes.

Finally, something I can Google.

I bring him up at every juncture in his life.

He reads like a saint.

A very successful saint.

Justin Fellowes received his M.D. from Harvard University. I remember that he'd left for the East Coast before Charlie died. I never knew when he found out about her death, or how.

He became a highly skilled and extremely reputable oncologist with offices in Boston and Manhattan, but apparently he has returned to his roots—he's now based in Beverly Hills. The most recent news on him is about his charitable organization, called JustInTime. Through his philanthropic ventures, he's currently helping a seven-year-old Bolivian boy, José Villalpando, who has non-Hodgkin's lymphoma. Dr. Fellowes has personally chosen José for a clinical trial in which he'll receive a new combination therapy for the blood cancer. José is at a hospital in New York and is reported to be doing very well, with his family—personally flown to the United States by Dr. Fellowes—at his side.

I stare at Justin's picture on his website: still very attractive, with hazel eyes, sensuous lips, and just a few wrinkles and streaks of gray in his full head of brown, curly hair.

This is the info that's most readily available.

Had Justin Fellowes ever wondered about what happened to Charlie?

Did he contact her family? Was he still in touch?

I'm surprised to realize that I've never heard of him, despite all his philanthropic work. Maybe he likes to fly under the radar. Maybe that's why he divides his time between LA and the East Coast.

Or maybe he feels some sort of guilt. For the way he treated Charlie.

By the time Charlie died, he'd been away at Harvard. But it wasn't fall yet—he'd left early. As if to escape.

Had he known something?

She was devastated when he left, but she, too, seemed to know that one day he'd go—more likely sooner than later.

I wonder …

I want to feel positive about his accomplishments and his altruism because it turns out that the boy, José Villalpando, is actually the eighty-seventh child with lymphoma from the developing world that Justin has assisted in such a kind, compassionate way.

But …

There are some individuals who experience guilt in a different way than others—in a way that can become a complex, obsessive kind of guilt that, in turn, can lead to a type of perfectionism. Like the kind of guilt a person might feel if he doesn't win a sports match, or get a job promotion, or eat the right things on a diet. In fact, anorexics suffer extreme perfectionist guilt. And so do some very successful people—it's what drives them.

Was Justin Fellowes driven by guilt? The guilt that can be incurred on a quest to be perfect?

Or did he project that need to be perfect on Charlie?

I still remember his comments to Charlie before she'd died. She told me, "Justin says my butt is too big for my prom dress."

"What?" I'd almost laughed.

Charlie was a tall, skinny girl; some boys used to call her "stretch."

She'd looked at me, a little forlorn, her voice seeming to trail her thoughts. She'd already turned around with her rear facing me, while pulling up on the underwear beneath her jeans, asking, "I've got a girdle on. Does it make my butt look smaller?"

I'd watched her pulling on the girdle, shocked she was worried about it.

Truly, she was thin, and beautiful.

If anyone had the big butt, it would be me.

I'd wanted her to feel better, so I said, "Yep ... your butt *does* look smaller."

"What a relief," she replied.

Then she giggled, a lyrical wisp of air and sparkle down the dull, brown-and-tan high school hallways.

I'd been reminded then of air and sparkle, but as I hear it now in my recessive memory, it sounds like a breath of hopelessness, as hollow as almost half the lockers belonging to the senior class out on independent study. And that's what we'd finally started talking about: school. A friend of ours, Kim Overland, who was a year older than we were, had gotten a job for school credit at an attorney's office in downtown Los Angeles; she wanted to be a lawyer.

Charlie was hoping to become a marine biologist.

I hadn't read the article on ecopsychology yet—but I was intrigued.

The issue of Charlie's butt was lost to talk of the next year—our senior-year internships, exams, whether we would get scholarships to college.

My landline rings.

It's after midnight.

I don't think Detective Whitney would call me this late.

It must be Hugo.

I won't answer it.

But when I check, I see that the number isn't his ...

I answer.

—m—

Anthony's voice is tight with restrained emotion. "I'm sorry, Emerald. I don't want to bother you. My mother was sleepwalking. She came in my room and started slapping my face. Started yelling about a cliff. Maybe it's the one in Majorca Point. I'm not sure. Now she's awake, and sobbing. What should I do?"

For a moment, I'm silent.

I put him on speaker.

Then I return to Google.

I resume my search on Abigail Pryce, and I see the lead story. The headline under her pale, pretty face reads: "The Murder of an Heiress." I listen to Anthony's tense, short breaths.

"Emerald?" he asks again.

I'm looking at Abigail but seeing Charlie.

I say, "Yes, Anthony."

"Would you be able to come over? I could send a limo for you."
I stare at Abigail ... Charlie.
"Is it electric?" I ask.
"No," he replies with a sigh. "Sorry."
"It's okay," I tell him. "I'll drive."

## 26

I pull up next to the white security hut just after 2:00 a.m.

A different white-clad guard, this one with a full head of wavy white hair, makes a call, nods silently, and opens the gate.

I make a slow entrance onto the red brick, around the cherub fountain. The lights of the enormous white house flood out of nearly every white-draped window and glow an almost unreal-looking white.

For an instant I get a preternatural feeling.

It seems to be a home of ghosts.

I brake and turn off the engine.

Waiting.

For who?

Charlie? Abigail?

The front door opens …

For a minute, no one's there.

My heart quickens.

But then Anthony steps out.

He looks to be a beaten man, depressed, forlorn, and lonely, with a bandage across his right cheek.

His mother must have slapped him hard.

What medication did Mr. Pryce say his wife was taking? Xanax?

To my knowledge there aren't any aggressive side effects to that particular anti-anxiety med. Did Mr. Pryce take her to another doctor? Was she prescribed something different?

I get out of the car. I'm in my usual cowboy boots and jeans, a light-blue organic cotton T-shirt—and still no phone. As usual, I stuff my other things—wallet and keys—into my pocket, suddenly aware that my typical MO gears me toward being ready to leave wherever I am at a moment's notice, which must be another consequence of living on a landslide.

I silently walk up the white marble stairs.

Anthony stays on the top step; as I get closer I can see his mouth is tight and crooked with an expression of sorrow.

I feel bad for him.

I feel …

Tenderness.

Before I've thought about it, I'm holding him, gently, and his face bows to meet mine, our foreheads touching, like a pyramid formation, finding strength in each other.

No … no … no … Esmeralda.

I tell myself, over and over.

Not good. Not smart. Not feasible.

His breath is close and sweet and warm.

No … no … no … Esmeralda.

His lips hover, closer.

No … no … no.

I step back, just an inch, but enough to stop the feeling.

The flow.

"Emerald," he whispers.

I shake my head.

Take a breath.

His mouth sets in a firm, sad line.

Then we turn and walk side by side into the blaringly lit ultra-white house.

## 27

We walk together past the hanging rugs and the suit of armor, up the red stairs that seem to stretch forever.

I whisper, "Are you all right?"

His voice is low, muffled. "I'm okay. She only slapped me. Her fingernail caught me on the cheek, that's all …"

I nod empathetically.

He continues, "And considering she's still got a pretty good backhand in tennis, she could have walloped me pretty hard."

I ask, softly, "What happened?"

He replies in a semi-monotone, "I don't know, Emerald. I was drifting off to sleep when I felt a shadow over me. I thought it might be Penelope. We don't …"

I nod, urging him on. I don't really want to know the details of his marriage. Or non-marriage.

He sighs. "But when I opened my eyes, it was my mother. She was standing above me, staring. I called out, and she started slapping my face. I grabbed her arms and pried her off me. I got out of bed. Then she started screaming about the cliff. And sobbing. My dad woke up and came running. He got her back into bed."

I quietly ask, "Is she taking any other medication besides the Xanax?"

He whispers, "I don't think so."

We're on the second-floor landing, walking down the white-walled hall to the closed white door. Anthony knocks softly.

Mr. Pryce opens the door.

Just like yesterday.

Was it really only yesterday?

Mrs. Pryce is back in bed, also just like yesterday, her tan face a stark contrast against the white silk pillow, her white nightgown slipping down off her tan shoulder.

She's asleep, I think.

But when I get closer and carefully pull her nightgown back up over her shoulder, she begins to shriek, as loud as a red-tailed hawk's prey in the night. I almost reach out to hold her but restrain myself—something I've learned how to do after years of hearing the cries of wild animals at night in the canyons near my home. I've learned that, sometimes, it's better not to disrupt the balance of ecology, no matter how much my therapist's heart longs to comfort and save. As cruel as it may seem, predator and prey were made to grotesquely challenge each other in order to survive. I also find that within the ecology, or the ecopsychology, of the human being, sometimes the best thing for discordant, unhappy individuals is to allow them, in metaphor, to hunt their own psyches, to eat, or be eaten, by their own conflicting emotions. These individuals might then have a better chance of survival because finally they can discover what they were pursuing: a hunger within themselves that they didn't know they had. Or they might become aware they've been victims, or victimized, maybe by their own fear, all their lives.

So, for a moment, I let Mrs. Pryce scream.

Obviously, there's a need that has gone unfulfilled, and it could be born of grief, or it could be signaling a deeper issue because attempting to harm one's own son, even if he's a grown man and it was by slapping, could signify something more serious.

Even dangerous.

On the other hand, I'm also the woman who puts water out for coyotes.

In the end, it's all about adapting.

One moment, one method works.

The next, you're sliding down a hill.

I may not hold her, but my eyes remain steady on Mrs. Pryce.

Her screaming ebbs, thinly, and she gives a tiny hiccup.

"I feel better," she says.

"Good," I say softly, and take her hand.

Mr. Pryce moves one of the twin white chairs from the sitting room over to the bed, and I sit.

He and Anthony stand at the foot of the bed.

Mrs. Pryce tightens her grip on my hand.

Anthony murmurs, "Would you like some time alone with Esmeralda, Mom?"

She nods, her eyes fluttering away from me in his direction, and before he can turn away, she sees the bandage on his face and asks, seemingly mortified, "What has happened to you, Anthony?"

She turns her face back to me.

Now there's no fear there, only anger.

"Look at me, Esmeralda," she demands. "What have my children done to me? What did Charlene do? What has Abigail done? And now Anthony? Their suffering will kill me. I am dying. Look at me. Do you see? Do you? I can't take it anymore. I am dying. Don't they understand?"

I watch, listen.

There are a few things running through my mind.

A stream of consciousness, which is often the way I connect with my patients, in a kind of sensing of their … inner nature.

Some remind me of water: swift, placid, shallow, or deep.

Some are trees.

Some are but a dandelion wisp.

Some are a solid acre of fecund earth.

I feel Mrs. Pryce as I've never felt her before. At one time, I thought I knew her well, or as well as a kid can know her best friend's mom. She always felt like a breeze, lyrical and pleasant, cooling on a hot day.

Now, she feels close to fire, burning down.

I keep hold of her hand.

She repeats, "Look at me. I am dying. They will kill me. They have killed me."

She's glaring at me.

I turn, but Mr. Pryce and Anthony have left the room.

Her tan face is scrunched into a prune-like visage of … *hatred*.

I hold her eyes, but I'm unnerved.

I'm wondering, analyzing: What could cause such a sharp, extreme shift?

I wonder and wait.

Finally, she grimaces and nearly spits out, "They took my baby, Esmeralda. And it's killing me."

I don't want to upset her, but I know that verbalizing her emotions can help. So I nudge her along. "You're talking about Abigail?"

She gives me a sharp look. "No, I'm talking about Charlene, of course."

I lay my hand on her forehead.

She seems on fire, but there's no fever.

Still, she isn't making sense, getting Charlie and Abigail confused. She may be suffering with dissociative amnesia. She's certainly experienced trauma, and an unconscious longing to forget the terrible things that have happened to her daughter and granddaughter would be congruent with her behavior.

I remind her as gently as I can. "Charlie committed suicide."

"No, no, no." She struggles to sit up. "They killed her, and now they're killing me!"

She doesn't have the strength to stay upright and falls back against the pillows. "Take care of me, Esmeralda. Take care of me."

I whisper, "You must get some rest."

And with that, her eyes shut, and she begins to breathe heavily.

Asleep.

An older, bereaved woman.

But has she become dangerous in her grief?

She doesn't seem to remember hitting Anthony.

Or does she?

Is she upset with Anthony? Why?

And what did she mean when she referred to Charlie's death as a killing?

She said: "They killed her."

They … who?

I t takes me a while to wake up.

My eyelids feel like lead. So does my body. I try to raise my right arm, then my left, but I can't. I worry that someone's holding me down, and when I lurch upright, it's with a shriek: *"¿Qué pasa?"*

I look around. My bleary eyes try to focus on a familiar object, but there isn't one. Except … how could I *not* know where I am?

Everything's *white*.

I'm in a white room, in a white-covered bed with a white head-board, and there are two white end tables, a white reading lamp, white carpet—even an elegant, thin white vase with a long neck that runs up to the top of a beautiful, singular white rose, yet I can't see the green stem, thorns, or leaves, just the flower. I take a deep, eager breath of its scent, but it doesn't have one. This seems to trigger anxiety for the efficacy of my other senses. I frantically cock my head and listen for a noise—a bird, maybe, or a vacuum cleaner … but I hear nothing. No chirp, no whir, no voices, no laughter: no sounds of life at all.

It's creepy.

Even alarming.

I feel as if I'm in a tomb.

I reflexively start to run my fingers along the sheets, needing a tactile signal to the neurons in my brain that I'm still *alive*.

But the white fabric is so smooth, so silky, like air, and I bite my lip instead.

Ouch.

Okay.

I'm still among the living.

But I've got to get out of here.

Now.

I flip my legs out of the bed, relieved that my jeans are still on, and my socks, and my light-blue cotton T-shirt.

I scan the white carpet and spot my cowboy boots in a corner by the door. I think of Sam and feel a little better.

I scan for a clock but don't see one.

I peer at the light coming in through the heavy white curtains; having been raised to be aware of the time by the cast of sun and shadows in the canyons and coves around my house because I was always losing, or breaking, my watch, I know it's almost eleven in the morning.

Good.

Not too late.

I can be home a little after noon—if there's "normal" traffic.

I get up and put my boots on.

I clear my throat, softly at first, then louder, as if trying to announce that a real live person is going to be walking down the halls of this mausoleum. I open the large white door with a flourish and see that I'm on the same red-carpeted floor as Mr. and Mrs. Pryce.

I begin to walk …

Fast.

I pat my pockets.

Hey …

Where are my wallet and car keys?

I go back to the room and look around. I can't find them anywhere.

Did Anthony do this?

Take my belongings so that I can't leave the house without seeing him? Which is exactly my plan.

I remember our foreheads touching last night.

We almost kissed.

Well, *that's* not going to happen.

At heart and soul, I'm a natural-born healer, and Anthony was ultimately reaching out to me in grief. It's common for people who've lost a loved one to try to replace that love with someone else—that's all last night's actions were about.

Now I want some time to think about his mother before I give him a diagnosis.

Really, I'd like to sneak out of here—call him later.

I stop, thinking I heard something.

Now I'm as silent as the rest of the house.

Very quietly, I turn around, on tiptoe, and …

"Ahhh!" I scream.

"Hi, Emerald," Anthony says.

"Hi, Anthony." I chirp like the bird I was trying to hear earlier, a baby chirp, as if I've been lost from the nest.

Oh, for crying out loud!

I don't need anyone to take care of me, to pick me up and return me to my nest, or to my common sense.

Anthony's cheek still has a bandage on it, though this flesh-hued strip is smaller than the one he wore last night.

Despite the tough-guy look the bandage affords him, he seems so unassuming—even for someone with so much money. Heck. *Especially* for someone with so much money. But none of that can compare to his marvelous green office building in San Pedro with the gray-water system.

So why does he live in this energy-sucking house?

Why the contradiction? The hypocrisy?

I sense it intuitively—something's disingenuous here, and it may be more than the white-washed walls.

I say, "Anthony, I must go. Do you know where my keys and wallet are?"

He nods. "They're in the drawer of the end table on the left of the bed as you walk into the bedroom."

I must turn five shades of red.

Here she is, folks. The very same girl from high school, only it's twenty years later ...

And she's still: "Match Head."

But Anthony, on the other hand, has no zits.

"No zits, Charlie," I scold in my mind.

Anthony's saying, "You were only going to lie down for a minute last night, but you must have been exhausted. You were asleep the moment your head touched the pillow. I hope you don't mind that I covered you with the blanket."

I *do* mind.

I don't need ... covering.

Before I get a chance to speak, Anthony continues, "Did you sleep well? Would you like something to eat? Maybe some coffee? Can I get you some coffee?"

My mind is still groggy.

My mouth is pasty.

I want to go home, but I also feel like doing a little detective work on my own. Whitney arrested Anthony, then released him—which leaves me with two unanswered questions: Why, and why?

I nod. "That would be great, a cup of coffee. Please. Then I'll be on my way."

# 29

We're in the white-and-black airplane hangar that doubles as a kitchen, and I'm sitting atop the same high black stool that I sat on when I spoke with Detective Whitney. As I recall her deep, bountiful cleavage in the black granite island's reflection, I look down at my own nearly nonexistent cleavage, and I smooth my strawberry-blonde hair away from my forehead and wet my lips with my tongue. Honestly, I do feel once again like "Match Head."

Hmmm.

I've got to get over that.

I smile brightly when Anthony brings me a large white mug of dark-roast organic coffee with the perfect amount of soy cream— exactly how I requested it—and as he sits opposite me, his mouth with the slightest upward tilt, I murmur, "Thank you."

His green eyes light up, just a little.

It gives my heart a hopeful pause to see this grieving man at least appear more at ease inside his own mind, sitting down, almost relaxed, because that feeling of denial and the forceful, panicked desire to run away that can come with severe bereavement is usually a longing to depart the confines of one's own hurting psyche.

We gaze at each other, and it's a comfortable moment, as if we've known each other a long time, which we have. But this feels like something more. I realize, again, that we're bonded by tragedy and grief. And maybe it's also that continued bond of growing up on the shaky, ever-slipping geology of Majorca Point, knowing that at any moment the rug, the floor, the very earth might be pulled out from under us. But if that happens—we know how to deal with it.

Don't we?

I have to ask him …

"Anthony?"

"Do you want some more coffee?" He immediately gets up to refill my cup, but I wave my hand over it. Is he trying to avoid my questions?

But then he sits back down, as if at my beck and call.

So I ask.

"Did you stay in touch with Justin Fellowes? After Charlie died?"

He looks down, not realizing I can read his face in the shiny black reflection—and what I see is disturbing. A sudden rage that immediately tightens his upper lip, his jaw clenching, his eyes clamping down, then opening, fierce in the granite.

I wait.

He doesn't look up for a while.

When he does, the anger is gone, but I know, because I could see, that he had to work hard to assuage it.

His tone is mild. "Justin and I are working together."

That takes me by surprise.

"Really?" I say. "I didn't know the two of you were friends."

"We aren't," Anthony says, then adds quickly, "I mean, weren't. Not after Charlie died. I blamed him."

"You did?" I say.

Anthony nods.

I do, too.

For a moment, we're silent.

I ask him, "So how did you end up working together?"

Anthony takes a swig of coffee. So do I.

He tells me, "We have a project. We're trying to partner with PWE. You know, Pacific Water and Energy."

"What are you doing with them?"

He gazes into the coffee cup. "It's part of the new division I'm heading up, DVI Green."

I nod, urging him on, wanting to know more.

"We're trying to make desalination less harmful to ocean life," he says. "See, in the desalination plants we have now, part of the process requires the cooling water intakes to use ocean water to cool their generators. The generators are massive, and they literally suck in the water, run it through the plant, and shoot the hot water out the other side. Discharge it. But what that does is kill everything that's in the water. All sorts of marine life."

I cringe. "Like a giant vacuum."

He replies, "That's right. It will suck in anything that happens to be swimming by. Then it pins fish—and mammals, too—against the intake screens, and they die from the pressure."

"That's awful!"

He nods, grim. "It traps the larvae, eggs, and juvenile marine life, too."

I mutter, "It kills everything."

Anthony nods. "Whether we've got drought or not, we can't keep taking water from the Colorado River, or northern California. We're up against a wall at this point. Something's got to be done. So Justin and I have been working on putting together a viable solution to southern California's water shortage problems. I think we may have found one."

I abruptly recall the flagrant waste of water going on in his backyard.

I want to ask him about it.

But I don't want him to think I'm here now as anything other than a friend.

A delicate balance.

I venture, "This sounds groundbreaking, Anthony. I have to say, though, it seems to be quite a departure from DVI's usual investments."

That anger flashes through his jaw again—it's quick, but I notice it. "Justin's spearheading this. He does a lot of philanthropic work, and water is—is one of his *issues*, I guess you'd say."

"Issues?" I lean forward.

"His foundation helps children with lymphoma, all over the world," he says. "He believes that contaminated water is the cause. He's working, as he says, to 'put himself out of business.' To end environmental cancers."

I hear a faint sneer in Anthony's voice as he relays Justin's mission, and I'm not sure why.

So I do what I do in session. I nudge, seeking more information.

"Sounds like a good mission," I say.

Anthony recovers. "It is," he says. "The idea is, we can take what we do here and replicate it in countries that need clean water."

Then Anthony turns toward the entrance to the kitchen.

I didn't hear him enter, but Joseph is standing at the door of the vast room. He clears his throat in a clichéd butler way but otherwise doesn't move a muscle, only his mouth, as he heralds, "Penelope would like to see you, sir."

Anthony mumbles, "Yes, Joseph."

I see he's sweating. Is it about Penelope? Or something else?

He murmurs, "I've got to go."

I nod. "Yep. I do, too."

"Thank you for coming, Emerald."

"You're welcome."

It's not until after he leaves that I realize that Anthony never actually answered my question.

*How did you and Justin end up working together?*

He told me everything but the how.

30

I don't see Penelope on my way out.

I do hear a faint sobbing from somewhere—perhaps from the recreation room.

Maybe she's standing before Abigail's graduation picture again.

The thought makes me sad.

I drive home from Santa Monica with my heart heavy; I'm tired and ready for a bath. And a peaceful night's sleep.

But it's not even two o'clock in the afternoon, and the workday traffic on the 405 is at a standstill.

*¡Ay, Dios mío!*

I'm stuck in traffic with no phone, unable to research that alternative-energy start-up, or call a friend, or send a text. Not that I'm an advocate of giving myself over to the temptations of a cell phone while driving.

I'm not—and I don't.

Except in unmoving traffic.

But now I have time to think.

To think of those poor children with cancer.

To think of Anthony and Justin, doing business together.

To ask myself, again, why? How did the two of them—Charlie's high school boyfriend and Abigail's father—end up working together?

With, it seems, only two dead girls to connect them.

I wonder if I'm longing for my phone—if I'm focusing on technology, my smartphone in particular—in order to distract me from the reality of tragedy that exists all around me.

The filth in the air, the ocean, the land.

Two dead girls.

A grieving father who is also a suspect.

A former boyfriend who isn't.

Why not?

I begin to mull in earnest: Who killed Abigail?

And why?

And what was it that she wanted to tell me?

*I really need to talk to you. I'm wondering if we can meet?*

Again I wonder: What did she want to tell me?

Wait—did she want to *tell* me something? Or *ask* me something?

I try to remember that first message, the one I erased from my landline's answering machine. *I need to ask you something.*

Did Abigail say those words, or am I remembering them differently? Caught in a fantasy cycle—telling myself the story that I want to hear—because I want to retain some control over my memories of Charlie? I want to believe that I have the answers about her. But what if I don't?

I'm jolted out of my own head when five different vehicles suddenly begin to honk at me because the car in front of mine has moved forward six inches.

I politely wave my hand at my five newfound enemies and pull forward half a foot.

I wave again in the rearview mirror.

Please, no road rage.

Please don't shoot me because you've had a bad day and are stuck here and it's driving you around the bend.

I wave again at the man directly behind me with the beet-red scowl who I can see is still cussing me out.

I take a conscious, soothing breath.

I keep glancing at the cussing man in my mirror.

His face is so puffed up he looks set to explode.

I begin to worry he'll cause himself a cardiac infarction.

He looks to be at a tipping point—he could have a heart attack, or he could punch my window in.

I wish he wasn't behind me—but there's no place I can go.

It occurs to me that no one's done a study on how many people make it through a traffic jam without harming themselves or another driver, only to do something scary and unexpected at home. How many wives, husbands, kids—or pets, for that matter—get beaten, or worse, after the inevitable traffic jam on the 405 freeway?

Ugh—I hate being stuck like this.

But I have to admit, I welcome the distraction.

Dealing with the traffic is better than thinking about Abigail and Charlie.

I've done that before, distracted myself from sorrow with whatever's been convenient at the time.

I try to recall what finally triggered the tears I shed for Charlie and my parents. What ultimately made me comprehend that no matter how much I trapped my grief inside my brutalized psyche and soul, my loved ones weren't coming back?

I remember ...

It was the day Sam was born.

I was at The Falling MP Stables with Dove, Shelley, and one of the best large-animal vets in southern California, a man named Dr. Tim Crowley, who's since moved to Virginia to treat Kentucky Derby contenders.

We'd found an abandoned palomino mare galloping, in a panic, down Majorca Point Road in the early morning. How she'd ever managed to dodge the oncoming workday traffic, we still don't know, but the Majorca Point PD had received a call about the frantic mare and in turn had immediately called The Falling MP Stables, alerting Dove of the situation.

Dove and Shelley had picked me up at my house, and we rushed down Del Mar Avenue in their wheelchair-accessible van to the main road, with just a lasso, a harness, a lead rope, and our own love of horses, which, believe me, horses can sense. When we caught up to the runaway mare, Shelley pulled over to the side of the road. She and I got out, while Dove stayed in the back of the van in her chair.

The frightened mare was scratched and cut by brambles and wire and who knows what else, and even though she was obviously pregnant, her ribs were protruding. But then, this was at the height of a severe recession, and a lot of people were simply letting their animals—horses and all sorts of other pets—go.

Shelley and I moved slowly, both of us whispering.

That's right.

Whispering.

Horses truly *do* respond to that, and the tone of it, the empathy.

We also had carrots in our hands, and peppermint. That must be where Sam gets his almost obsessive predilection for the candy—he had it in utero.

It worked.

The mare, trembling, dehydrated, scared to death … *came to us.*

We fed her and slipped the harness over her head, and I walked her all the way back to The Falling MP.

Dr. Crowley wasn't very optimistic. In fact, he thought the poor mare wouldn't make it past a day or two.

But even her traumatized condition hadn't elicited a tear from me.

It was Sam's birth, three weeks later.

Nine years ago.

Seeing a new life, his wobbly legs, and knowing that he really shouldn't have made it, and his mother shouldn't have made it—that was what brought my sobs bursting, and I didn't stop weeping for a week, every time I saw him, because I'd realized, deeply, that the best things in life, the most valuable, *can't* be controlled.

They can only be nurtured—if they're lucky enough even to occur.

And the worst things in life?

The land sliding out from under your feet?

They can't really be controlled either.

Just endured, lived through—hopefully.

My eyes mist at the memory.

Then I wonder …

Does the question of control keep coming up for me, especially about Charlie, because, deep down, in my unconscious, I still wonder: Could I have controlled what happened to her?

Could I have saved her life?

I realize I was young, and I didn't know what she was going through.

Okay.

But …

What about Abigail?

Here comes another barrage of unasked questions.

Why didn't I meet her sooner? Her voice sounded like Charlie's. That should have spurred me to act quickly. So why didn't I try? Was I afraid?

I know … I know.

This is what happens in a traffic jam.

The body can't move so the mind starts *streaming*.

Stream of consciousness.

That red-faced man is still fuming.

I wave at him again.

And, abruptly, a memory surfaces in my mind's eye.

Twenty years ago.

I see Justin Fellowes, the cute, buff, *nice* Majorca Dolphin, at a mid-spring night's baseball game, waving at Charlie from the dugout. She eagerly returns the wave, throwing her head back to laugh, not a wistful note to be heard, just happiness.

I was smiling, too—for her.

Then I'm seeing something more.

Justin's long-lashed hazel eyes are on me.

He's waving at Charlie, but his eyes are on …

*Me.*

# 31

By the time I get home, it's nearly dusk, and I'm exhausted and annoyed (more so than usual) that there isn't more high-speed rail in Los Angeles, especially on the Westside.

Instead, the 405 just keeps getting more lanes.

I step out of my Ford with a huff and almost fall—my legs are actually numb from sitting in the same position for so long.

I rest my hand for a second on the hood of my car; it's hot to the touch.

My mind feels a bit slow.

The intuitive feel that I often have for my own home, and the moving land around it, is muted. Dull.

I blink my eyes, trying to make them open wider, as if I've been asleep for a long time.

I look west and see the sun sinking into the ocean.

Redder, reddest …

With a slight wobble to my step, I make my way down the dirt driveway to my doorstep, and by the time I get to the front door, everything's pretty dark. I guess I should have left the car's headlights on for a moment, just in case the coyote is thirstier, and hungrier, than

I originally thought and attempts a rare, risky move on a human for sustenance.

But when I feel around for the shadowed lock and turn the key, the door opens: no problems, no bumps in the night.

I turn on the lights.

I nearly faint.

The interior of my house is ...

*Destroyed.*

I frantically move through each room.

The contents of the old ranch cupboards and drawers in the kitchen have been ruthlessly emptied all over the floor. The scuffed brown faux-leather couch in the living room has been rolled over, and the bottom has been sliced down the middle with a knife or something equally as sharp, the stuffing flung everywhere. The bookshelves have crashed onto their sides, and the books, most of them collected by my dad, look as if they've been assaulted, their spines broken, yellowing pages ripped apart.

Then, my bedroom: It's been annihilated.

The bedding is strewn about the room, it climbs up the curtain rods, over my built-in desk, under my swivel chair, over my file cabinet, then runs all the way to the bathroom like toilet paper streamers. My files, bills, personal papers, and flash drives are scattered all over the bed. My laptop is lying open on the bed, too. The bed itself has a jagged slit in the center of the mattress, and my pillows are in shreds.

I'm breathing fast.

I run back to the kitchen and look past the entryway closet, down the hall at the dark green tarp that shields the house from the construction on the second bedroom. I'm amazed that it's still there, held down by the large concrete blocks—not even a ripple of air disturbs it.

Whew.

Even with the terror of this happening to my home, I'm relieved I don't have to put the tarp up again; it really was a lot of work.

I practically slide down the hallway wall and find myself sitting on the second bedroom's mattress.

That's nice—one piece of furniture that doesn't have stuffing erupting from it.

Except … wasn't it sitting on its side in front of the hall closet?

Didn't I reprimand myself the other night for blocking the small space when I'd pushed it out of the second bedroom?

I quietly stand up and edge, with my back against the wall, to the front door, away from the closet.

With my car keys in hand, I get one foot out to the front step, then the other—and before I see it, I smell it, a cloying, sweet scent, like antiseptic perfume, and then I glimpse a large hand holding a light-colored rag. I put the image and the smell together and realize I'm being attacked with chloroform. I shove my keys out, trying to stab the hand, and I must hit my target because I hear a low male voice yelp, then feel the hands tight around my head.

Then, all goes black.

—⁂—

At some time during the night, I wake up, on my back, unable to move. I can see nothing; my eyes are like welts, swollen, as if I'd been beaten, and they keep involuntarily shutting.

All of my other senses seem to have vanished.

But even though I can't see it, can't smell it, can't feel it …

I can …

Hear it.

I know where I am.

Next to the jacaranda tree.

My mother's tree.

And …

I can hear her.

"Don't move, *mi niña*," she whispers through the leaves. "Be still, very still. *Te quiero mi niña*, Esmeralda."

I whisper back to her in my mind. *"Sí, Mamá."*

Then I feel a rough, fetid-smelling tongue licking my face.

I can't help but feel relieved that my senses are coming back.

But I keep my eyes closed.

Is it the coyote?

"Be still, *mi niña*," my mom repeats. "Don't move."

A hot, dry nose nudges at my arm.

Oh …

*Mierda.*

There are *two* coyotes.

I hear a voice drifting down the slope, male, the same man that yelped when I stabbed him with my keys, but I can't hear what he's saying.

A flashlight runs over my body. The glare creates a red hue in the lids of my still-closed eyes.

The coyotes continue to lick me.

Another male voice, this one with a higher, nasal tone, almost squeals. "Ah … coyotes! Coyotes are eating her!"

The flashlight abruptly turns off.

The man who had the chloroform seems to move closer. This time, I can hear him clearly when he says, "Back off, Esmeralda. Or next time, it'll be *your* turn to jump off that cliff."

The coyotes stop, as if listening in the dark.

After that, I hear footsteps and, from farther away, a car's engine— it sounds like a mid-size sedan—not a hybrid.

The coyotes return to nuzzle my neck.

I can't help it. I'm terrified. I whisper, *"Mamá?"*
Nothing.
She's gone.
And then, so are the coyotes, suddenly—vanished.
I try to get up, but I'm pointed headfirst down the slope, and the blood feels like it's literally pooled in my sinus cavities.
It takes me a long time, but I roll onto my stomach, face in the dirt.
Then, trembling, I get onto my hands and knees. It takes me even longer to turn my body around so that my head is facing up the hill, toward my house.
I think I must lose consciousness a couple of times.
When I wake up later, I'm back at my doorstep.
And it's morning.

C all me crazy.
        Why should I care?
        Because …
    I'm not cleaning this mess up without placing blame where it's due—on Detective Suzy Whitney.

    After all, what do I have that's worth ransacking my house for? Worth killing for?

    And Detective Whitney is the only one who knows about that piece of cassette tape I found.

    Unless someone saw me find it. And watched me bring it home.

    Is it possible?

    Either way, I want Whitney to know what's happened.

    I crawl into the kitchen, fumble over a frying pan, and struggle to grip the open drawers beneath the counter. As I work to pull my body up, I see my underwear, tossed but still somewhat stacked. I think, for a moment, it's interesting they didn't dump my panties on the floor—which at least indicates that it wasn't a panty-raid sex-crime type thing—right?

    I cling to the recycled counter, grab the phone, and fall back to the floor, almost hitting my jaw on the still-open panty drawer on the way down.

Then, I call the ...

Bitch.

There, I've said it.

I dial 911, get the Majorca Point PD, ask for Detective Whitney, and when she finally comes on the phone, I practically foam at the mouth, saying, "Two men were at my house last night. They knocked me out with chloroform. They almost killed me."

"Calm down, Green."

She doesn't sound as alarmed as I'd expected, or hoped.

"You're not making any sense," she continues.

"Next, I'm going to call KLAT," I retort, "and let them know there's been a crime committed here. A crime that's linked to the murder of the heiress Abigail Pryce. Then, I'm going to make sure my face is front and center in those cameras, and I'm going to give them my professional, and personal, opinion as to what those creeps were after."

There's a pause.

"Which, in case you've forgotten," I add, "is the piece of evidence I called you about. The evidence your own people failed to find at the crime scene."

Another pause. I know she's trying to resist, but she can't.

"Do you still have this evidence?" she asks finally.

"You'll have to come here to find out."

I hang up.

Then I call Hugo.

—ɯ—

It's almost laughable.

They arrive at the exact same time, as if racing each other to the scene.

I can't say for sure whether they started from the same location. After all, Detective Whitney could have been connected to me from anywhere, and I called Hugo on his cell phone, so who really knows if they were cavorting somewhere? But when they pull their respective (or non-respective) cars into my driveway—his green Hummer, her chartreuse (yep, chartreuse) mega-SUV—they nearly collide.

Hah!

Maybe they do belong together. Two gas-addicts living off each other's fumes. Now, that adds a new dimension to "'Til death do us part."

I'm sitting on my front step under the glare of the morning sun with a nearly empty glass of water in my right hand and three apple cores lying at my feet. I feel a little better.

I haven't washed my face or brushed my teeth or hair—I don't have the energy for that yet.

I watch Hugo and Detective Whitney get out of their gas-exhalers.

They barely acknowledge each other.

I wonder, for a moment, why I always suspect Hugo of having an affair with this woman? Just because they're cooperative when it comes to their careers doesn't mean it goes beyond that. It occurs to me that Detective Whitney may be trying to manipulate me into feeling exactly that—wanting me to feel jealous, insecure, on edge.

Instead of being played by Hugo, have I been played by Whitney instead?

I shake my head.

I'll have to think about that later.

Hugo comes running, making a big show of concern.

He gets down on his knees and feels my forehead, asking, "Are you all right, Ez?"

I say, "I don't have the flu, Hugo."

His eyes look bewildered, then flash with irritation. "You've still got your salsa."

But I see there's a hint of a smile on his lips—and relief.

My face remains solemn—mostly because it feels numb.

I ask, "How long does chloroform last?"

Hugo shakes his head.

The earth abruptly tremors for a few seconds.

Another quake, a little larger than usual.

But Hugo doesn't seem to notice; he just looks a bit pale.

Maybe he's sensing not the tremor but Detective Whitney.

Suddenly she's casting a shadow behind Hugo, like a hawk coming in for the kill.

But it's not going to be me.

Not this time.

I ask a still-kneeling Hugo, "Where's the rest of your crew?"

As if on cue, a KLAT van spews dust up the hill.

Behind it comes a black-and-white cruiser.

Whitney raises both arms, presumably so the detectives in the cruiser can see her, but in my lingering state of being anesthetized, she looks more like an attacking peregrine falcon, and I cower for a second, then sit up straight and boldly look her in her dark designer shades. Hugo watches this for a moment, seeming confused by the almost palpable tension of estrogen and female posturing.

I realize that he's clueless.

Either that, or aroused.

I must unconsciously shake my head because he looks worried again, and he repeats, "Are you all right, Ez?"

Whitney snaps, "Quit with the small talk. What's going on here, Green?"

I feel more comfortable now, having them both here, using them as a type of leverage against each other. I reply, "I need your investigators to go through the house and look for clues, Detective.

Two men were here last night. You'll see they tossed the house looking for something, but I don't think they found it. I probably interrupted them when I came home. They grabbed me and knocked me out with chloroform. When I woke up, they told me I'd be next to 'jump' off the cliff if I didn't back off."

Her voice is laced with disgust. "What exactly do they think you need to back off from?"

I stare her in the sunglasses. "Isn't that *your* job, Detective?"

I can't see her eyes, but I sense her anger. "I've already warned you about hindering this investigation, Green. What is this evidence you think you have?"

Now I'm enjoying this a bit. "It's a shame you weren't more interested in it when I left you a message about it, Detective. Does it always take a near-death experience to get your attention?"

I turn to Hugo and say, "Since Detective Whitney isn't concerned with my well-being, to assure my safety and to assist in furthering the investigation of the murder of Abigail Pryce, I'm giving you permission to bring in your own investigative team. I'm also offering an exclusive to the story as to what, if any, relevance this event bears on the case." I take a breath and allow a meaningful pause. "It would be ironic, wouldn't it, Detective, if at some point later in this investigation *you* were found to be impeding it?"

In an odd way, I suddenly feel very fortunate to be able to pit these two, a TV news journalist and a homicide detective, against each other. The two professions are notorious for despising each other but also needing each other, at times so desperately that they'll put all supposed morality aside and, as the old saying goes, get into bed with each other to get what they want.

For a second, I wonder how they could not be sleeping with each other.

They stare at me—for the moment, quiet.

Stunned, I believe, is the right word.

Finally, Hugo stands and turns to Whitney. "Any news on Abigail Pryce is big news. If you don't plan to follow up on this possible lead, I'll bring my own team of independent forensic experts up here. But, of course, it's your call."

I'm looking up at them, their profiles remaining in shadow as the sun is still behind them, rising over the peninsula.

Whitney looks down to address me, her voice a monotone. "Okay, Green, I'll get our forensics people into your house. Don't go back in until I say it's clear. And don't touch anything."

Hugo turns toward me and says, "Please, Ez, sit in the van. Lie down and rest."

Whitney demands, "Where's this evidence you said you had? If you still have it."

How long did it take her to get back to me? And only because my house was broken into and I was nearly killed?

It seems so long ago, but it was only yesterday afternoon that I found this piece of plastic, riding Sam to the park next to Charlie's cliff, looking for a clue that might tell me who killed Abigail.

Looking for a key to my own past.

I reach under the front step. There's a hole under the stone, dug long ago by a gopher or a possum, or maybe a rat. Not the kind of hole you'd want to stick your hand inside—which is why it's such a good hiding place.

I take a deep breath, search with my fingers, then I touch it, the baggie with the broken piece of cassette tape.

I pull it out, grabbing hold of the bulge inside the bag.

What were the two men last night looking for?

This?

*Or something else?*

# 33

Detective Whitney is wrapped up ... coiled up ... in her own world again, and she doesn't notice I have a plastic bag in my hand. She repeats, "What's this alleged evidence, Green? You're wasting my time here."

Hugo has carefully stepped around me. He peeks inside the house and mutters, *"Ay ... Madre de Dios."*

I extend my hand out to Detective Whitney. The recycled plastic bag is actually glistening in the sun.

I realize it's been compromised as evidence, but if I hadn't taken a second look down at The Point, it wouldn't be here; *her* people sure didn't find it.

I say, "Well, at first, I thought they were after my cell phone, Abigail's message, but you still have it, right?"

She merely shrugs. "It's been entered into the evidence chain."

I expect her to acknowledge that she knows that Hugo called me fourteen times, and maybe, for half a minute, it had become a point of contention between them—but she reveals nothing.

Hugo, on the other hand, does an actual mea culpa.

It's obvious, to me, that he's relieved because he believes my phone's in the crime lab.

I grin up at him.

But he's not smiling, especially when Whitney turns to motion to the men in the cruiser and I silently mouth, "Fourteen calls?"

He shrugs—but his forehead is so tense it's bearing down on his nose.

I shrug, too.

He rolls his eyes.

I roll mine.

Then, finally, Whitney examines the bag, moving in closer. "What is it?"

I reply, "I don't know. But it was down at the cliff. Buried a little—wedged into some bushes."

She snatches the bag, peers at the plastic shard.

Her voice draws out in intrigue. "Part of a cassette tape."

She looks at me, but I still can't see her eyes behind those huge, Versace shades.

"Brady," she calls over her shoulder.

"Yes, Detective Whitney," my favorite cop answers, with one of his usual amiable grunts.

"I need to get this to the lab."

She looks back at me, smiling with a big, wide, red mouth.

Again, I feel as if I'm being assessed for food-worthiness.

This time, I think the predator senses good eats.

Yummy, happy food.

She practically purrs, "Thank you, Dr. Green."

Okay—now she's a cat.

I'm a mouse.

Cute.

I try to get up and groan.

My neck and shoulders are killing me, and so are my wrists.

Those jerks last night must have dragged me by my arms down the hill to the jacaranda tree so they could continue searching my house for the phone or this piece of plastic or … whatever it is they wanted. I really have no idea.

Hugo notices my distress. He darts in front of Whitney and gently lifts me, from under my armpits, to a tentative stand.

I look over his shoulder to the detective.

But she's already turned her back and is standing up the driveway with Brady.

I finally notice that her long legs are exposed by a short, red-leather miniskirt, with a short, matching jacket.

Who wears that kind of getup at eight in the morning? Unless she was out on the town the night before and hasn't had time to change.

Was she with Hugo?

He's still holding me, and my voice sounds a bit tight when I say, "You'll have to do the camera news thing with me *now*. After that, I've got to go lie down."

"In the van?" he asks.

"At The Falling MP," I say.

"Okay, *mi amor*."

"No, don't *mi amor* me."

"When are you going to trust me?" he whispers.

I reply as honestly as I can. "I don't know."

34

I give KLAT a pretty good show.

I have to—my freedom and especially my safety might be depending on it.

I still haven't asked Anthony for his attorney's name. However, I don't think an attorney could have saved me from the men who wanted to kill me last night.

I stand in front of the open door to my house. A woman with the KLAT news crew moves about with a handheld camera, adroitly filming me, Hugo, and the CSI team as they enter the debris-strewn hallway. I relay the events of last night as accurately as possible, given the fact that for much of the upheaval, I was unconscious.

Hugo's made a deal with Detective Whitney that he won't disclose anything that could undermine the investigation, including that the two attackers mentioned "the cliff" and that I would be next to "jump." I've also been asked to refrain from blurting that they wanted to "kill" me. In return, she's promised she'll do thorough evidentiary collection and keep me posted on her investigation of the break-in.

Hugo is cordial to her, but brief, and she barely looks at him.

In contrast, he's almost solicitous to me.

He's trying to prove something, I suppose.

That he cares for me?

Sure, maybe he does.

But I can't help but wonder if an exclusive on this story is what he's been after all along. Wasn't that the reason he came up here the other night? Because he knew that something involving me was about to happen, and he wanted to be first to get the news of any further development in the De Vos–Pryce heiress murder?

That would ramp up ratings at KLAT for a few days.

I sigh, worn out.

I still haven't brushed my hair or washed my face since heaving myself up the side of the hill last night, or, for that matter, after being licked by the coyotes, and while the woman with the camera bobs and weaves in a seeming attempt to zoom in on every blemish, imperfection, and blotch on my face, I consider mentioning the two wild canines—but decide against it.

Their eerie presence is just too close to the utterly preternatural hushing voice from the jacaranda tree.

My mom.

I believe she ...

*Came to my rescue.*

Even with the tumultuous and truly agonizing last couple of days, my psyche is comforted by the sense that my mom is with me.

When I'm done with the interview, I see Shelley parked at the crest of my dirt driveway in a white van—new, with a hybrid engine, and even though it's big, it gets forty-two miles per gallon in stop-and-go traffic.

Now, why couldn't Hugo have gotten something like that?

Oh, stop, Esmeralda.

It will never happen: A cad is a cad is a polluting cad.

I surmise that Shelley's waiting to take me up the road to the small ranch house that she shares with Dove, which sits on a rise just above the stables.

Hugo must have called them.

He helps me into the passenger seat and whispers, "You mean so much to me, Ez. You must be careful. Please."

Shelley gives him a nod. "She's going to eat, sleep, eat, and sleep some more."

Hugo raises my right hand to his lips and kisses it, gently.

Tenderly.

Later, in the guest room at Shelley and Dove's house, I sleep for more than ten hours after gulping down a homemade, blueberry-and-banana almond-milk shake. I dream that Hugo is kissing me, tenderly, on the mouth, next to a Majorca Point cove ...

When I wake briefly, I will my unconscious to switch off that dream.

Quick.

I slip back into sleep and dream about my mom.

My beautiful mother, RosaMaria Nieves-Green, was born in the United States. When her mother, my *abuela*, was a young woman, she'd worked for a wealthy American investor named John Temple, who'd helped build one of the first hotels in the tourist area of Cancún in the early 1970s. She'd originally been hired to work as a maid but, in just a few months, had shown such a unique talent for flower arrangement that Temple had sponsored her to come to America. He went through all the proper legal channels so she could gain a visa, and finally citizenship, to help design the interior of a Latin-themed restaurant he was opening in downtown Los Angeles.

My *abuelo*, originally from El Salvador, had escaped a terrible civil war there and moved to Los Angeles, where he found work as a truck driver. One day, he delivered some supplies to the restaurant where my *abuela* was in charge of the color scheme—he had brought the paint.

The rest, they say, is history.

I dream …

It's a long time ago: My *abuelo, abuela,* and my mom as a pretty little girl are riding in the front seat of an enormous, shiny blue cab, hauling an immense semi-trailer behind them, coughing and choking on the thick smog of the latter twentieth century, stuck in traffic on the infamous 405 freeway but smiling happily, even joyously—after all, the air pollution was in America, and nothing could ever really be wrong in America.

Even smog.

I wake up.

Clear my throat.

I look around, seeing heavily shadowed white walls, afraid for a moment that I'm back at the Pryce mansion. But then my eyes catch on the floor-length blackout curtains with the hand-embroidered, fluorescent green-and-purple designs of horses jumping over moons. I sigh and relax, then put my head back on the soft pillow. Earlier, I must have literally fallen into this bed for the first truly satisfying sleep I've had in a week.

Has it been that long since this dreadful mess began?

Thinking of messes—I groan.

My own house must be even more disheveled than it was after the two men tossed it, since I've never known a forensic team to be tidy.

I lie in bed, pulling the bright, multicolored quilt—with each square depicting more embroidered horses jumping over fences, shrubs, and streams—on top of my head.

I don't want to get up.

I don't …

I focus instead on the muffled sounds of a working stable in the early morning: horses whinnying after being turned out to the lower enclosed field to eat grass, socialize, and run; the scraping of a stall being cleaned; a laugh shared between the two stable hands, Ernesto and Franco; the steady, pounding gait of a canter in the outdoor ring, followed by the staccato bumping of a trot.

Shelley must be already outside and training.

Then I think I hear Sam's whinny.

I get up.

—⁓—

It seems I sleep in my clothes a lot these days—when I step out of bed, I'm looking at my jeans and the light-blue T-shirt I wore to the Pryce house ... when?

The night before last?

Hmmm.

That's a bit disgusting.

I need a shower.

I open the door of my room, the house quiet, like the Pryce house, except every white surface of wall in this hallway is covered with ribbons, medals, and photos of horses, riders, and Shelley and Dove. I'm there, too: a large, framed picture of me when I was in my twenties, kneeling down with Sam as a colt.

I can't help but grin.

He was such a spunky little guy.

A survivor.

I head toward the kitchen.

Dove's in there, sitting in her high-tech wheelchair, spinning around on the hardwood floor, making coffee, toast, and tofu.

I swear she's just about to do a wheelie when I enter and say, "I can't believe I slept for so long."

She spins around, her body and red-blanketed, atrophied legs looking so tiny, especially when compared with her large, wide face and open, gregarious smile. She's waving a wooden spatula at me, ordering, "Sit, Esmeralda. Sit. You must be starving. I've made you my latest, greatest specialty: tofu scramble with virgin olive oil, a hint of vinegar, capers, olives, and tomato. All of it organic. How does that sound?"

Dove's a vegan, too. Shelley goes out for the occasional turkey burger.

I'm salivating.

I reply with gusto, "Yum."

Before I sit down at the round wooden table covered with a cheerful-looking lemon-yellow tablecloth that matches the curtains on the window above the large, old-fashioned porcelain sink, I ask, "Can I help?" But I already know full well that Dove never allows anyone to do anything in the kitchen.

I sit and tell her, almost fiercely, "Dove, you're an angel."

She chortles. "You *are* hungry."

She prepares the food for me and then, with one hand on the controls of her wheelchair, slowly steers over to me, her other hand deftly placing the plate on the table.

"Oh! I forgot the toast."

She steers back to the counter, retrieves the multigrain toast, and brings it over with aplomb.

I can imagine her suddenly bursting up from her chair—and dancing—though it could never happen.

I pick up an antique silver fork and take a bite.

She sits to my side nearest the stove, looking content as I eat with practically as many adjectives as mouthfuls.

Then, when I'm finished, she stares at me with her bright, almost beady brown eyes and says, "What have you gotten yourself into, Esmeralda?"

I raise my head to explain, but she cuts me off.

"Whatever it is—it must stop," she orders. "You could have been killed by these men ... whoever they were." She pauses. "Do you know who they were?"

"No," I answer, almost forlornly.

She nods firmly and continues, "You mean the world to me, and Shelley, and Sam, and your friends and patients. You're a *good* person, Esmeralda. Shelley and I are determined to keep you safe, and as much as I know how you feel about Gabriel ..."

"Hugo," I correct her, a little too quickly.

"Hugo." She sighs. "He cares about you deeply. He stayed here last night for—it must have been six hours—just to see if you might wake up and need him."

"Six hours?"

"That's right." She nearly admonishes me. "He's a decent man. I know, I know ... he's a *man*."

She smiles for an instant.

So do I.

"But he'd lay down his life for you." She returns to her serious tone. "And Hugo, Shelley, and I think it would be wise if you stood back from this ... murder ... even if it does have a connection to your friend Charlie. It's become too dangerous."

I lower my head as I finish my toast.

Dove sits quietly, waiting.

When I look up, it's with genuine appreciation because, in many ways, she's like my mom, and I need to hear that someone cares enough to take the risk of telling me, "No."

But I was also a bit of a rebel growing up, particularly with my mom, and you can take the rebel out of the child sometimes, but it's difficult to take it out of a green psychologist—we're always rebelling against the traditional psychoanalytical system.

So ...

I purse my lips and breathe out slowly.

Thinking.

Breathing.

Thinking.

With Dove, as with Hugo, as with almost any circumstance—psychological, emotional, or ecological—that comes my way, I always try to be completely honest if I don't know what the heck it is I should be doing. Finally, I say, "Let's just see how things go."

Spoken like a true Majorca Point girl.

Let's just see how much the land slips ... today.

Now, *that's* what I call living in the moment.

# 35

W hat do you mean I can't go in there yet?" I demand, standing at the doorway to my home, which is still cordoned off with bright yellow crime-scene tape. If the forensic team was still inside collecting evidence, I could understand, but no one's there. Apparently they finished late last night and won't be back.

According to Lieutenant Brady.

He's been here in his black-and-white for who knows how long.

It's after noon, I've taken a shower and borrowed some clothes from Shelley, and I'm ready to tackle the ominous job of cleaning up my house, but Brady's not letting me inside.

Truthfully, if I don't get in there soon, I'll lose my motivation.

The place must be absolutely *gross*.

I bluster, "This is an outrage!"

Brady grunts; then, after shuffling his polished black shoes in the dust and dirt, he climbs the driveway up to his car and calls somebody on the radio. I can't make out a word he says, but when he ambles back down the driveway, his shoes begin skidding on the gravel, and he practically yelps, "Go ahead. Detective Whitney gave the okay."

I wonder whether this is one of the detective's strategies to keep me in check—by emphasizing that she's got control of my life, and my house, even from afar, or if it's simply one more indicator of the time lag between reality and bureaucracy.

I guess there's about a fifty-fifty chance of one, or both, explanations being correct.

I rip through the yellow tape with my uneven fingernails and open the door.

I carefully tiptoe over the mess in the hallway and take a right turn into the kitchen, where I step over the frying pan, then pick up the phone from the floor, where I must have dropped it yesterday, and call Shelley and Dove at the stables, just as I'd promised, to let them know I'm safely inside.

Then I take a big inhalation and stand there.

Disillusioned.

I take another big breath and thank God, Goddess, the great universe, and my mom and dad, that I'm not ...

Dead.

The place is *that* wrecked.

What were they looking for?

Would they have truly killed me?

It's a warm day, but I'm cold, and my arms are wrapped tightly around my torso, my jaw rigid with chill.

I whisper, "Charlie?"

But the chill's not the manifestation of spirit.

Just terror.

No big deal.

It's at that precise moment I hear a surge of voices and footsteps at the front door.

Suddenly, at least ten people are in my house. They carry trash bags, mops, brooms, scrubbers, pails, and environmentally friendly cleaning products. It's my second family, the core of The Falling MP: Shelley;

the stable hands, Ernesto and Franco; and a close-knit group of riders: Ann Portnoy and her husband, Mark Portnoy; Giovanna Regal; Darcy Belle; Morgan Aventura; Eddie O. Wilson and his son, Jack.

Dove is back at her house, preparing dinner for everyone.

I almost burst into tears.

I have such good friends.

But this is typical of The Falling MP, and a credit to Dove and Shelley, because they've created a place where we can form the kind of strong, lasting bonds with one another that helped create the part of our country's history that resonates with the spirit of the land.

They help me.

Ann, an accomplished Western and English rider, keeps the mood light as she sweeps up shards of broken glass in the kitchen and chats about a horse she used to own that would stick her tongue out and spit every time someone tried to groom her. "She just didn't like to be cleaned up. Like a child who hates taking a bath. And, to top that off, she used to roll in the mud, too!"

"What a character." Darcy laughs. "I remember my first horse— Winnie, an older dapple-gray mare—was best friends with a goat. The goat would follow her around the pasture and into the barn, and when I'd saddle up and go into the ring for a lesson, that goat would stand at the rails, bleating, crying, until Winnie came out."

Eddie is bagging armloads of couch and bed stuffing, and he comments wryly, "Horses with good homes. Good owners. I used to work on a ranch in Idaho—long time ago. I was taking a year off college. I was on a search. The man who owned the ranch used to get real angry—who knows at what? His wife? His life? I never knew. But he used to take it out on the horses. I'd watch him run his finest quarter horses into barbed-wire fence. He'd be up in the saddle, spurs kicking in their ribs, forcing them into that sharp, spiked wire again and again until the blood was flying everywhere. Sometimes the horse would be so badly injured, he'd shoot it. Then he'd go for about a month calm and happy as hell. Until he wasn't. And he'd be running a horse into the barbed wire again. I ran away from that place, returned to college. I never looked back."

We've all stopped, listening.

Morgan, a twenty-four-year-old law student, says, "These days, in most states, he'd be in jail for animal cruelty."

We all nod.

We don't say it—but we know it.

There's a definite correlation between how a human treats another species and how a human treats himself, or herself, and others.

We work hard the rest of the day.

Sure enough, by dinnertime, the place is put back in order not that I've got a bed or a couch or pillows that have any stuffing in them—but after a truly delicious and festive meal of soy tacos, rice, black beans, guacamole, chips, salsa, and Dove's homemade corn tamales filled with apples and cinnamon, I return to my house with Shelley, Ernesto, Mark, and Eddie. These four friends are going to spend the night in The Falling MP van, taking turns guarding the house, but first they come inside with me and scrutinize every corner of every room. They also look behind the dark green tarp to the open space of the second bedroom, making sure all's safe.

It is—or as safe as it can be.

Shelley has offered to give me her pistol—but I don't want it.

Not yet.

Maybe I'll take it tomorrow night, when they all aren't watching over me from the van. It's occurred to me, quite a few times in the last twenty-four hours, that even though I've never fired a weapon, if someone really plans on killing me—I could be persuaded.

I pace for a while, back and forth, around the house, fusing with it, trying to sense a harmful presence.

Finally, when I'm feeling at ease, I give a thumbs-up to my four friends that I'm okay, then I lock the door and also the rarely used dead bolt, sliding it into place with a precise thud.

That sound makes me feel better, too.

I walk around the house again, noting the furniture that survived the attack, already training my mind to forget the pieces that didn't make it.

Slipping land.

Slipping reality.

It happens.

But I'm still *alive*.

I'm starting to feel almost upbeat.

I kick my boots off in the living room, where my friends dragged the still-intact second-bedroom mattress, and, although I leave my clothes on (at least this time they're clean), I cover myself in a navy-blue sleeping bag with a soft, cozy red-and-blue plaid lining. It was given to me by my dad when our family went camping one summer near Big Bear Lake.

I've made some hot chocolate, and I watch TV.

The two intruders upended my medium-size flat-screen from its stand against the wall and opposite the couch, but they didn't break it, and I surf past most of the near-midnight fare to KLAT, wanting to see if they've gotten any more info on the Pryce murder.

I've got good timing.

Right in front of my eyes is …

Me.

—⚉—

I'm staring at the pores on my nose.

I feel a flush of embarrassment swell up my face to the top of my head.

I scold the woman who was filming me yesterday: "Oh, please. You couldn't have given me a break? I'd just spent the night with coyotes!"

I turn the sound down.

But keep watching.

The camera zooms in on my puffy eyes.

My dry lips.

The freckles on my chest.

My hint of cleavage.

How ...

*Inappropriate.*

As if he hears my thoughts, the phone rings, and I give it a glance, recognize the number, and pick it up to say, adamantly, "Hugo."

"Yes, Ez."

"How come all of KLAT's reports on everything, including murder, are spiced—no, no, laden—no, no, *infiltrated* ... with SEX."

"*¿Cómo?* What do you mean?"

"I mean, how come that camerawoman absolutely ... lingered ... on my breasts when I was talking about my house being broken into, and—"

"How come you don't appreciate that I got your story on the news in the first place?"

Here we go—the questions.

Back and forth.

"How come you don't realize that this kind of ... sensationalism ... is a bane to women everywhere?"

"How come you don't realize that we have to play the ratings game just like everybody else?"

"How come you don't realize ..."

I pause.

"What?" he prods.

I'm still silent.

Thinking.

Breathing.

Remembering the close-up of poor Abigail's lifeless body after the Majorca Point PD pulled her up the cliff, the black wire basket cutting into her pale, smooth skin.

The tiny blonde hairs on her arms.

This time, I visualize the deep scratch on her palm.

But, still, something's bothering me about the image.

I hear, of all people, Whitney's voice. *That scratch is not consistent with the injuries she sustained when she went over that cliff.*

What?

"What?" Hugo keeps repeating.

I look back at the TV. A commercial.

I let out a sigh. "Nothing, Hugo."

"Are you all right?" he asks. "Do you want me to come over?"

"No, thanks."

"Do you want me to stay on the phone with you?"

I look around at my dark house, the TV the only light in the clean but nearly barren room.

"Yes," I finally say.

I turn off the TV and lay my head down onto the sleeping bag's inlaid red-and-blue plaid pillow, the phone resting next to my ear as I stare up at the ceiling.

Sleepily, I ask him, "Why did you call me fourteen times?"

I hear him groan. "I still don't trust your friend Anthony Pryce. Don't trust him, don't like him. I was worried."

"You were worried?" I whisper. "Or you're a control freak?"

He groans again.

I sleep.

At three in the morning he wakes me.

"Ez?"

My eyes fly open.

My tongue's thick and pasty, and I can barely form words. "Who's there?"

I hear his voice on the phone.

"*Mi amor*, you're snoring."

I say, "Don't … *mi amor* … me."

"*Mi amor*," he says again.

I sleep until daybreak.

## 36

Over the next few days, I make my house livable again.

I'm trying to stall it from slipping. Or I'm trying to stall my house from slipping from my own consciousness because I can feel that holding it up, holding this illusion of its continued e xistence up, is getting harder for me. So, slowly, like taking a warm bath when the muscles are aching, I allow myself to relax the pressure of mentally cultivating a future with something that can't last, and in doing so become aware that a part of me is still, after all these years, trying to keep my parents alive, and to keep Charlie alive, too.

Ultimately, I'm trying to keep alive a way of life that doesn't exist anymore.

But I love my house.

I love so much about that lost way of life.

So I try to adapt, yet again.

I try to figure it out: how to hold onto the best of both worlds.

The first thing I concentrate on is the furniture.

I've always adored my old, scuffed faux-leather couch, even though it was most likely produced with every environmentally toxic chemical known to humankind in the twentieth century. But my dad used to sit on it, his legs crossed, playing the guitar and singing, even teaching me the alphabet that way. So I want to save it.

What can I do?

There's no stuffing for it.

The entire underside was slit with the attacker's knife, or knives, as were the cushions, and the innards were haphazardly tossed around the living room.

Thankfully, they didn't harm my antique oak four-poster bed. It was my mom and dad's bed, passed down from my dad's family, shipped all the way from Ireland. But the eco-friendly mattress I bought for it a couple of years ago is ruined—ripped apart. The pillows were hacked, too.

Good thing I wasn't asleep in bed when my attackers arrived.

I have little doubt they would have stabbed me right along with the mattress.

After they'd found what they wanted.

Whatever that was …

I'm standing in my bedroom, cringing, looking at the remains of my organic cotton sheets. My Falling MP friends tried to fold and stack them neatly in a corner, since I'd wanted to pick through everything and see what was at all salvageable.

But they're shredded.

Again, I cringe.

My eyes search for a moment of respite.

Find it.

Amazingly, my laptop endured the assault, and someone from The Falling MP put it back on my built-in desk, and it's ready to go.

I sigh.

My laptop and TV—the plastic stuff—survived with nary a scratch.

I feel very ambivalent about that because as much as I abhor plastic, I love the technology.

Another eco-conundrum.

The rock and the hard place.

So I try to figure that out, too. Or at least try to make the technology work for the environment, somehow, and it does—I Google myself up the key to fixing my toxic couch with eco-friendly stuffing.

Or foam.

—m—

The "BiOH foam" is shipped to me the next day, arriving in a truck that states on its side that it runs on natural gas.

Life is good.

Or getting there.

I insert the pieces of soy-based foam that has no harmful chemicals and, most important, no "BPA," or flame retardant, into the torn couch. I'm feeling both energized and foolish. I also found out that even though I've been concerned about BPA getting into my body via things like water bottles, I didn't realize that the BPA in the foam in most furniture will escape as dust and make its way into every corner of a person's house or office and, then, into her body.

Right.

Have a little immune system compromise with your loveseat.

I almost happily sew the jagged tear together with near-matching, dark-brown organic cotton string.

At dusk, sweaty, my fingers red and sore, I take a tired step back, assessing my inexperienced handiwork.

I like it, in a grotesque way.

The mutilated couch is once again whole, and even though I can see the brown, stitched-up scars—so what?

It's been recycled.

And it proves, once again, that there's opportunity in adversity—or in nearly ending up a slasher victim.

Or a coyote's meal.

Or, for that matter, a person learning that cancer can be caused by the chemicals in her home, or her yard, or the water coming out of the tap.

That makes me think of Charlie, of her whispered voice: "Water…"

What did her warning mean?

And then I realize I'm connecting the two—hearing that one word in my head, remembering Charlie's warning to me all those years ago: *Stay out of that water.*

Somehow I know that it's all connected; I just can't think of how.

Charlie and Abigail falling from the same cliff.

Abigail contacting me before she died: *I know we've never met before, but you knew my dad's sister, and … well, I really need to talk to you.*

And then another voice intrudes—I hear Penelope, accusing Anthony: *If you hadn't allowed her to get involved with that documentary … that environmental documentary …*

Abigail and her documentary. Did she discover something that Charlie also knew? Something that someone didn't want her to know?

But who?

The question goes round and round in my head.

I can't figure it out.

Yet.

I whisper, "I'm going to try, Charlie."

I'm just not sure how.

Over the next few days, Hugo calls me every morning and night.

He tries pleading, anger, frustration, concern, and finally, blatant sexual entreaty to sway my thoughts over to his side—but I resist him.

For now, anyway.

—m—

Anthony calls me, too.

He tells me he saw me on the local CBS, NBC, and ABC news channels, and that makes me wonder, for a moment, if the English-speaking stations carried it because of the near-exposure of my breasts.

I've become so cynical.

I don't want to be cynical.

I mull this over while listening to Anthony.

He's been promised that Abigail's body will be returned to the family for burial within four days.

"I hope you'll be here, for the service."

He sounds so lonely and vulnerable.

"Of course I will," I tell him.

Then he asks me to come again today, to look in on his mother, and I have to decline. "I'm sorry, Anthony. I've just got to take some time for me."

"It's safe here," he offers. "I worry about you being alone there. After being threatened like that."

"I'll be okay."

There's a pause between us, and I think of Abigail again, of the documentary. Could that cassette have been related to her work? Was it even related to this case at all?

Again I think it must have been trash, simply unearthed from its burial spot after the last quake.

But it didn't look weathered, as though it had been out in the elements for more than a decade.

It looked shiny. Almost new, except that I don't even know if they sell cassette tapes anymore.

I decide to ask.

"Anthony, this is going to sound strange, but did Abigail have any cassette tapes that you know of?"

His long pause makes me wish I hadn't asked until we were in the same room. You can hear a lot in a voice, but you can see that much more in a person's body language and facial expression. Now, over the phone, he has time to recover, and he says smoothly, "A cassette tape? No, I don't think so. Everything Abigail had was digital. You know kids."

"I guess so," I say.

"Why do you ask?"

Now it's my turn to try to recover. I take his lead and say, "I'm doing an article on the effects of digital media on teens. Attention spans, social lives, and the distance it creates between them and their environment—that sort of thing. I didn't mean to pry about Abigail—I'm sorry. I'm just collecting anecdotal evidence where I can."

He doesn't buy it; I hear new tension in his voice when he says, "I need to go check on my mother. Take care, Emerald."

He's been using my old nickname all week, but hearing it just now gives me a chill.

—⁓—

I try not to think about the case as I spend a few hours at my built-in desk, on my laptop. I find a green stock I like—this one is a new company with a couple of reputable environmental names on the board, and they make high-tech, non-toxic, extremely strong equipment to repair water and sewage systems. I learn that the federal government may award a large contract to this company to overhaul much of the nation's antiquated wastewater infrastructure before a complete disaster takes place.

There seems a true symbiosis in that.

But Majorca Point probably won't see any federal assistance since, conversely, we've managed our precarious situation wisely, mostly because we're always threatened with infrastructure breakdown as the land may slide at any moment.

Yep. We citizens of Majorca Point have stayed one step ahead of a wastewater catastrophe—because we've had to.

Thus, ironically, no government help will be available to me.

I'll still need to make the money to pay for the pipes.

But this is a stock I can comprehend, from a life experience point of view, as well as an ecopsychological perspective, since the very *idea* of tons of raw sewage making its way into the drinking water, as well as the streets, will tip the Washington vote toward funding the overdue project.

That's my bet.

The name is Rialto World Energy.

I decide to buy some of the company's stock—just not yet.

I'll only buy after it's been beaten down in price, as it most surely will be before it goes back up.

Experts say: Buy low, sell high.

That's what I try to do, too.

But what the experts don't tell you is that a stock that's being watched for a "breakout" to the upside (due to something like a government contract) will most likely go lower before it shoots up because so many market-makers (those frantic-looking men and women you see on the stock exchange trading floor waving their arms around and screaming out bids and asks), want to get in—for cheap— and they'll purposely beat it down. They might pay other people to bad-mouth it on Internet stock chat boards, or put out negative rumors, playing all sorts of shenanigans that can't be traced. Then, when everybody in the so-called "know" has bought in for relative pennies, they'll "pump" the stock back up with positive news.

It's a game.

A lot of the time, it's a dirty game.

But it's also very much like nature because nature is dirty, rainy, too hot, too cold. Gray days that sometimes seem to go on forever. Floods, earthquakes, drought, tidal waves, typhoons, monsoons, hurricanes.

Nature has never been a perpetual "day at the beach."

Now, with climate change, everything is just that much more extreme.

That's the perspective I take when buying and selling stock.

I look for the bad weather.

There's opportunity in it.

Maybe the most important thing to remember is that the stock market absolutely, completely runs on a "fall down and get back up" premise.

My forte.

So now I'll just wait for the falling-down moment.

Then, like I always do, I'll get back up.

—◆—

The next day I spend outside.

I ride Sam and fuse with the slipping land that I love. The land that I understand because it's like me: adaptive but stubborn. In a way, we've shaped each other, since it was my *abuelo*'s hands that built my house, and while I continue to rebuild it, chunks and pieces of both new and old foundation now make safe, shady homes for fox and

rabbit and squirrel.
   And snake.

—⁓—

   Detective Whitney doesn't call me.
   Remarkably, it turns out to be a truly blissful three days.
   Also in that time, on the peninsula that I cherish as it shifts, shakes, and slowly crumbles, sliding down to the waiting arms of the Pacific Ocean, I realize: I'm ready.
   For what?

## 37

I don't know from where it's going to come.

Or from whom.

But I can feel it in my soul, my psyche; it's coming with a stealthy message of perception.

"Listen …" the jacaranda whispers.

I sit beside the beautiful, tenacious tree, so like my mother. She was a gentle, loving woman. Very pretty, with dark brown eyes and valentine lips—that's what my dad used to say, which made her blush and smile. But she was also the one to literally carry him up this hill when he fell and broke his ankle while planting some purple Mexican sage along the border of our property.

Mom.

I miss you.

I carefully pat the dry, ashy dirt around the base of her tree. The lilac-colored blossoms are gone for the year, but next year they'll return.

And she is always with me.

"Listen …" my mom whispers.

And then I hear it—what I hadn't been able to hear in the moment but can now hear clearly.

Anthony's voice.

*I worry about you being alone there. After being threatened like that.*

How did he know I'd been threatened?

He said he'd seen me on the news—that was how he knew what happened.

But I'd been forbidden to mention the threats on the news.

Still, somehow, he knew.

How?

Was he behind this?

My body had known, even then—the shudder I felt when he called me Emerald. The body always knows: the biology of nature.

I don't know what to do.

Call Detective Whitney? It's not as if she'll listen to me.

And what real proof do I have?

He will say he *assumed* I was being threatened—isn't that the natural assumption when one's house is torn upside down, that a deeper threat is lurking somewhere?

Besides, I still can't quite fathom that Anthony had anything to do with his daughter's death.

Even if the police seem to think so.

The phone rings.

I still haven't gotten another cell phone. I've kept in touch with my patients via my landline and will see Jonah tomorrow.

"Go ..." The tree whispers in the still, almost sweltering morning air.

I stand and run up the slope, sweat bursting from my pores. The sun, hotter today than yesterday, is breaking another southern California heat record.

I answer the phone, longing for a cooling breeze.

My voice trails with disappointment when I hear Hugo on the

other end of the line—but who did I expect?

My mom?

Charlie?

A ghost?

Hugo's preamble is chatty.

He's up to something—I can tell.

Hugo's not much for superfluous chit-chat. For crying out loud, now he's even asking me about the weather. I'm completely on guard.

"Okay, Hugo," I say with an edge, "what's up?"

"What do you mean?"

"Why are you behaving like a salesperson?"

"You think I'm trying to sell you something?"

"Are you?"

"Why would you think that?"

I almost tear at my hair and ask, "Can't we ever have a conversation that doesn't involve grilling each other?"

"I thought you liked that ..." His voice sounds almost morose.

I sigh. "I do," I answer truthfully. "But only sometimes."

We're both silent for a minute.

I stand at my recycled-glass kitchen counter, looking out into the living room toward my now BPA-free couch, then past it through the sliding glass doors, the sun glaring up to the middle of the cloudless, bright blue sky, and my eyes reflexively seek the shade underneath the porch's faded brown canvas awning. I find some relief upon the small wicker table, that place where Hugo and I had our last moment of tenderness.

That is, before I was interrogated about a murder I know nothing about.

Or do I?

I hear Hugo say something about a night out.

"Tomorrow night. Hollywood. At the Kodak Theatre. For the

LAMAs—the Latino Annual Media Awards."

It sounds like a date, a real date.

I'm quiet.

I need to focus on the moment.

The slipping, shifting moment.

"The awards start at five," he continues. "First the awards, then to Rascals, that new Latin-Asian–Middle Eastern fusion place. I'll pick you up at—"

"Wait," I cut in. "I haven't said yes."

I can't give in this easily.

He waits.

I finally answer, "Thank you, Hugo. I'd like to go. But I've got patients all day tomorrow, so I'll be running a little late. Can I meet you there?"

I *do* have patients all day.

I also don't want to lie to him about how I feel. About him. About whether he's been sleeping with Detective Whitney. About his Hummer.

He tries to hide the disappointment in his voice. "That's fine."

I pause for a minute, considering just asking Hugo about these things. Is he as attracted to Whitney as she, apparently, is to him? Do I really mean as much to him as he says, once you take the De Vos–Pryce news out of it? And how can he continue to drive that Hummer when the world is facing unprecedented climate change? Is he just one more male marking his territory with his gargantuan carbon footprint?

But I don't ask him any of these things. Instead I say, "How about if I take the Metro Rail to Hollywood, and you can give me a ride home?"

Oops.

I quickly add, "Just a ride home. That's all."

His tone sounds a tad less dejected. "Okay, Ez. I'll have someone meet you at the door."

"Great."

We hang up.

I walk to the bedroom.

Open my closet.

Grateful, thankful, incredulous that the intruders left my clothes alone.

And then it feels suddenly good and delicious to be caring about …

Climate change? Electric cars? Slipping land?

No.

What … dress … to … wear.

## 38

I take the Los Angeles Metro Rail, an ever-growing work in progress, which is great—soon we might be able to cut the smog in this city by half.

Now, if they could just build some rail to take the place of the 405.

First, I park my car at the Green Line station in Redondo Beach, a sprawling beach community about three miles north of Majorca Point. I ride in the fast, smooth train just a short way, then change to the Blue Line in Wilmington, and finally transfer to the Red Line.

I'm dressed to the ninety-nines—at least for me.

I've even got a handbag—a tiny black one—attached to my wrist with a stretchy black band.

I must look like I'm on my way to the proverbial ball.

But nobody seems to notice.

This is LA. Everybody's dressed in their own version of hip, or chic, or get-out-of-my-face-before-I-kill-you attire.

There's that cynicism again.

I really never wanted to go that route.

But it's been a long day.

A hard day.

Especially with Jonah.

As I sit on the train, speeding along, never once having to pay attention to a stoplight or a car in front of me or behind me, I bow my head, close my eyes, and try to relax. When the Red Line train stops in Hollywood, I actually have to shake my head to wake up. I slowly make my way out of the station, through the crowds to the entrance of the Kodak, still feeling half-asleep.

Suddenly, lights are popping off in my face from all directions.

For a moment, I think I'm being attacked.

Then a hand is on my elbow. I turn, and it's Hugo, and he's smiling, waving at the eager crowd that stands behind a red velvet rope. We walk up a long, lush red carpet, and it's amazing what a few cameras can do. I feel (almost) entirely rejuvenated. I even begin to strut, just a bit, in my clingy, black, backless, nearly-to-the-floor-length dress. I have to admit—this dress isn't that eco-friendly. But I usually tread very softly on the earth. I try my best not to purchase many toxic items—from toilet-cleaner to clothes.

Still, I never said I was perfect.

And tonight I needed to wear a not-a-care-in-the-world dress. I needed the release of pressure, the lift up, because I feel low.

And it's not only my worrying and wondering about Anthony.

I feel as if I failed Jonah today. Not that I haven't experienced this unpleasant sensation with some of my other patients. As a psychotherapist, you learn that, no matter how hard you try or what theory you practice, you'll still sometimes fail your patients. It's only through hard-won experience that I've come to know the best thing to do after therapy has gone awry is something completely different. I've got to try to change my own perspective to then, I hope, understand what I missed in the session.

Jonah's session.

Well …

Strutting it on the red carpet in low-cut, skintight, poly-based material is *different*.

I try to enjoy it.

Hugo, of course, picks up on the incongruity of our phone conversation of a few nights before as he whispers in my ear, "You look beautiful, Ez. You gonna be mad at the press if they take a few pictures of your sexy, *muy caliente* body?"

I turn to him and smile. "Yes. But that will be then, and this is now."

In the moment, it's the only way I can get through most of my slipping life.

I giggle, a little, entering the Kodak.

*Having fun.*

—⁓—

We sit with our arms touching.

Hugo looks dashing in a black suit, so silky it shines, and it matches his nearly black hair and eyes.

This evening, I can't help feeling a joyous pride in my heritage, in my mother's family: So many of these intelligent, glamorous, successful people come from a similar background as my own. Most are second- or third-generation immigrants, and their parents or grandparents probably risked losing their lives, homes, and families in México or Central America to come to *El Norte* to work hard, very hard, at the most menial jobs—the jobs no one else would want—to assure their progeny could have a better life.

I watch as a tall, thin man, the owner of KLAT, is presented with a lifetime achievement award. The presenter, an older, beautiful, well-known Latina actress, who I remember was nominated for an Oscar a few years ago, jokes easily with the enormous audience as if we were all in her dining room for an intimate dinner party. In fact, the atmosphere, even in this large venue, is warm and convivial. There's a feeling of accomplishment, but more than that, I think, there's also a sense of home.

A sense of being accepted.

By our peers, as well as the many other races, cultures, and ethnicities that applaud, laugh, and embrace.

I laugh and applaud along with the rest. Hugo's hand clasps mine whenever it rests on the arm of the seat, and he holds it to his lips many times, smiling sideways at me, his eyes bright but serious.

My heart is doing the hypnotic rhythm of the ...

Brazilian samba.

A two-four beat.

Luscious.

I let him hold and kiss my hand.

I smile back.

I don't have to think about what might transpire later.

I'm feeling *good*.

Then I hear a familiar name—and I think I must've heard wrong.

I quickly look over to the stage.

I hear Dr. Justin Fellowes being announced by another Latino presenter: the mayor of Los Angeles.

I nearly stand up so I can better see Justin Fellowes walk to the stage.

I can't believe he's here.

I turn to stare at Hugo, but he doesn't seem to grasp the significance of this moment for me. And how would he? He doesn't know that this man was once Charlie's boyfriend.

In fact, nobody knows.

Just me.

He was a secret—an older guy, just by a year, but Mr. and Mrs. Pryce were strict back then. Especially with Charlie.

So I was the only one who knew.

And Anthony.

I almost forgot …

She *had* to tell him—he caught her sneaking out of the house one night to meet Justin—and they made some sort of bargain with each other. To keep each other's secrets.

And as far as I know, they both did.

Or did they?

I watch Justin Fellowes take the stage. He doesn't look all that different, despite the years that have passed. He's still lean and muscular; his hair shows a few streaks of gray, but other than that it's still full and curly; his jaw's still square, and, yes, I remember—his chin's still ever-so-slightly dimpled. He takes the steps with athletic zest, two at a time, and when he gets to the podium, he shakes the mayor's hand, then, with both arms, exuberantly reaches out and hugs him.

Some people in the audience get to their feet, clapping and cheering.

The mayor moves back, and the doctor stands before the audience, his handsome face slowly tilting, his smile abruptly verging on sheepish, his arms and hands postured at his sides, palms open as if emptying his pockets of material wealth, his sleeves even a bit too long, as if to suggest a complete lack of interest in façade. His entire persona seems to bespeak the utmost humility.

I'm flabbergasted.

Charlie's heartthrob has become a near …

*God.*

The crowd is still cheering.

Finally a few people sit, and then so do others.

He leans into the microphone.

We wait for him to speak.

He begins, his head still tilted in a kind of unspoken servitude. "Years ago, when I took the Hippocratic oath, I also swore to myself that I would use my opportunity for knowledge as a gift of service to those who'd been abandoned, even brutalized, by an uncaring, unseeing world."

Justin looks out to the crowd for a moment, silent, and when he speaks again, there's a powerful emotional waver in his voice, almost otherworldly, as if by treating those people who were less fortunate, he's been forever transformed.

A dark screen is lowered behind him.

The crowd waits, hushed.

The first image is of thick green vegetation and what appears to be a swamp. The caption below reads: Nigeria. As the camera, clearly handheld and maybe even a smartphone, moves in closer, I see something dark, brown-black, and bubbling up from the surface of still water. The person holding the camera wades into the water, and we watch high, yellow boots lift in and out of the oily muck. It must be oil. The camera pans out from the swamp to a crisscross of worn-looking pipes, huge things, broken and leaking. The camera pans out farther to the surrounding land, and we see a small village, clotheslines in the breeze, children playing. We see that some of the kids are playing next to a very large, bubbling pool, that there are many pools of the toxic stuff. But the children play next to it as if it's fresh water.

Justin narrates, his voice booming, "This is the Niger delta, where many oil companies laid pipelines for oil forty or fifty years ago. Now, the pipes are breaking. The oil companies do nothing."

My mind is whirring.

Oil, polluting the water ...

Water—one of his *issues,* as Anthony told me.

Anthony and Justin, in business together.

But why—especially if DVI, Anthony's company, is one of the companies that does this sort of damage that Justin is so against?

Justin waves his outstretched hand at the terrible, disturbing image, and more like it follow: oil spills, oozing earth, dead dolphins on ocean shores, and frail, sick-looking children. The images seem to move faster and faster as they cover more territory—in Africa, parts of Asia, the Middle East, South America, and Central America.

Then, we abruptly cut to a montage of some of the same frail children we've just seen, but this time they're in American hospitals. They appear to be undergoing treatment for cancer, their hairless heads bowed to cuddle stuffed animals or to draw pictures with crayons, and when they look up at the camera, it's with the special smile that only children seem to have—one of innocence and pure optimism. Soon, we see the same kids, healthy and happy, with hair beginning to grow on their heads, playing outside at a picnic underneath a big white-and-green banner that hangs between two enormous eucalyptus trees. The banner reads: JustInTime.

Justin Fellowes's charitable organization.

I'm so caught up in the joy of the finale, I barely notice the lilting music in the background, but when I finally do, tears spring to my eyes.

I'm thinking about Charlie.

I'm thinking about Abigail.

Both are dead.

But, thankfully, these beautiful children are alive.

What did Charlie and Abigail need to survive?

There's a wisp of insight connecting in my mind.

Something …

The crowd is making a connection between compromised ecology and compromised immunity.

And I am, too.

Hugo's got a hold of my hand.

He's mouthing, "What's wrong?"

I realize that my heart is beating rapidly, that my palms must be sweaty. Something is connecting in my mind ... I'm just not quite sure what.

The music stops.

The crowd's applause swells, feet stomping, cheers verging on screams, and Justin is trying to speak, waving his hands, waiting.

Hugo's got my fingers to his lips. He's whispering in my ear, "Why are your hands so cold?"

I shake my head, trying to silently placate him.

The crowd begins to hush. Justin moves closer to the microphone and says solemnly, "The most powerful images in this film were taken by a talented young documentary filmmaker and dedicated environmentalist—Abigail Pryce."

There are a few cries of disturbed recognition from the audience.

My heart pounds in my head.

All this time, Abigail had been working on a documentary—with Justin Fellowes.

Why didn't Anthony mention this? Or even Detective Whitney?

Justin must be a suspect.

Right?

He can't hide behind his philanthropy—not for murder.

Justin declares, "We will never forget you, Abby."

The crowd starts to clap again, this time with temperance and dignity.

I look at Hugo, but his face is blank, other than his concern for me. He must not have known about this connection either.

So clearly Detective Whitney isn't spilling all her info to Hugo.

I watch as, once again, Justin spurs the audience into another blast of spontaneous, vigorous energy. He raises both of his hands into the air, his too-long white sleeves sliding up past his wrists, and shouts, "If we all work together, we can reach the heavens!"

It's then that I can hardly believe my eyes.

I see ...
*A deep, red scratch.*
Across his knuckles.

# 39

I cannot tell Hugo.

Even when the award ceremony's over and the glittering crowd seems to roll as one giant wave across Hollywood Boulevard to the western side of Highland Avenue, to the latest trend-setting restaurant, Rascals. Even as we all hungrily partake of uniquely inspired Latin-Asian–Middle Eastern tapas, things like sushi with goat cheese and soy-and-mango salsa—I don't tell him.

Not about the scratch.

It was more like a gouge, between his knuckles.

I think …

My eyes must have deceived me.

Justin Fellowes is a good … amazingly good … man.

Is it really so farfetched that he would work with Abigail on his documentary? He and her father are business partners, after all.

I'm not going to jump to conclusions.

I'm not going to jump …

… *next time, it'll be* your *turn to jump off that cliff* …

I try to conjure the voice in my mind.

Was it Justin Fellowes?

No. It can't be.

Justin Fellowes has more important things to do than destroy the inside of my house, chloroform me, and then try to kill me.

Doesn't he?

I try again to remember that voice, and all I can hear is Charlie's: "Water…"

Maybe I'm trying to make Charlie's wistful … *ghostly* … voice … Valid.

Because that may be what a part of me wants.

I want my friend's voice to be *real*.

As if she never died.

I shake away the voices, bring my mind fully back to the present.

I'm standing near the center of the room, nibbling on broccoli tempura wrapped in grape leaves with a hint of aioli mixed with soy sauce. It's *fantástico*. I make sure I give an occasional smile to Hugo while he has the obligatory chat with his producer. His eyes sparkle back at me. Dinner will be served soon, but so many of the LAMA guests are obviously more interested in the party, and it appears the tapas and cocktails will prevail over a regular sit-down affair until much later.

Especially when the music starts.

I didn't realize I was standing right next to the dance floor, and I quickly move aside as couples from every direction assail the polished wood. The band, which seems to have appeared out of nowhere, is beginning with a famous Latino hip-hop artist doing his rendition of salsa.

He's got a terrific voice, and I find myself moving to the deep Afro-Cuban beat.

There's an arm around my waist, and I turn to dance with Hugo— we both know the steps—but it's not Hugo at my side.

Justin Fellowes pulls me close.

"Esmeralda Green," he says in a low whisper to my right ear. "I'd recognize you anywhere."

Again I try to discern whether his voice matches the one at my house the other night.

But the thing is: Both voices are out of the context of real life.

One at a too-loud Hollywood party.

One in pain and angry at being stabbed with car keys.

Not your normal daily fare.

I respond, "I'm happy to see you, Justin." And it's true. I *am* happy to see him, and I really hope that he's the saintly visage of goodness that everyone believes him to be. I smile up at him, and then, as a couple of incredible dancers move in our direction, I clasp his right hand to move us out of the way.

I must admit, I want to feel his hand, just for an instant, to find out if there's a cut there. But I'm definitely not expecting him to ask in a flirty tone, "Would you like to dance?"

I'm still holding his hand, tightly.

My fingers searching for a scab, a wound—something.

He leans his chiseled face closer to my cheek, saying, "Come on, Esmeralda. For old-times' sake."

And with that, he sweeps me onto the floor.

I catch Hugo's eye—or eyebrow—it's cocked at an unsettlingly high angle.

Anger? Jealousy? Intrigue?

I blow him a genuine, heartfelt kiss.

Then spend the rest of the dance spinning like a top.

When the music ends, my hair's in my face and my dress is twisted and—to my near-horror—almost exposing my left breast. I quickly adjust the shiny, poly-based material, grumbling to myself that it's the last time I wear a non-organic dress—it literally feels as slippery as the oil it's made from.

Justin's still close, his body pressing against mine. He gives me a flashing grin, and then his handsome face clouds, and in a longing voice reminiscent of Charlie's wistfulness, he says, "You're gorgeous as ever, Esmeralda. To me, you'll always be sixteen. Those were … beautiful days."

I don't know what to say.

It confirms my memory.

Of how that day, on the baseball field, he'd looked past Charlie to me.

How he'd never loved her the way she wanted him to. The way she deserved to be loved.

He always had his eyes elsewhere. Looking for something more. The greener grass.

Is that what he's doing now?

By partnering with Anthony?

What does Justin Fellowes have up those long sleeves of his?

Every part of me knows something is wrong—and I think Justin senses it.

His lips brush against my cheek.

I glance down for another quick look at his right hand.

Nope.

No scratch. Not that I can see, anyway.

He gives me a small, sad smile.

Then he turns and walks away.

—⁂—

It's only as I make my way toward Hugo and look down to make sure my tiny black handbag is still attached to my wrist after all that spinning, that I notice …

A spot of red.

Just a smudge.

Right there on my palm.

Is it blood?

Well …

Maybe it was the good doctor after all.

Nursing a jab made by a desperate woman with her keys?

I feel depressed.

I don't want to believe it, you see.

I want someone from my past, Charlie's past, to be happy and successful and passing on the things we felt were important in high school.

Saving the planet.

And children.

No … no … no.

I rub the smudge, and I'm comforted when it disappears.

After all, it could have been from a scratch of my own from that night. Or it could be a smear of lipstick.

It just can't be Justin who did that to me.

It's just got to be somebody else.

—๛—

Hugo and I dance the night away.

I don't mention the spot of red on my hand.

I purposely don't look at Justin Fellowes.

When Hugo and I aren't dancing, he's procuring me more of those vegetable tempura tapas wrapped in grape leaves. I can't seem to get enough.

I'm also running down every possible scenario in my mind.

Justin wanted me killed because … I had Abigail's message on my phone. But she didn't reveal anything. She certainly didn't mention anyone's name. But he doesn't know that. Or … he wanted to kill me because he knows I have that chunk of cassette tape. Which may or may not be anything related to Abigail at all.

I eat more.

Dance more.

No … I just can't believe the attacker at my house was Justin. It doesn't make sense, mostly from a common-sense point of view: Even if he did have something to do with Abigail's death and wants me to back off, why would he go to my house himself? He's a rich, famous person. Like Anthony, he has people for that sort of thing.

Like Anthony. When I think about it, either of them could've hired people to come to my house and threaten me.

Hugo and I dance and dance.

We consume a gallon of water.

We laugh, and embrace, and kiss.

I'm finally ready to take a ride in Hugo's Hummer.

Maybe in more ways than one.

He really is so … *hot*.

But I'm saved from my indiscretions by …

Another murder.

## 40

The crime in Los Angeles seems to fluctuate with the weather—and there have been studies to show that when it's unseasonably warm, crime jumps dramatically. I've actually been asked by several universities to teach an ecopsychology class pertaining to just this kind of phenomenon: extreme temperature and how it affects human behavior. But honestly—sometimes it seems preposterous that I'd be asked to teach this in schools.

*Of course* the weather affects our moods.

Most of us are aware of that.

Too bad it takes the scientists forever to catch up with human, especially women's, intuition.

As an example, I'm able to intuit almost immediately, when Hugo's phone vibrates, that something's wrong.

Hugo takes me to the side of the dance floor and quickly reads the text message on his phone. I watch as his eyes get wider and his mouth cuts a sharp, deep line. When he lifts his face, his head is already shaking.

"What?" I ask with growing dread.

He can't hear me, the music overtaking my vocal chords.

He grabs my elbow and leads me toward the front door.

"Christi Shah," he says.

"What?" I ask again, feeling my stomach knot.

"She's dead," he replies, not looking at me now but making big swinging gestures with his hand above his head to a group of people just sitting down in an adjacent room for dinner. He's mouthing, *"Venga. Venga. ¡Vamos!"*

"What happened to her?" I demand.

"That's all I know right now," he tells me. Then, "I've got to go, Ez. Sorry." I can almost see the wheels in his head turning, his thoughts moving in every direction, but somehow he's also able to make arrangements for me. His voice comes in rapid spurts: "It's too late for you to take the Metro Rail, too dangerous. This is Phaedra." A young, petite black woman with a symmetrical face and smart, quizzical eyes appears at his side. "She's one of my assistants. She'll drive you home."

Phaedra nods.

"Wait ..." I say.

Not liking him ordering me around. Not wanting to be stuck in a car and obliged to make small talk with Phaedra either. I've got questions. I'm adamant. "I want to know happened to Christi Shah."

But he's gone.

Literally gone, with his crew. Disappeared out the door, into the nighttime crowds on Highland and Hollywood. I poke my head out the door.

"Hiya, beautiful."

I'm nearly run over by an Elvis on stilts.

Right behind his towering, gold-chained figure is a red-and-blue costumed Spiderman. He's followed by one of the Three Stooges— what was his name, the guy with the blond hair?

It doesn't matter.

All I can really see in front of my eyes is a memory of a nice, dark-haired woman in a short white dress, surrounded by green plants and sustainable fixtures, weeping for her boss's daughter.

Christi Shah. Dead?

*How awful.*

Tall Elvis smooth-talks: "Do you want some free passes to the Hollywood Wax Museum?"

"No," I whisper politely.

For me, when I feel this upset, I usually search for nature to fuse with—it soothes me—remarkably.

Always has.

But this is the city, and practically every character ever to appear on a movie screen is out on the streets, most of them probably out-of-work actors getting paid minimum wage to dress up in various costumes to hawk free passes and tickets to shows. Then there are others who are mildly, or more so, dysfunctional and feeling at ease with the ensuing Tinsel Town chaos on a near-tropical October night.

Spiderman's hissing, making a "spidey" sound. A little bit of spittle hits my face as he hisses through his small, white teeth, "I've got tickets to a new TV sitcom. Buy one, get one free."

Then Hugo's assistant, all five feet of her, gets in front of me and barks, "Hey! Get your spit outta here."

Then she turns to me and says brightly, "Are you ready to go?"

I look at her.

This tiny woman could probably take me down—and I have no doubt Hugo's instructed her to do just that if I try to elude her and take the Metro Rail back to my car.

I sigh.

"Okay," I finally answer.

Spiderman's still hissing and spitting as we walk onto the sidewalk, but after a ferocious-looking scowl and a semi-karate move from Phaedra, he scurries after tall Elvis, trying to crouch under the man's long white coat.

I follow Phaedra to her car, thinking about Justin. Now there doesn't seem to be a need to call Detective Whitney to tell her my theory. Even if it were possible that he'd killed Abigail, he could not have been the one to murder Christi Shah. He was here all night, in plain view.

Or was he?

I'd stopped looking at him—but was that because I really wanted to? Or because he slipped out during the festivities?

## 41

I've been quiet, mulling over the death of Christi Shah in my mind, and Phaedra is having a running dialogue with herself as we take the Santa Monica freeway west toward the 405—just how many times have I driven that insidious freeway in the past week?

Now she's talking fast, something about Greece.

"My mom named me Phaedra because she saw it on a billboard for jeans, or cigarettes, or something provocative and sexy and all that. I don't think she ever knew what it meant, that it was the name of a character in Greek mythology. She just liked the way it sounded. After she died, I had so much grief. I went searching for a place to vent it, and I was lucky I found an acting class instead of alcohol or drugs. I enrolled in the UCLA theater program and auditioned for a play in my junior year called *Hippolytus*. And what do ya know? There was Phaedra, in this ancient play by Euripides. Have you heard of him?"

I nod, vaguely.

However, I'm merely pretending to listen.

It's not that I don't like Phaedra—I do. I've only just met her, but she drives a Toyota Corolla hybrid, and that's good enough for me.

But I'm trying to hear my own inner voice that is weaving round and round: Who killed Christi Shah? Was Anthony involved? Or Justin? And who killed Abigail? And why?

I have a lot on my mind.

I have no desire to discuss Greek mythology right now.

I just want to be alone with my own conjecture.

My own Greek tragedy.

But Phaedra continues, "There are three versions to the story of Hippolytus—did you know that?"

I shake my head.

"Yeah. It's kind of like *American Idol*, voting on different outcomes, only two thousand years ago. See, this writer, Euripides, wrote two versions that had Phaedra dying. One, she committed suicide because she felt ashamed at having been in love with Hippolytus, who was actually her husband's son."

At the mention of suicide, I can't help but take more notice.

"Two, Phaedra committed suicide because she felt guilty for causing the death of Hippolytus because apparently he was killed after she lied and said he raped her."

I'm listening.

"But in the third story, Phaedra didn't die. She felt ashamed for being in love with Hippolytus, but she didn't kill herself."

I ask, "What did she do differently in the third story? How did she stop herself from committing suicide?"

Phaedra glances over and gives a wry smile. "She *endured* it. That's how we interpreted it at UCLA. She didn't give up. She endured the shame and guilt and name-calling—all of that nasty life stuff. She handled it."

My breathing is quicker.

It abruptly occurs to me that Charlie may have killed herself because she felt shame.

Shame that Justin was capable of degrading her?

And she couldn't handle it.

Could it be?

I don't know.

*I blamed him*, Anthony had said about Justin, after Charlie died.

Was Justin really to blame?

Charlie seemed stronger than that.

But then, Justin's comments about her butt are never going to be okay with me, and her response to it is always going to be disturbing.

My mind, ever the adaptive traveler—shifts to Abigail.

Abigail didn't commit suicide.

She was pushed.

Was Justin to blame for this, too?

I ask, "You said Hippolytus died?"

Phaedra nods, hands firm on the wheel, voice steely. "He sure did. But only in one version. In another version, he was resurrected and made to be a god in a forest. A beautiful green forest."

I remember, again, how Justin disappeared before Charlie's death. As if to escape any possibility of guilt, or blame.

Then, as if resurrected, he went on to Harvard, to eventually save the lives of hundreds of children.

Phaedra says, "I suppose Hippolytus, even if he did get to come back as a resurrected god, suffered."

"What do you mean?" I ask.

She grins. "He got used by an older, wiser woman. I think Phaedra was probably a cougar for her time. Know what I mean?"

I smile a little and nod slightly.

Still, why would Justin harm Abigail?

It really doesn't make much sense.

Yet when nature's integrated with the human experience, I believe, all sorts of messages, signals, and ideas that we'd otherwise disregard as completely random and nonsensical come to light.

Just like the tribal women of hundreds of years ago would understand that seeing a dead bird on the side of the path could be a sign of coming disease.

There are signs.

People are part of nature, too.

We forget that sometimes.

But the twenty-first century Phaedra driving the car may have just signaled something ... meaningful.

*Prescient.*

—⁂—

We arrive at the Metro Rail parking lot in Redondo Beach.

She beams her headlights at my little hybrid Ford in the shadowed darkness, and I thank her sincerely for the ride, and for the insight—though I've told her nothing about Charlie and Abigail. But when I get out of the car, I ask, "Why are you working with Hugo now? Did you decide not to pursue acting?"

She laughs, her slender, smooth neck rippling with mirth.

"I'm still an actress. I'm breaking in. But being somebody's personal assistant during the down times sure beats waitressing, doesn't it?"

I realize this woman's got no doubts about herself.

She knows what she needs to do to stay ... vital.

Then, I finally understand what I missed in Jonah's session, too.

I'd been distracted—with everything that's happened—and I'd missed a whispered reference to his mother, having been concentrating on making sure his stirrups were long enough, since I swear he grew in the week I hadn't seen him.

Now, I mentally kick myself for not asking him about it.

For not following his lead.

With kids suffering from PTSD, an adult's wandering mind can signal abandonment just as quickly, if not more quickly, than an actual, physical disappearance.

Had Charlie felt abandoned, too?

I think of Phaedra and the play, and this brings me back to Justin. Maybe, for all his success, he hasn't been able to outrun his guilt after all.

Maybe, like Hippolytus, even if resurrection is possible, we still suffer.

Hmmm.

Best car ride I've had in a long time—considering I just wanted to be alone.

Says a lot for carpooling, doesn't it?

42

The next day—I get a new phone.
I choose the color orange.
It somewhat matches my hair.

Okay.

I'm vain.

What's going to happen when I get that first gray hair? Are there any organic dyes? Henna?

I don't even know.

I'm sitting in my car in a nondescript parking lot outside a phone store in Torrance, on hold for Hugo.

I could have texted him, but I have *questions*.

When he finally comes on, he gives a light smooch into the phone, and before I'm able to stop myself, I smile.

Then I must cut to the chase. "I haven't seen anything on KLAT, or any of the other news channels, or anywhere, about Christi Shah. Does that mean she's all right?" I ask hopefully.

"I'm fine," he says. "Thanks for asking. I had a good time last night, too. Do it again? *Sí, mi amor*. Any time."

"I did have a good time, Hugo," I emphasize. "But I—"

He tells me, "Save your breath. I'm sorry, but Christi Shah is dead. The press is downplaying it. On orders from—"

My tone sounds more snide than I intend when I say, "Let me guess. Detective Suzy Whitney."

"Her, too," he affirms. "It's mostly the De Vos family. Because Christi Shah worked for your friend Anthony." When he mentions Anthony's name, I notice that his tone, too, sounds snide.

For a moment, neither of us speaks.

The driver's side window is open barely an inch, and I stretch my neck and breathe in the fresh air from outside, not wanting to turn my car on just to open the window more. But it's also getting hot, the sun starting to beat onto my windshield, and the air smells like stagnant car exhaust and fast-food burgers and fries.

I wrinkle my nose and get to the next question. "Could you please do me a favor?"

"Not about Christi Shah."

"It's not about Christi Shah."

"Who's it about then?"

"Am I bothering you?"

"No. I only know that sometimes you're too inquisitive for your own good."

"That sounds like good ol' fashioned machismo to me."

"It's not, Ez. But just because you know some of the players in this *malo*, very *malo*, bad business—doesn't mean you should get involved."

I have to say to myself three times: He's not a creep. He's only worried about me … He's not a creep. He's only worried about me … He's not a creep. He's only worried …

Then, he surprises me.

"Okay, Ez. What's the favor? I can't promise anything. But I'll listen."

I know when I'm being thrown a bone—and I take it.

"Could you find out if Detective Whitney knows about that witness, the one who saw Abigail with someone on the cliff? Have they provided any other info?"

"Oh, Ez…"

I ask, "Why not? I just want to know why Abigail was up on the cliff. That's all. You know …" I pause.

He says, "What, Ez? *¿Qué pasa?* Too much subterfuge—even for you."

"Thanks a lot," I reply.

He says, "Come on … what else?"

"I want this murder solved, even if I have to solve it myself. Not just because I know some of the people, as you're so fond of saying. I don't want to have any more visitors at my house, or anywhere, who want to kill me."

"That's why I don't want you involved—"

He's abruptly cut off by a radio, or mic, in the background. When I can hear him again, he tells me in a near monotone, "I've got to go."

"Hey!" I call into the phone.

"Okay," he barks. "I'll look into it."

He hangs up.

"Thanks," I whisper. "*Gracias.*"

## 43

I have no intention of dismissing Christi Shah's death—or Abigail's—and I don't care if the almighty De Vos family doesn't want anybody poking into their private lives.

We're talking about *murder*.

And the next one sure won't be mine.

I'm still sitting in the parking lot outside the phone store. Though I'm breathing in the smell of burgers and fries—things I don't eat—I'm beginning to salivate anyway. I open my glove box and search for a snack. I usually keep some nuts in there: good for the heart, and tasty.

However, I sometimes like them un-heart-healthy: salted.

Oh, well.

At least I'm not dressed in a poly-based product today but one of my usual, comfortable organic cotton T-shirts, this one a bright turquoise with short sleeves.

I think while I'm eating organic cashews.

*Ay, Dios mío*, they're excellent.

Apparently I'm so comfortable in my loose jeans, I eat the whole bag. But that's okay …

I've got a plan. Well, not really a plan, but I'm going forward with it.

It starts with calling Detective Whitney.

Not to ask her about the witness. That's more sensitive information and needs to come from Hugo. I don't want her to know just how much I plan to investigate.

But I can let her know that I plan to investigate just a little.

To my surprise, she takes my call.

"What is it, Green?"

"Nice to hear your voice, too, Detective," I say.

"What do you want?"

"I've been wondering whether you found anything of significance at my house. Prints, fibers, DNA ..."

"We've got the lab working on it," Whitney says. "That's all I can tell you."

"Did you find prints on that cassette, for example?"

"The lab found some partials, and they're working on it. Again, I can't—"

"This is evidence you have thanks to me," I remind her. "Don't I have the right to—"

"To impede a criminal investigation?" she interrupts. "No, you don't. Is there anything else?"

"I'm curious about Justin Fellowes," I say.

A pause.

"What about him?" she asks.

"I understand he was working with Abigail on a documentary just before she died."

"What's your point, Green?"

"I'm wondering whether he's been questioned, that's all."

"Of course he has," she says irritably. "He has an iron-clad alibi for the night Abigail was killed."

"So he's not a suspect?"

"No, he's not. He was in surgery all day and at a charitable event that evening. Hundreds of witnesses."

For a moment, I'm relieved. Then I realize that this doesn't exactly mean he's innocent.

"That reminds me," I say, "I saw Justin Fellowes at an event last night myself. With Hugo."

I pause here, just to let this sink in. I can't help it.

Then I continue. "It occurred to me how easily he could've slipped away. You know how it is—make a speech, everyone sees you, everyone assumes you were there the whole time. Might make a clever alibi, don't you think?"

"He's been cleared, Green. Now, if you're done wasting my time, I've got work to do."

She hangs up.

Hmmm.

I'm not sure that was helpful, but I feel better having put it out there.

But I'm still not any closer to getting the answers to my questions ...

One: Why was Abigail up on the cliff?

Was she meeting someone? Or was she looking for something?

Two: Did that cassette belong to her? And if so, what was on it?

*The lab found some partials.* Detective Whitney must know, or soon will, who handled that cassette.

Which might answer the why. Maybe I need to give Hugo a longer list of questions to pass along to the detective.

But, for now, I can make a start, with a little help from Google and my new smartphone.

I search for the documentary Abigail had been working on, the new one that had gotten Penelope so upset.

I search under Abigail's name, under Justin's, under JustInTime. Even under DVI Green.

Nothing.

I do find her name—she is associated with the film Justin had showed the night before, just as he'd said. But with nothing else.

Maybe this is normal—that there would be no information about a film that's still in production.

But it's as if it doesn't exist at all.

And I'm not sure how normal *that* is.

Yes, definitely time to add to my list of questions for Detective Whitney.

But then, how's Hugo supposed to get this information? Am I actually setting him up to spend time with *Suze?*

He's a big boy. He should be able to handle it.

Which moves my mind back a few paces to Phaedra's explanation of why the Greek Phaedra didn't kill herself in the third play by Euripides—she'd handled the pressure in her life. So, speaking of handling pressure, of course Charlie was strong enough to deflect Justin's criticisms. I remember when she used to deflect the criticisms that came toward *me*.

I was the one with insecurities, starting in elementary school. I abruptly recall when a group of girls—they were nine, a year older—called me …

"Two-tone Barbie."

"What?" I reacted with a small shriek. "What do you mean?"

One of the blondest children I'd ever seen in my life, a girl named JulieAnne Johnson, stepped forward on the playground in her Madonna-type outfit—black leather and white lace in fourth grade—and snottily replied, "You've got red hair and always-tan skin. Redheads are supposed to be really white with freckles. It's weird."

I just stared at her, blushing like a torch.

I may have a perpetual tan, but I've always turned red as fire when embarrassed.

I almost ran, but Charlie suddenly came to my side to say, "You still play with Barbie, JulieAnne? *That's* weird."

Miss Madonna turned on her heel, and she and her blonde gang walked away.

Charlie had always been really adroit at the verbal comebacks.

I've digressed, but somehow …

I think all of this is connected.

Charlie's strength. She would never have killed herself over something as insignificant as Justin's comments.

But no one has ever guessed why.

Or no one has ever come forth with a theory.

Secrets.

Like Abigail's secret.

*You knew my dad's sister …*

She knew something about Charlie.

Something she wanted to tell me.

I open my eyes, stare up at the blue sky, and see an itinerant wisp of cloud that looks as if it's putting tiger paws out into the ether.

Leaping—to the sun.

Or …

Off a cliff.

Maybe they're sometimes one and the same.

I hear Charlie's voice: "It *is* connected, Emerald. Think … "

I'm ready to call Hugo.

I have more questions.

## 44

I end up leaving a vague message on Hugo's phone.

Then I leave one on Anthony's.

I'm hoping he can tell me more about that documentary.

His voice sounds warm and unassuming. It's hard for me to believe he could have anything to do with the murder of his daughter. For that matter, it's hard to believe Justin Fellowes could have anything to do with her murder either.

I don't *want* to believe it.

Which, in an ecopsychological metaphor, signals that I'd better stay on my guard.

Nature doesn't operate according to human desire. We just want it to. Especially these days—as our human population gets bigger and more demanding, the things we expect from nature are so *unnatural*. We want clean drinking water, so we pump raw sewage into our lakes, rivers, and oceans. We want more food, and bigger chickens and cows to eat, so we pump them up with all sorts of chemicals and create antibiotic-resistant disease. We want to base the world's economy on oil, so we pump it into the air and get climate change.

We want … we want … we want … a miracle.

Or we want some news agency, or government agency, or bureaucracy, to tell us everything's going to be fine.

I'm on my way home, taking the back way through San Pedro, and I suddenly jerk the Ford into a parking lot.

I stop the car, fuming.

*I don't want a miracle.*

I want some *real* answers.

I pull forward, looking around.

I feel a chill in the heat of late morning.

I'm in the DVI Green parking lot.

I hadn't realized, when I pulled over, that I was at Anthony's office. Or maybe I had.

It's Saturday, and the white-clad valet isn't here.

I slowly drive the car over to park in front of the indigo-blue door.

I get out of the car and walk up to the stream of water that cascades down the three-story building. This time I notice that, at each level where the water pools, there is moss on the concrete, small grasses, and even tinier flowers. They must serve as water filters of some kind—for the gray water.

I gently touch my fingers to these little marvels.

They look so perfect.

And clean.

We get used to it in Los Angeles, the fine particulate in the air that turns every surface, even moss, black with toxic dust.

I look at my fingertips.

There's nothing there but my own skin.

For a moment, I think about skin.

Abigail's pale, smooth skin on the night she was found dead.

Charlie's bloody skin, cut up by rocks.

I feel a hand on my right shoulder and almost scream.

"Hello," says a voice.

247

I turn, my keys clutched in my fist, the biggest one, the one to the Ford, out and ready to jab.

But the person in front of me is a tall Indian woman in a traditional sari. Looking up at her large, sad eyes, I put down my key-fisted hand.

"I didn't mean to startle you," she says in low voice. "I am Sumitra Shah. I take care of the gardens."

Her voluminous eyes are very dark and moist, and there's a familiarity about them. "Are you related to Christi Shah?" I ask gently.

"She is—was—my niece."

"I'm so sorry for your loss," I reply softly.

She nods, silent. Her chest trembles beneath the lavender-and-white sari. She opens her hands to expose a small piece of yellow rag, maybe a dish towel. I see that it's covered with dust—that particular gray shade of particulate from the city and the Long Beach Port. She smiles, sweetly, almost tenderly, and tells me, "I came to tend to the moss, and these tiny gardens. I have always done so. Once a week, I would visit Christi here, and we would go to lunch. Mr. Pryce would also allow me to go inside and tend the plants in the building. I told him, the first time I visited Christi here, that the whole building reminded me of a sacred grove in India, where I'm from."

"Sacred grove?" I ask.

"Yes." She nods. "In India, for thousands of years, we've tended to our sacred groves. They are sanctified areas of forest, some small, some large, that grow throughout the country, and they're protected. For each grove, the rules may be different, but most prohibit the felling of trees and the taking of materials. Some communities still have laws which will punish a person with death if they should harm any of the plants or trees."

She clutches the dish towel to her breast, and I watch her stop herself from sobbing with a firm, purposeful lowering of her head.

When she looks up at me again, she whispers, "Lord Krishna,

forgive me, but I wish that whoever has done this to Christi will suffer." Then, with a determined, resolute grace, she steps past me and murmurs, "But not the moss banks here."

She softly brushes the dust from another concrete level of tiny garden, then turns back to me and asks, "I wonder if anyone is watering the plants and trees inside?"

I stare at her, feeling utterly helpless.

I look up at the three-tiered building, taking in all the small levels and pools that inhabit the concrete.

"I don't know," I answer. "Is the building open?"

"No." She shakes her head. "Soon after Mr. Pryce's daughter passed away, he told Christi he no longer needed her to come in."

"He did?" I ask, surprised. "He gave me the impression he was still working on a plan with PWE."

I say it more to myself than Ms. Shah; however, she tells me, "I think he is closing this building. He told Christi he will sell it."

"Have you learned any more about what happened to Christi?"

Sumitra shakes her head. "Nothing. Who would do such a thing?"

"I can't imagine." I pause, then venture another question. "Did you ever notice anything unusual when you came to visit Christi?"

She shakes her head again. But she appears to be thinking of something, and she says, "Christi told me that Mr. Pryce has been—angry. She said that he and Abigail had a fight recently."

I feel my heartbeat quicken. Was Christi the witness Detective Whitney was talking about? Did she know something she shouldn't?

"A fight about what?"

"He was angry about the film she was making. With that doctor."

I hold my breath, waiting.

"Something about how the film wasn't true," she continues. "He didn't like that doctor, Christi said. He said the doctor was responsible for his sister's death."

*I blamed him.*

I'm still holding my breath, feeling dizzy, waiting.

"He said he had proof. A tape or something." Sumitra shudders. "She told me it was terrible, to see family fighting like that ..."

"Was it a cassette tape?"

"I don't know."

I look around. The building is deserted, the parking lot empty.

I ask, "Do the police know this?"

"I don't know," she says again. "I think they spoke with Christi, but I cannot be certain."

If Christi heard Anthony fighting with Abigail—a possible motive—who would want her dead more than Anthony?

Was it possible?

I look at Sumitra, and I know I can ask no more questions. Her eyes welling up, she says, "Someone should make sure the plants inside get water."

The tears begin to stream down her face.

My own eyes begin to sting.

"I'll make sure they get water," I promise her.

She nods again and turns, continuing to clean the tiny gardens.

I get back in my car.

My new phone is ringing a staccato beat that I don't like—it's too frenetic. I'll have to change it.

It's Anthony.

I answer.

## 45

There's a definite sense of tilt to this day.

On the long drive north on the 405, I keep checking the news for a local earthquake, thinking that the off-kilter, queasy unease I feel could be related to geological instability.

Now, sitting here in the De Vos–Pryce family's Santa Monica mansion, I'm tempted to sum it up as emotional instability.

Or maybe it's a combination of the two.

Aren't most things?

I look around, as if the contrasting colors reflect the theory.

I'm surrounded by white, white, white, but everyone's dressed in the blackest of black, at this exquisite memorial to Abigail Pryce. There's another poster-size picture of her, this one with her beautiful face thrown back, laughing, and she's standing in a white halter dress amid a vast expanse of white and yellow daisies. It hangs just a tad … tilted … over the white, highly polished marble fireplace in yet one more large white room that I've never seen before.

All this whiteness still reminds me of a mausoleum.

I'm half-expecting her casket to be rolled into the fireplace.

I feel nauseous again.

I grab onto the smooth edges of the white metal folding chair beneath me with tight fingers, my head held rigid, facing the front, watching the minister, a man in a black suit and a white tie.

He seems to tilt in my vision.

It's just a sense, really.

When Anthony called and asked me to come, I agreed.

I'm here to say good-bye to Abigail. And to Charlie, again.

Most of all, I'm here to keep an eye on Anthony.

Or did he ask me here to keep an eye on me?

All of a sudden, the whole room seems to tilt.

I grip the chair even tighter.

I don't know if it's a geological bent or the angular, aching descent of emotion for these forty or so mourners, or my own, sometimes fearful perception of death—but it's extremely uncomfortable.

Or who knows? Maybe I'm having a stroke.

Whatever it is, I keep fighting to hold my head straight.

However, as the minister continues his bountiful speech of earthly praise for Abigail and her most deserved comfort in heaven, I must finally allow my head to bend in an attempt to compensate for the ecopsychological tilt, if nothing else. The very disturbing, ecopsychological sensation of predictable life slipping, slipping away.

Something's not solid to me here.

Not stable.

Not that murder could ever be stable.

Anthony gets up from his chair in the first row and walks slowly, morosely, to the place where the minister stands. He looks as if he's aged ten years since I've seen him, his back almost bowed, tilted.

His life has been turned upside down.

My heart skips a beat in empathy.

Which I mustn't let sway me because I've had to force myself to realize …

I've had to *forcibly* put myself on psychic, steady ground and realize that Abigail's death, and now Christi Shah's death, point to Anthony Pryce.

When I called Hugo to tell him about the argument, he agreed that it is suspicious. He didn't have any information for *me*, mind you, but he did let me know that Anthony was the number-one suspect. Enough of a suspect that Detective Suzy Whitney would be here, at this memorial.

I look quickly behind me.

There she is, wearing a shiny black suit, standing very still behind a gleaming mahogany table that holds an abundance of white roses.

I wonder if she's here to intimidate Anthony, or to arrest him again.

I look around the room and notice that Justin Fellowes *isn't* here. Hmmm.

Wouldn't a man who shares the same passion for ecology, who had taken Abigail under his wing—wouldn't he come to pay his respects?

Or did the De Vos family keep him away?

As usual, I've got more questions than answers.

I'm not even any closer to assuring that those trees and plants inside the DVI Green building in San Pedro will get watered.

Yesterday, when I spoke to Anthony, he could barely put a cohesive sentence together. He was talking about Abigail's body being returned, that there would be a memorial at his house the next day, asking if I could be there, as a friend. It was not the time to discuss trees. Or to ask whether he'd killed his daughter and Christi Shah.

So here I am.

Tilting—or trying not to.

As Anthony begins to speak, a piercing wail comes up from the front row, and I know without looking that it's Penelope De Vos. Then she is rising to a frail, wobbly stand, her waif-like body wrapped in a black, geisha-type dress, her dark eyes smudged in thick black mascara, which is dripping trails of black down her pale cheeks. She lifts a slight, almost translucent hand and points at Anthony, sobbing, "You … you …" Then she holds both hands to her nearly bald, white-blond head and collapses to the floor.

For a moment, no one moves.

Everyone's stunned.

But it's also that slow-motion southern California inaction that sometimes casts its thick-minded dispensation on our masses—just before an earthquake.

I pay attention to those things.

I've seen it time and time again.

Earthquakes make for extreme emotions and slow reactions.

I watch.

Anthony is the first to break the inertia. He goes to her, lifting her carefully, like a crushed white flower, and gently carries her in his arms to a long white sofa near the entrance to the room.

I see that Detective Whitney has moved with him, along the back of the room, staying near the wall but making a clear signal with her presence that Anthony will not be trying anything tricky in this white crypt without her knowledge.

Or that's what I surmise.

Once Penelope is laid down on the expansive white leather couch, Anthony returns to the front of the room to eulogize his daughter.

But again he's interrupted, this time by his mother.

Mrs. Pryce still sits in her chair, and I can see only her tan jaw and the back of her head, resting on her husband's big shoulder. Her gray hair is softly curled and fanning out in static tendrils onto his black suit. She begins to chatter, "You're killing me, Anthony, every person in this room is killing me, don't you see what is happening to me, why do you keep doing this to me, you must all want me dead, dead, dead …"

Her words seem to come in ripples of sound.

My sense of tilt increases.

I have an abrupt headache—the kind of sinus headache I usually experience just before it rains or quakes. I've always been sure earthquakes could be felt in the atmosphere.

And now, the scientific community, running years behind, has finally discovered the Lithosphere-Atmosphere-Ionosphere Coupling Mechanism, a "new" theory that stipulates that in the hours or days leading up to an earthquake, colorless, odorless radon gas is released from the stressed fault, and once it reaches the upper atmosphere, the radon gas strips the air molecules of their electrons and splits them into negatively and positively charged particles. These charged particles, called ions, start attracting condensed water in a process that releases heat. Scientists can detect this heat in the form of infrared radiation.

Sound complicated?

It's not, really. The pressure of heat and moisture in the earth is released and ultimately creates heat and moisture in the atmosphere.

And it affects my sinuses.

Next stop, I hope: The scientific community will document the emotional effect of earthquakes on human beings. Not that they haven't had a chance to do that with animals and their erratic behaviors during earthquakes. But then, as Shelley would say, there are still so many people out there who believe animals have no emotions.

Bottom line: I have a headache.

I rub my forehead.

Look up.

Still, no one's moving.

Not even Anthony.

But the room looks brighter—whiter, if that's possible.

*Extreme.*

And then, there's a quake.

A sharp jolt. Short, but perceptible.

Tangible.

It stirs everyone into reaction.

A woman exclaims, "Did you feel that?"

"That was a four-pointer—I'd bet on it," responds another woman.

A young man chimes in. "Yeah."

"Felt like it was right out in the Santa Monica Bay. Could be a precursor to something bigger," an older man says matter-of-factly.

The usual southern California earthquake dialogue that can either normalize the situation or cause a panic. This time, neither happens.

Instead it's just that odd feeling of tilt again.

We're all quiet once more, as if no one here has a claim to the experience—except the most aggrieved because they are suffering the earthquake of the soul.

As if in testament to that, Mrs. Pryce resumes her agitated chatter. "I've been killed by my family, killed by every member of my family, over and over, and I know they want me to die a thousand times …"

She begins to sob.

I make myself stand, my head still throbbing, and I move my feet, as if through mud, to the front of the room.

Anthony looks at me with heavy desperation.

I sit down in his empty chair and hold Mrs. Pryce's hand; her fingers are like ice.

I look at her.

She stares defiantly into my eyes.

"You're killing me, Esmeralda, you're killing me even more than anyone else, you and Charlene, killing me, the two of you, the things you do, I'm dying, dying, don't you see?"

I look up at Anthony, still standing at the front of the room, arms at his sides, silent, waiting.

His mother repeats, "You're killing me, Esmeralda, killing me …"

The earth moves again, and Abigail's picture literally swings.

Oddly, it makes her look even happier: as if she's *dancing* in the field of daisies.

It's another jolt, a little smaller than the first.

But most of the mourners are getting themselves out of their chairs, moving in the direction of the front of the house.

I hear Anthony mutter under his breath, "Go, go."

His mother, still sitting alongside Mr. Pryce, who almost appears to be sleeping, squeezes my hand and asks sharply, "I didn't cause them all to leave, did I?"

I look at her again and reply, "No."

But I can see that this is not the right answer. Not for her.

She grimaces at me and whispers, "Yes, I did."

It's at that precise moment that I make contact with knowledge that I'd since buried, with Charlie, long ago.

"Oh, Charlie," I whisper to her in my mind.

My wistful friend.

Longing for …

Truth.

## 46

Like one of those old-fashioned cameras that emits stark white light illuminating everything in its path, my mind flashes to a memory of Mrs. Pryce on the Majorca Point soccer field. Charlie and I belonged to a team for a season when we were about fourteen years old. In my memory, I see Mrs. Pryce in a pink-and-yellow floral print dress, standing with her weight on one slender hip while her fingers delicately turn some small, shiny pearls around her neck. She works on them like rosary beads, a tearful catch in her throat as she leans in to the coach—what was his name? Coach Braidswell—to say…

What's she saying?

We're taking a water break, and I've come back to the fountain on the side of the field for a second drink, and then I've got to adjust my shin guard because it's itching my leg like crazy, but when I hear the tremor in my best friend's mom's voice, my ears quicken to the sound, and I focus in on their conversation.

She's explaining in a low, quavering voice, "I worry about her, Coach Braidswell. All the time. I'm afraid she doesn't have very long. I'm so worried. I'd die for my baby. Sometimes I feel as if I could *die*."

I'm still scratching underneath the shin guard, but my eyes are turned upward and sideways, and I catch a pat on her shoulder from the coach as he tells her in a hushed, compassionate voice, "Please, Mrs. Pryce ..."

"I feel like you know so much about us. Please, call me Gracie."

"Gracie ... please. There's gotta be other doctors. Hey, if you want I can ask my brother. He's gotta friend—"

"*No.* Our doctor's good. I just needed someone to talk to. I'm sure you understand."

"Any time, Mrs. ... Gracie."

"Thank you," she replies, voice stronger.

That's when they both see me, crouching by the water fountain.

Mrs. Pryce looks shocked, while the coach shouts, "Ten laps around the field, Green!"

But I'm already sprinting away as fast as I can, running away from this ... this ... *strangeness.*

What were they talking about?

Mrs. Pryce didn't actually say Charlie's name.

But then *who* were they talking about?

There weren't any other *she*s in the Pryce house.

Except maybe Charlie's grandma?

No ... Mrs. Pryce said she'd die for her "baby."

Can't be grandma.

Okay ... then ...

The family dog?

*Yep—that's it.*

Mrs. Pryce loves that dog ... Mandy.

She's a girl.

Oh, no.

Poor Mandy.

*Pobrecita.*

She doesn't have very long to *live?*
Is that possible?
I'll ask Charlie.
No.
I won't.
Because Charlie doesn't know. She hasn't said anything about it.
And she would say something if she knew Mandy was sick.
She *would.*
Charlie always told me everything.
Until she couldn't.

—w—

I'm still holding Mrs. Pryce's icy fingers.
It turned out that Charlie didn't always tell me everything, did she? Like when she planned, a few years after I overheard that conversation, to jump off a cliff.
I look up at Anthony again.
He knew some of her secrets. He knew about Justin, for instance. Did he know anything else? Anything that I didn't?
He says, "In case there are any more aftershocks, let's move the memorial to the backyard."
"Yes, dear." Mrs. Pryce complies.
A snore comes from Mr. Pryce.
He *was* sleeping—though that can be fairly common for some people during earthquakes, too. The atmospheric pressure seems to make them abnormally tired. It's been suggested that it's an evolutionary trait: Don't move; danger's coming.
But isn't that kind of like being a deer caught in the headlights?
Abruptly, I also think of the Pryce dog, Mandy.
A cute little cocker spaniel.

She was hit by a car, wasn't she?

Not more than a couple of days after that soccer practice.

Maybe that's why I'd forgotten about the conversation between Mrs. Pryce and Coach Braidswell ... until now. Because the dog had died, and any questions I'd had about Mrs. Pryce's fears concerning her baby who didn't have long to live were answered.

So swiftly, really.

Too swiftly.

I gently try to extricate my fingers from Mrs. Pryce's icy hold, but she grips me tightly, her fingers creeping up my forearm, trying to pull me down.

She grips my hand all the way to the backyard, jabbering again, "You're killing me, every single one of you, don't you see, can't you see what you're doing to me, but all you think about is yourselves, isn't that right, isn't that right, isn't that true?"

I remember Charlie's warning…

*Stay out of that water.*

*Promise me, Emerald.*

*Don't swim in that cove anymore.*

As I lead Mrs. Pryce to the backyard, I'm struggling to make connections in my mind.

Abigail and Justin.

The documentary—which Penelope and Anthony both hated.

DVI—which pollutes the planet, one dollar at a time.

DVI Green, trying to do some good.

To make up for—what?

As Mrs. Pryce rambles on, it occurs to me that maybe she is talking about the water, about DVI. That maybe she is making more sense than anyone else.

*Promise me, Emerald.*

# 47

The rest of Abigail's memorial takes place in the Pryce backyard without incident.

The many household staffers quickly carry the white folding chairs outside, while others urge the mourners from the front drive to come around to the back of the house. They placate the guests' anxiety about another earthquake with freshly brewed coffee in gleaming white china, and we all file onto the brilliant green grass to our neatly arranged seats, exhibiting more energy and confidence than when we were inside.

Being out in nature can do that.

Albeit a highly managed nature.

No slippage here on this perfectly level acreage.

The turquoise pool glistens in the background as Anthony is finally able to eulogize his daughter without interruption.

Penelope and Mrs. Pryce both appear calmer and remain quiet, though since I've been returned to my third-row seat I have a marginal view. But I can still make out Penelope as she wraps her thin, black-clad arms around her tiny torso, then closes her dark eyes and seems to meditate. Mrs. Pryce's head is once again resting on Mr. Pryce's big square shoulder, but this time, out here, her gray hair's no longer electrified by static; it lies smoothly on her tan neck in a soft curl.

Out here, the feeling of tilt is gone.

I'm vaguely trying to ascertain whether it's because the seismic activity has diffused the pressure within the earth and no more radon gas will be released (at least for today), or because we're all feeling unconsciously, instinctively safer outside, with no ceiling or chandeliers to come crashing down atop us during a substantial temblor?

Whatever it might be, geology and psychology seem ameliorated in the morning sunshine, and although sadness still streams among us like a psychic river, there's a collective sense of letting go and relief.

The tilt is gone.

For the moment.

Later, when the memorial is over, the mourners are led to a gracious reception within the front sitting room, the one that I first entered a week ago—has it really only been a week? I make my way over to Anthony to give my good-bye because I won't stay, can't stay, not even for a minute longer. I've tried to help Charlie's family. But I'm lost as to what else I can do—and as I get in the line of guests waiting to give their condolences, I realize there must be at least ten people ahead of me, so I discreetly turn around. I'm thinking that I will try to catch Detective Whitney here, while I can.

So she doesn't have another chance to ignore my calls.

This time, it may be too important.

I find her on the front step, as if she's keeping watch, approving of everyone who tries to leave.

"Hello, Detective," I say with as much cordiality as I can muster, hardly in the mood for playing cat-and-mouse, or shark-and-dolphin, or snake-and-squirrel, or alpha dog–submissive dog, or any other kind of game that she and I have become masters at strategizing.

But she surprises me.

"Hello, Green," she replies in a cool hush.

Standing next to her, I suddenly feel like a child in my black flats and sleeveless black bamboo dress with the little tie in front. The dress suddenly reminds me of the old-school baby-doll look that I actually hated. I wonder, for a moment, if I shouldn't invest in some tailored suits, like Whitney, because they sure look kick-ass. I'm almost compelled to ask her what her suit's made of—organic or poly-based material? Then I realize I'm trying to claim the moral high ground because in the looks department, she's really got me out-dressed. Which shouldn't matter to me and usually doesn't. But she's just so *muy guapa*. Truly gorgeous. So as I continue to try to discern the source of the shine that reflects off that exquisite form-fitting black suit as she shifts impatiently from one heel to the other in the late morning sun, it takes every ounce of self-esteem I have to say, "I've got another question for you."

Several questions, actually, but I'm thinking I should ease into it.

She brushes me aside. "I've had enough of your butting into my investigation, Green."

I remember, back when I was in the police cruiser at the DVI building in San Pedro, how I channeled the squirrel in response to Whitney's rattlesnake, and it seems the best way to deal with her now, so I attempt it again, kicking up some sand, forcing the rattler to divulge information about herself. "I'm sorry, Detective Whitney. I'd never want to get in the way of your investigation. Listen, I know how devoted you are. And I'm grateful for it."

She stares at me, intently.

"Which is why I'm wondering what Abigail discovered about DVI and its environmental practices that got her father so upset?"

I can feel her sizing me up. Is she contemplating how tough it would be to swallow me whole? How long I'd take to digest?

"And I know that this seems to make Anthony the main suspect,"

I continue, "but I can't help but feel that Justin is involved somehow."

She replies tightly, "Get back inside, Green."

Nope. She's not going for it. No matter how much sand I kick up.

But I try again. "Did you know that Justin and Charlene Pryce used to be an item?"

She looks at me sharply. It's clear that she didn't know.

"I didn't think so," I continue. "It was a secret. The Pryce family seems to have a lot of secrets, don't they?"

She flips her blonde hair and glances out toward the driveway as if something there has caught her attention, but it's clear that she's still listening.

"And I can't help but think there must be some reason they've kept this a secret," I say. "I mean, why wouldn't they have disclosed this past relationship to the police? Especially when they all blame Justin for Charlie's death."

She looks at me again, then covers her surprise quickly. "That's enough, Green. I need to get back to work."

She struts into the white marble mausoleum.

But I can tell I've gotten to her. That she will be unable *not* to consider this.

And so my job here is done.

Squirrel-like, I make a scruffy line to the nearest white-clad valet and the keys to my Ford.

48

I can't get away fast enough.

Go, go, little squirrel.

Save your acorns, make it through another winter.

Just one problem, though.

I really haven't been as bright as a squirrel.

I haven't had the forethought that every squirrel on the planet utilizes and many a human being ... does not.

Or, as my dad used to say, "Esmeralda, it really doesn't take a genius to figure out that if the human species keeps eating and building and populating the planet at the rate we are now, we're going to run out of resources, and probably at the very worst time. Like a squirrel in the coldest of winter. But then, a squirrel's got more forethought than that—a squirrel would never let that happen."

I'm out of gas.

"Sorry, dad," I say silently.

I'm a few blocks away from the Pryce mansion, taking a left turn on Fourth Street, making my way toward the entrance of the 10 freeway when I casually glance at my gas gauge and realize the tank is empty.

Now here's the thing with a hybrid such as this Ford: Once the gas runs out, the battery will kick in and give a gas-free ride for miles, maybe fifty or more. So I flick a switch next to the odometer to see how far I can get with no gas, and the digital reading comes up: zero miles. It seems I've been driving on the battery for a while and paying it no mind.

I've gotten so used to barely having to fill this car with gas that I've apparently forgotten that I *ever* have to do it.

My dad used to warn me against that, too.

Taking for granted what comes easily, to the point of forgetting its relevance altogether.

Like the ocean, clean air …

Now I've got to find a gas station, when I really want to get out of Santa Monica. The earthquake tilt might be gone, but, somehow, I can feel that danger still lurks.

Okay.

I put my foot on the gas pedal, gently, as if that will assure the car makes it to the gas station.

Where is the nearest one?

I search my memory.

I think it's on Wilshire, right? I should try to make a U-turn on Fourth Street and head north to Wilshire.

Nope. Not a good idea.

There's a cop on a bike—I won't make a U-turn.

I know. I'll drive in and out of one of the Santa Monica city parking structures, to head left.

*Bueno.*

So I go in and come out the entrance of the parking structure, and instead of heading south, I turn north, and I just make it across the pedestrian walkway when the Ford begins to chug, then falters.

The gas is … totally … gone.

The fumes are gone.

I'm in the middle of busy Fourth Street.

I get out and, with my right hand on the steering wheel, I push the car.

I grunt and put my full body weight into it.

Thankfully, I'm in good shape from walking on the beach and up and down the sliding hill, and the car is small, so it's not that heavy.

I smile sheepishly at all the people behind me, a couple of them honking. Even if Santa Monica is known to be one of the most environmentally conscious cities in America—the library is green; the courthouse is green; the restaurants, movie theaters, and markets are green—there's still a staggering amount of traffic on its streets. Although in the local drivers' defense, many of their cars run on some type of alternative energy, and as I push my car over to the side of the road, I can see that most of the cars around me are either hybrids or electric. Some of the drivers, however, don't seem that understanding when it comes to my predicament. In fact, a white Bentley pulls up next to me, taking up the illegal middle yellow line, and a face pops out—to berate me, I suppose.

To my surprise, it's Penelope De Vos.

"Hello, Dr. Green," she says breathlessly as the electric window rolls halfway down, then abruptly stops. Her skin looks so pale in this late-morning light, it could be alabaster, and her eyes are still as black and smudged as tar. She attempts a smile, but her lips begin to tremble, and I can tell she's going to start weeping.

Joseph, the butler, is behind the wheel, with white-gloved hands on the steering wheel and a white cap on his head, which he takes between a thumb and index finger and tips, ever so slightly, at me.

Penelope wheezes a bit. "Can we help you?"

I tell her, "Don't worry. I'm almost there." And I am. I push my car into a red-curb space between parking meters, knowing I'll get a ticket, but what else can I do? I suppose I could wait with the car and call a roadside service company to have someone bring me the gas. But that could take an hour, and I would have put yet another carbon monoxide–emitting car on the streets. Nope. I'll just walk to the gas station and hope they don't tow my Ford away before I get back.

Penelope breathes heavily. "Please, Dr. Green, let me help you. You've done so much for my in-laws during this time. They're the only parents I have left. I worry about my mother-in-law. Please, I could drive you to a service station. Please, I ... I ..."

Tears are in free-flow down her pale face, and she wipes her thin, too-white hand across her gaunt cheeks. The black eye makeup smears in wide tracks of sorrow down to her delicate jaw, and I feel suddenly protective of her: She's a child, a victim of arrested development. Too much luxury, not enough life experience.

Meanwhile, cars have begun blasting their horns at us. Odd—no Santa Monica cop on a bike comes to ticket the Bentley.

Hmmm.

Perhaps they *know* the Bentley. Well, maybe that will save my car a ticket, too.

"Okay, Ms. De Vos—"

"Call me Penelope."

"Okay," I repeat and grab my keys from the Ford's ignition.

More horns blare.

Joseph gets out of the car, runs to my side, and opens the door.

Penelope slides over.

I get in.

The doors shut.

Joseph nearly revs the engine, and the horns recede as we enter the traffic heading north to Wilshire.

I reach for my black wrist purse, but it's not beside me.

*Mierda*. Double, triple *mierda*.

I groan. "Oh, no. I left my purse in my car."

Penelope lays a pale hand on my light-brown hand.

"Don't worry," she whispers.

I want to go home. I want to ride Sam on the bluffs and immerse myself in the earth's beauty. I want to …

Instead, I ask a question.

"Ms. De Vos—Penelope—I thought you would still be at the memorial. Is it over?"

She stares at me, almost glassy-eyed.

For a moment, I wonder if she's forgotten who I am.

Joseph answers for her. "Mourners will be able to pay their respects all day," he says.

Which doesn't answer my question, but I let it go.

There's another, more important question I need to ask.

"Penelope," I say, "I remember when you mentioned the documentary Abigail was working on. With Justin Fellowes?"

I can see the gas station on my left as we crawl in the traffic toward Wilshire, but as much as I want to get back to my car, I'm hoping she'll answer.

Penelope turns to me and begins to weep again, her eyes streaming more black down her pale, hollow cheeks as her tiny, translucent hand reaches for mine; again, I'm reminded of a child.

"I'm sorry," I say. "I didn't mean to upset you."

Her daughter is gone. Her husband may have murdered her. Where is my compassion?

Sitting next to Penelope, I sense a bird, a broken-winged bird.

Her head droops forward.

I'm wishing I'd never gotten into this car, never opened my mouth.

Joseph steers past the gas station.

I stare at the gas pumps with longing.

Now that's a first.

## 49

As I sit in this $100,000 luxury automobile, asking nosy questions of one of the richest women in the world, she opens a small refrigerator and offers me orange juice, soda, milk, champagne, a gin and tonic, and homemade chocolate chip cookies.

The traffic on the Pacific Coast Highway is relentless. Beachgoers are out in huge numbers during this October weekend heat wave.

I could have retrieved the gas for my car and been home by now— or been on the 405—which is a more familiar nemesis.

Penelope opens a console in the center of the backseat. "This is my secret stash. Would you like some?"

I look at the bottle. It's ornate and looks as if it's got real gold lettering. It's French, I think.

Penelope opens it. The smell that wafts up from the glass is a mix of lavender and pepper.

And here I thought the exotic scent that usually surrounds her was perfume, or a new kind of breath mint.

She takes a churlish swig.

I note that she just showed more energy for that gulp of vodka than she has for anything else. Other than blaming Anthony for their daughter's death.

The way he blames Justin for Charlie's.

She hands the bottle over to me like a pirate.

I almost expect her to growl, "Arrggghh. Shiver me timbers."

I decline as gracefully as I can. "No, but thank you. It looks very good."

She takes another gulp.

Puts the cork back in the ornate bottle.

Secures it back in the console.

Then, once more, her head droops, and she's lost to the world.

Maybe I'll wait a few moments before rephrasing my question.

Or maybe not. "I don't mean to upset you," I say again, "but I was curious about the documentary after seeing Justin Fellowes the other night at the LAMA event. He was so proud of Abigail and her work."

Penelope seems to come to life again, like a windup doll, and she snorts. "She had no business working on that film. It's all his fault."

"Whose fault?"

"Anthony's, of course. He should never have let her work on that film. To put our family at risk like that."

"At risk?" Like the good psychologist, I nudge her along with a question.

"She didn't understand," Penelope says, reaching for her special bottle again. "She was only doing what kids do. Trying to make a difference. No ... she just didn't understand." She begins to weep again.

"Understand what, Penelope?"

"If only she'd given me that tape," Penelope continues, sobbing. "I could have explained everything. Everything would have been okay."

I feel my body freeze, not sure I'm hearing her correctly.

*If only she'd given me that tape.*

Penelope takes another drink, her hand unsteady, then abruptly turns to me. "Would you like some water, Esmeralda?"

I don't want to break the spell, so I nod. She retrieves water from the fridge, in an individual bottle—I hate those. So much waste. She hands it to me.

"You were saying? About the tape …" I turn the cap and take a drink, trying to seem casual. There doesn't seem to be a safety seal on it, but at least this means she's recycling the bottles.

"Tape?" she asks, as if she'd never mentioned it.

Had I heard wrong after all?

I take another drink. It's flavored water, raspberry.

"About the documentary," I continue, slowly. "Was it about Justin's work in … in … "

My words seem to crawl toward Penelope, so slowly, but I can't make them move any faster. She simply stares at me.

I lean back in the car seat, suddenly so tired that, like Penelope, I can't seem to keep my head up.

Charlie's voice comes wafting through my mind. She whispers, "Water … "

"What?" I'm silent, but my eyes fly open.

I notice Joseph watching me from the rearview mirror.

"Promise me, Emerald," Charlie says to me.

"What?" This time, I blurt it out loud.

I look forward to Joseph again, but my vision is blurry.

I hear Penelope's voice. "Joseph! It's not working!"

Joseph makes a nasal whine, panicking.

I've heard that whine before …

Penelope snaps, "Do I have to do everything *myself?*"

She rustles around.

I can't seem to move.

She stuffs a white kerchief under my nose.

And … I'm … gone.

50

I wake.

Or maybe I'm not awake.

My eyes are shut. I try to open them, but my eyelids are too heavy to lift. It's the same sensation I experienced at my house, under the jacaranda tree on the night the two intruders nearly suffocated me with chloroform. Only this time, I'm not quite as zonked out.

Maybe Joseph used too much last time. No wonder he's usually so quiet—he's been afraid to talk. Because now that I've heard him in panic mode, I'm 99.9 percent positive that the butler was one of the attackers that tore my house apart.

I'd recognize that whine of desperation anywhere.

But who was the other attacker?

It must have been Anthony. Right?

No, he would use his people. Like he used Joseph.

Whoever it is, will he … kill me?

Today?

I try to think effectively, but my mind's still fuzzy. Wherever I am, I'm alone, for the moment. I want to shout for help, but as the fog starts to clear from my brain, I realize my lips are practically smeared across my cheeks, and I must have a wide strip of heavy-duty tape plastered across my mouth.

Crap.

At least I've still got my black dress on—I can feel the soft organic cotton against my body—but when I wiggle my toes, they're free, my shoes gone. I reflexively try to stretch my legs but can't—they're bent and pushed up against my chest, and my hands are tied with what feels like rough-hewn rope in front of my knees. I'm bunched up like a pair of dirty socks, stuffed in the back of a drawer. Or, since my back is against a wall, and my toes are butted up against an opposite wall, maybe it's a broom closet.

I force myself to breathe—deeply.

Breathe. Breathe.

Calm. Calm.

My heavy eyes are still shut and stinging, but I'll never give Joseph or Penelope or Anthony the satisfaction of tears.

Or fear.

Nope. I *won't*.

Breathe.

Then, I smell ...

*The ocean.*

Nature.

Fuse with it. Fuse, fuse, fuse.

I breathe in the salty effervescence of the great and wondrous water—the birthplace of all things—and my spirit begins to light. We are friends, the ocean and me. We have a relationship, just as I do with every beloved entity in my life, and with that thought, the wind that perpetually rides the sea's undulating crest, obeying her every command, building in strength for a tumultuous storm or insouciant gust, brings me ...

Two more scents.

Not close to me, not yet, but near enough to waft beneath the closet door.

I know that it's Penelope De Vos—I recognize her breath, which carries the hint of lavender and pepper.

It is always there—with Penelope.

Usually light, airy.

But now it's heavy, as if she doused herself in the expensive vodka. Now, the scent of the ocean has lit up my neurons, and those odors elucidate for me the depth of Penelope's despair.

I'll bet she has drunk ... a lot.

And so the ocean has given me a means of escape.

Or a start, because now I know ...

Not only has Penelope been drinking.

She is very likely ... inebriated.

## 51

I wait in the dark.

What else can I do?

Finally I'm able to open my eyes, and as they adjust, I can see that I'm definitely in a small closet—no brooms, just a skinny-looking vacuum cleaner in a corner and little else. I stay very still, making no groans or pleas, nothing to give my captors any clue that the chloroform has worn off. It's probably worn off a bit early for their purposes. Which are—what, exactly?

Was it something I said? Was I asking too many questions?

Or was it something Penelope said?

Yes, the tape.

They have kidnapped me, to kill me.

Because I know about the tape.

Even though I actually know nothing about it at all.

Maybe they won't hurt me after all. Maybe they just want to scare me. Like they did that night at my house.

No, I realize: They want to kill me.

*I have no blindfold on.*

Of course, I already know who drove me here—but they don't

care that I'll be able to recognize anyone else involved when they retrieve me from this closet. Obviously, they have not a care in the world about me pointing them out to the police in a lineup. No worries at all—because I'll be dead.

Will the money wipe everything clean again? As clean as their shiny white house?

I breathe in the ocean.

If these are my last moments, or hours, I will fuse with the water and ride a spiritual blue wave to heaven. My dad will be there, and my mom, on a beach in our small cove, our fringed blanket spread out on the sand. We'll be singing ...

I distract myself with these more pleasant thoughts.

Maybe they'll sing "Rock Me on the Water" by Jackson Browne. That was a favorite. My dad was a big fan of the singer-songwriter— he used to say that Browne was one of the first eco-lyricists, that he'd put him right up there with Henry David Thoreau. He loved singing the melodic call to protect the earth. My *abuelo* would hear my dad strumming away and mutter in Spanish, "With all the gringos in the world, why did my daughter have to marry a hippie?"

Wow.

I haven't thought of *that* in a long time.

My mom and dad had lived at my grandparents' house, my house now, while my dad put himself through college, and he'd also paid rent to my *abuelo* by doing what seemed like a hundred odd jobs: plumber, handyman, waiter. He'd even worked for PWE. I remember that the PWE had given him the not-so-unpleasant task of collecting water samples from the inlets and coves that line The Point's coast. That seemed fitting because he was studying marine conservation.

I sit bunched up in the closet, fusing with the ocean, recalling things I haven't thought of in decades.

I breathe.

My *abuelo* would become so upset every time my dad went down to the coves to collect water samples. He'd be irate, really. My *abuela* would whisper, "*Cállate*, Ernesto. Please, be quiet. He's doing his job. What is your worry?"

I'm thinking to myself: What *was* his worry?

I breathe.

My reverie is broken by the sound of a door opening. Strong footsteps made with cushy, athletic soles, possibly a man's, enter the house. I hear keys being casually dropped into a container of some kind, making an almost musical ping.

I half expect to hear a voice boom, "Daddy's home!"

But there's nothing, only the same energetic footsteps walking on wood floors, then down exactly three wooden steps, and there's a faint reverberation, as if the room that the footsteps have descended into is vast.

I listen for Penelope and Joseph.

*Where are they?*

The scents of lavender and pepper aren't as heavy as they were, as if, like parasites, they followed their host to another room.

The footsteps stop.

*Is it Anthony?*

The questions suddenly rise like a tide within me.

Have Penelope and Joseph forgotten I'm here?

Was Penelope so drunk that she passed out somewhere?

What if they forget they've left me here?

## 52

I nod off again.

The chloroform is still making me groggy. But in my meditative fuse with the ocean, I've let my mind go to another place, as if floating in placid, turquoise waters. I breathe and rest and wait for the optimal moment to become aware. Ready for anything.

Or almost anything.

A vicious shark.

A friendly dolphin.

A white, transparent jellyfish—drunk and prone to stinging.

I'm not going to anticipate too much—I'll move with the slipping land and swelling sea, and when the moment's right …

Then the closet door opens, and I'm pulled to my feet.

Here's the moment.

Now I'm awake.

I'm standing, held upright by strong arms that forcefully pull off the rope that was binding my hands. Then these arms roughly yank my hands around to my back and bind them there while a knee pushes at my butt, and I stumble forward.

What do I do?

I struggle to open my heavy eyelids again while angrily trying to shout past the tape that's still smeared over my mouth: "Mmm-mmm-hhh-mmmm!"

I hear a deep, concerned voice say, "Don't hurt her."

I'm immediately, reflexively placated.

That's ... scary.

I push my eyes open.

The house is shadowy, almost dark.

But I know who it is ...

Justin Fellowes.

The saint.

What is he doing here?

I've assumed I was taken back to Penelope's house.

But of course, that's not possible.

*Mourners will be able to pay their respects all day*, Joseph had said.

I must be in Justin's house.

Why would Penelope bring me here?

Justin continues, "It is good to see you, Esmeralda. I will always remember that. How good it was to see you."

He sighs, his tone as wistful as Charlie's own.

It's not comforting.

I feel he's telling me good-bye.

In his beautiful way.

I watch his handsome, cleft-chinned face as it tilts to the right, just as it did on the Kodak stage.

He smiles at me in that same sad, bittersweet way.

I look at his hands, but I see no marks.

He smiles again; his hazel eyes crinkle at the edges.

Behind him, a thick, black curtain begins to open, very slowly, almost sensuously, and Justin opens his arms as the brilliant sun streams into the room.

The view is one of the best I've seen—and I've seen many—but this one must have cost more than anybody I've ever known has had to spend.

Now that the curtain has disappeared into the wall somewhere, the ocean appears to extend her full-bellied grace right up to the seamless window that must run the length of at least a third of a football field—it's that long. But even though the shimmering Pacific mesmerizes tantalizingly close, as if we could all just dive in, it's probably about a quarter mile away.

Justin is still smiling, beatifically, like a king.

I fight to stay aware. Ready.

Being a southern California native, it takes me only seconds to scan the wide Santa Monica Bay to know almost exactly where I am: up very high in the Pacific Palisades, that wealthy celebrity community that inhabits a hill just off the Pacific Coast Highway.

Gauging the distance between the house and the Santa Monica Pier that juts famously into the sea with its colorful spinning Ferris wheel, I can tell we're not far enough north to be in Malibu. But the house, which appears to be an enormous Mediterranean villa, is upon a towering cliff, and I can't see any other houses directly below the forever-window, so I'm guessing the Fellowes mansion is somewhere high above the old Getty Museum.

I start mulling over the possibility of escape.

I must trust the ocean.

I must trust the slippage of time.

The time, the wave—will come.

*Right?*

Meanwhile, someone's still got me from behind. I'm pretty sure it's Joseph—it can't be Penelope because the hands that squeeze my tied wrists are extremely large and strong—and I'm being firmly held at the top of three highly polished wooden stairs. The wood itself is a deep rose color and so dazzling it looks as if it might be Brazilian cherry or *jatobá*, the procurement of which is a major force behind illegal logging in the Amazon rainforest.

Justin's still in the vast room below, seemingly immersed in the *jatobá* floors that run alongside the remarkable window, broken only by carefully placed pieces of luscious, dark Asian furniture, probably teak, much of it inlaid with what appears to be ivory.

He sees the direction of my eyes and utters, "Rhino horn."

Amazingly, the saintly doctor winks.

"It's also used as an aphrodisiac."

That's when I see the Justin I knew at the baseball field, waving at Charlie but looking at me.

He's still here, inside the saint, yearning to break out

Wanting attention.

And now, I realize, he's actually posing in front of the ocean vista.

I watch as he extends his right arm, broadly sweeping in front of the sparkling glass, and I'm reminded, once again, of his charismatic stage persona at the Kodak Theatre. I'm almost expecting a huge movie screen to drop down and delineate the touching, momentous story of America's most heroic and generous oncologist.

I find the slow, insidious revelation of his narcissism seeping through his cultivated façade of altruism sickening yet fascinating.

I'm also struck by the level of his deceit.

But why should I be?

This is the man who complained about Charlie's butt being too big—he had it in him all along.

This is where that possible guilt complex got him ...

He became a hollow perfectionist.

Now, the critical hero.

They exist all over the place.

But Justin's done better than most.

He waves his arm again, and suddenly the window, without a sound, rises into the ceiling.

Justin stands, beaming.

The ocean breeze cascades into the room, almost completely overwhelming the lavender and pepper scents that still hover.

My eyes track the vista, catching on the inlaid rhino tusk, and I'm wondering, truly wanting to know, what it must be like to support the slaughter of an endangered species in order to feel a sense of material accomplishment, or so-called beauty. Though according to most eco-psychological theory, throughout much of the world materiality and beauty have become one and the same thing, which then makes it very daunting to presume the global population will ever start to conserve as avidly as it consumes.

But still, I don't want to be cynical.

Even, apparently, on the day of my death.

I keep eyeing the tusk, trying to strategize … to find a way to get myself out of here, when Penelope enters the room.

She's loaded to the gills (yep, I did intend that sea-creature pun), and in a drunken whirl and stumble, she runs into a black, heavily polished Steinway Grand that appears small in a far-off corner.

She's changed her clothes from black to stark white, some kind of clingy, sheer material, and I can see the pale tinge of small nipples under the mid-thigh-length dress. For an instant, mostly because it's so overt, I'm compelled to wonder how she's managed to make her nipples appear almost completely white.

She exclaims, "Ouch! That really hurt! Joseph? Where are you?"

"I'm here." Joseph, the ever-dutiful retainer, replies in a polite monotone from just behind my left ear.

Justin sighs. "Pen, darling, Joseph's busy. Why don't you be a good sweetheart and sit down?"

_Pen, darling?_ Now when did that start?

Are Penelope and Justin having an affair?

"Okay," she breathes. She plops down onto the wood floor, cross-legged and with no apparent underwear—even so, her crotch is white, too.

Is she white *everywhere?* What has she done to herself?

My eyes move back to Justin, who's shaking his head.

"Poor little rich girl." He sighs. "We didn't know much about that growing up, did we, Esmeralda?"

I just stare at him.

He goes on, "No, we had to get ours the *hard* way. We had to earn it." He looks out the long expanse of open window that leads to an equally long slate balcony, then back to me, his hazel eyes twinkling.

"You've done some nice things to your grandpa's house. Nice eco-upgrades. You've worked hard, done well." He smirks, and I realize that he must have been one of the men who attacked me, which explains not only how he knows my house but also explains the blood that rubbed off on my hand the other night. So I *had* jabbed him with my keys, even if I still can't see the wound.

He goes on, "But do you have any idea how hard I've had to work to earn the kind of bucks for this?"

He's waving his arm around again.

"Do you know how hard it is to try to compete with old money?" He cocks his head in Penelope's direction. "To get what they have? And it's a joke, Esmeralda. In the end, it's a pathetic joke. Because most of them who are born with it don't want it. No. They want something else."

He drops his arm and looks at me. "Do you have any idea how much cash it takes to treat children with cancer? Lymphoma? Do you know how much cash it takes to bring them and their families to an American hospital, to try to heal their disease and also to heal their hearts and souls? Only to send them back to the toxic desecration that brought them to me in the first place?"

He gives a subtle grimace.

"Sometimes you have to do bad to do good, Esmeralda. The ends justify the means."

I have no idea what he's talking about, and he seems to comprehend my confused look. He continues: "We all know that DVI has been poisoning children all over the world. That those antiquated pipes they laid in Nigeria leak oil like sieves. But did you know it's been happening *here*, too?"

He throws his head back and gives a sorrowful moan. "No, I bet you didn't," he says. "You see, no one did. No one except Charlie."

I stare … unbelieving.

*Stay out of that water.*

*Promise me, Emerald.*

"She made me a cassette tape before she killed herself," Justin says. "Said she had to tell someone. Told me all about it. I was the only one who knew—or so I thought."

He turns on one heel and gazes out the window again. "Turns out her dear brother Anthony also knew all about it. And he's a lot like me. He's a businessman. He saw opportunity, just like I did. Of course, we're also different. Very different."

Something about his tone sounds menacing, and, almost as if to highlight that effect, Justin walks a few paces and turns again. "So what does Anthony do? He uses what he knows to force his way into DVI via this poor little rich girl. Talk about marrying up. But of course, that was all well and good with the De Vos family. Spilling oil is just fine with them—but spilling secrets? Not so much."

Justin gives a wry little laugh. "And what do *I* do?" he asks. "I get a medical degree and treat kids with cancer. Struggle to pay off medical school and to keep my clinics running."

Again he looks straight at me. "That doesn't seem fair, now, does it, Esmeralda?"

He seems a man caught in transition—one foot in deception, maybe even murder, and one in the realm of conscience, compassion.

I stare ... watching ... thinking more than ever of the need to escape.

But I'm also nearly hypnotized by this transitory quality he exudes.

I think, now, he embodies the duality of humanity.

The positive and negative. Or the so-called good and evil.

*The moral confusion.*

"So it only seemed fair that Anthony support JustInTime. And, while I had his attention, we started up DVI Green, too. You know, the ocean needs a lot of cleanup." He takes a deep breath and lets it out in a long sigh. "So what if I skim a little off the top? I work hard, too—harder than Anthony Pryce ever worked. I deserve all this ..." He waves his arms around the room again. "I deserve it far more than Anthony Pryce."

He turns my way again. "Wouldn't you agree, Esmeralda?"

He's looking at me as if expecting a response.

I move my eyes up as if to say yes. I want him to remove the tape from my mouth, and it works. Justin nods to Joseph, who reaches his hand around my face, picks his short, smooth fingernails at the tape on my cheek, and swipes it off my mouth with one swift, dizzyingly painful movement.

It takes me a moment to find my voice. "Why did you kill Abigail?"

He laughs. "You're mistaken, Esmeralda. I did not kill Abigail Pryce."

"Then why is this documentary of hers such a secret? What did she find out?"

"What she *found out,*" he says, "is exactly what I wanted her to find out. I put her on the trail—unbeknownst to her, of course—of DVI's contamination issues. A little harsh, I realize—no one really *wants* to know their parents are destroying the planet—but it couldn't be helped. Anthony was getting a little stingy with the cashflow, you see, and I needed for him to be *convinced*."

So Anthony did kill his own daughter.

He didn't like what she found, and he wanted to protect the family business.

From the floor, Penelope cuts in, her voice thick but determined: "You never should have brought her into this," she says, raising a trembling hand to point at him. "You had all you wanted. You had me."

"Penelope, darling, I think you know by now that love doesn't pay the bills. Love doesn't pay for those children's surgeries."

Justin turns back to me. "I needed a steady influx of cash to keep JustInTime going," he continues. "So that was Abigail's job. And she did it well. She confronted her father about DVI, and they got into a nasty fight about it. All was going as planned."

"I would have given you the money, as much as you wanted," Penelope says.

"Sure you would have," Justin says. "And your husband wouldn't have had any problem with that, right? Wouldn't have suspected us of having an affair? Wouldn't have, say, leaked our affair to the media to discredit me and my work? No. I knew what I was doing."

"She wasn't supposed to *die!*" Penelope wails.

Justin glares at her—then averts his eyes. "No," he says, "she wasn't."

Penelope's voice slurs. "But *you* wanted more money, Justin. You wouldn't let it go."

Justin spreads his hands out again, the practiced gesture of humility. He says, his voice softer now, "I wanted it to save those children."

Penelope's head is resting on her chest, but she jolts it up. "What about *my* child?" she cries. "What about *my* daughter?"

For a moment, no one speaks.

Justin finally says, "Tell Esmeralda what you want to be, Penelope."

Penelope's eyes droop, and I can barely make out her whispered, "Noooo ..."

Justin says, with a tone of disgust creeping into his voice, "Tell Esmeralda your *true* desire."

He sweeps his arm over toward Penelope.

Her head is wobbling, her legs still crossed.

He goes on, "What she really wants to be is *an angel*. She wants to appear like a spirit, don't you, Pen? She thinks it will make her more *spiritual*." He pauses, shakes his head. "That's why her skin is bleached. Her entire body. I mean, *everything*."

Penelope says nothing, and Justin adds, "While she's bathing the world in oil, she wants to appear as white as an angel in a Christmas movie."

My mind feels like putty.

I'm making no sense of this.

Then Penelope struggles to her feet. "It's your fault," she accuses him, wobbling on her bird-thin legs. "You poisoned her with all your high-and-mighty ideas, turning her against this family. My family built DVI with its own sweat and blood—and thanks to you, my own daughter was trying to bring it down!"

"She was a smart girl, Pen," Justin reminds her. "She made her own choices."

"But you gave her that tape," Penelope whispers.

"The tape doesn't matter," he tells her.

"Yes, it does," she cries. "That tape ruined everything!"

"No, it didn't," he explains patiently. Then he looks over at me.

"You see, Esmeralda, after Abigail was killed, the cassette tape that she'd so conveniently found in my archives went missing. Now, since I am not her murderer, I have no idea what happened to it. I can only imagine that her father disposed of it, which was why he killed her in the first place."

I hear a gasp of anguish from Penelope, and then she begins to cry.

"Fortunately, I was one step ahead," Justin says. "I told him that there was another tape. That our dear Charlie had made three of them. One for me, the love of her life. One for her dear brother. And one for her best friend, Esmeralda Green."

Now it's my turn to gasp.

"That's right," Justin says, nodding. "You have the third tape—at least, Anthony thinks you do. Which might be why he's been so chummy with you lately. He probably wants to get it from you without killing you. He's got too much blood on his hands already."

My voice is raspy when I ask, "So he killed Christi Shah, too?"

Justin leans down, as if to share a secret. "No, Esmeralda, that was the work of yours truly."

I stare at him in disbelief.

"I hated to do it," he continues, "but when Anthony was released from jail for Abby's murder, I had to make sure he ended up back where he belonged. Killing off a witness usually goes a long way." He looks over at Penelope with digust. "Pen here is a little too loyal to her husband, it seems. Gave him an alibi, didn't you, darling?"

Penelope lifts her bald white head, her eyes trying to focus, and breathily declares, "Abigail called me …"

I think of the phone call I received.

*I really need to talk to you. I'm wondering if we can meet?*

I ask, "She called you—when?"

Penelope slips back down to the floor, but this time she makes an attempt at modesty, stretching her legs out in front of her, pulling her

dress down her rail-thin thighs as she repeats, "My baby called me …
I only wanted to get that tape back … "

Penelope tries to stand, her hand on the piano bench, but each time
she pushes herself up, the legs of the bench skid on the polished rose-
colored floor, and Justin, in an abrupt show of anger, barks, "Pen, stop
it. You'll ruin the wood."

"She called me from the cliffs," Penelope goes on. "She was there,
looking around, she told me … and I went there to try to get the tape
back. Just give it to me, honey, just give it to me …"

Now she's waving one hand around while putting all her weight
on the other, until she crashes down onto her elbow.

It looks painful.

But she doesn't seem to notice.

"And then I grabbed it, but she wouldn't let go," Penelope says.
"I pulled on it, and I heard the plastic crack. But she still wouldn't let
go; she was pulling so hard. And then she slipped. She went flying
backward … flying … over the cliff."

She begins to weep.

I can only watch her helplessly  I'm still tied up, after all  but
then I notice that Justin is staring at her, too.

And I realize: He didn't know.

"It was *you?*" he whispers.

"She would have ruined us … ruined our family … "

Justin looks shocked. "If Anthony hasn't got it, then what
happened to the tape?"

She looks up at him, raising her chin. "I destroyed it," she says,
defiantly.

"*What?*" He approaches her, kneels down to the floor to look her
in the face. "Do you know what this means? Without that tape, we
have nothing. Nothing!"

Penelope is striving to hold herself upright with her hands on the floor. She says in a quavering but forceful voice, "Our job is … to be redeemers. We are the De Vos family … we can redeem ourselves and be angels and cure all the bad things. Even the bad things my daddy did. I know we pollute the ocean. I've been to our board meetings. And you know what? There's no oxygen in the ocean. Not anymore. Not off the world's coasts, not even our coast! That one right out there in that pretty blue water … "

She gets herself back up on both hands, wobbles a bit, and, with tears still streaming, blares, "It's got no oxygen. Did you hear me? NO OXYGEN."

I shake my head.

As inebriated as she appears, her plea for the ocean isn't lost on me.

Justin's response is low, commanding: "Enough."

I watch him.

There he is, waving his hands in front of his cherished view, and I realize, like the eco-shrink that I am, that the ocean, the supreme giver of life to this earth, has become, for the narcissist Dr. Justin Fellowes, nothing but a mirror.

Whether it's the Niger Delta or the Santa Monica Bay, he finds his own reflection there—nothing more.

It's his money maker.

His *green*.

Penelope is standing unsteadily in bare feet that I notice are so white they're almost blue. "My baby! I want my baby girl!"

Justin stands before me, solid on his sneakers.

But he's beginning to crumble internally.

His façade is … slipping.

Penelope holds her hands to her stomach and begins to dry heave.

I attribute it to the alcohol, until she cries to Justin, "*You're* the one who killed her! She wouldn't have had that tape if you hadn't gotten her involved!"

She starts to run, feebly at first, then stronger, faster, until she stumbles. She falls to the floor in a frenzied pattern of white, and her head hits the polished wood with a loud crack.

For a moment, all is still.

The blood slowly blossoms from her nearly hairless scalp, spreading from a delicate patchwork of blue veins to dark red rivers along the rosy hue.

Joseph drops my hands and goes to her, brushing by Justin as if he were nothing but a fly on his sleeve.

Justin turns toward her, too.

I quickly work my wrists, wiggling them loose from the rope.

My long-ago days of Western horse showing with the lasso have sure come in handy lately.

The bindings fall from my hands, and I skillfully hold them so they won't drop loudly to the floor.

Got them.

I breathe a sigh of relief, right into Justin's angry face.

In his rage, he's forgotten Penelope.

He's got his hands around my neck.

He stands on the stair below me.

"Don't worry, Esmeralda," he says, breathless with the effort of holding me tight. "Your death won't add too many years to Anthony's sentence. And you'll just go to sleep, nice and quiet, and never wake up. They'll find you at the bottom of the cliff. Just like Charlie. A fitting conclusion, wouldn't you say?"

I struggle to get free, and it angers him even more.

"And Anthony won't know what happened to that tape you supposedly have. When I tell him I've got it, he'll do whatever it takes to keep it quiet. Yes … everything will go back to normal."

I try to pull away from him, and he grips my neck more tightly.

Shaking me.

*Strangling me.*
No ... no.
No way am I going *down.*
Not with these people.
Not today.
I knee him, with every bit of thrust I can muster, in the balls.
He howls.
I run.
Like the wind.
The sea.
Like ... Sam.

## 53

I become Sam.

I fuse with my beloved horse, my kindred spirit, and with the force of wildness, docile no more in the face of danger, I run, I gallop—through the open window—I whinny and jump from the balcony, seeing myself in his golden fleet of foot and light of grace. I am Sam, the sun horse, flying up to the bright orb, landing on a dirt hill, and I run, fierce, proud, able, and wise through all these years of human servitude, and I run faster, my long mane sweeping behind me, my legs strong as the many millennia of pulling the till and the carriage, carrying the warrior, the explorer, the builder, the cowboy, the spirit of East and West, North and South, and the birth of all civilization—none of it could have taken place without me.

I am Sam.

I am breaking free.

I'm sobbing as I run: "Sam ... Sam ... "

I'm scratched by bramble.

Pounded by stone.

There are shots fired.

Loud pops.

I hear Justin: "Kill her!"

But the bullets stream past me in silver.

And I keep going.

Running.

Leaping.

Until I pitch onto a road—agonizingly hot black tar—and my hooves feel unshod and vulnerable, hurting.

I whinny and wince, and there she is …

Waiting for me.

"Green!" she yells, and pulls me into the waiting vehicle, her own chartreuse SUV: Detective Suzy Whitney.

—⁂—

I'm next to her in the front seat, and she cries out, "*Get down!*"

I'm still fused with Sam, coming out of the trance, and I feel like a horse whose legs are cast—spread beneath me in the confines of a stall—and I can't get up, but it turns out that's a good thing, as Whitney shouts again, "Get your head down!"

I do.

A hailstorm of bullets pounds the SUV.

I hear a return of gunfire from somewhere right above us and a loud, sickening wail.

Justin? Joseph? A cop?

I don't know.

I lift my face up from the console.

Whitney's blonde head is crooked beneath the steering wheel, her cleavage falling against the black lace camisole underneath the black silk suit.

My face is hot.

Burning.

I feel terrible.

Silly, silly squirrel.

"How—" I begin to ask.

Someone—it sounds like Lieutenant Brady—shouts, "All clear!"

The detective is staring at me with those piercing baby blues, and her wide, red lips narrow into a biting scowl. "I hate to admit it, Green, but you were right. I had some officers do a little more digging into Justin Fellowes and found a lot of problems with his charity's financials. And his not showing to the memorial service seemed a little odd, too. So I was just on my way over here to question him when I saw Penelope's Bentley in the driveway. I made a call to Brady for backup, and we were about to go in when you came running out of the house in a hail of gunfire."

I'm impressed.

For someone who seems to relish control, she's giving me a roundabout, but genuine, pat on the back.

And I'm humbled, too. "Thanks," I say. "I owe you one."

"Damn right," she says, and I think I detect a bit of a smile.

Who knew?

54

I'm feeling full of myself.
Putting my own narcissism on display—because we're all capable of it, just some more than others.
The thing is: *I don't know I'm doing it.*
That's ...
Not *bueno*.

—⋙—

It's been two days since Justin Fellowes squeezed his so-called healing hands around my throat.

And today I'm with Jonah Brown, my red-haired, consternation-browed, nine-year-old patient who might just grow up to be a narcissist himself, with possible hostile, even violent tendencies, because unfortunately, as the statistics show, the abandoned children in our world—or for that matter, most over-pressured, under-parented children—grow up feeling extremely insecure. Subsequently, they also grow up having an inner void to fill.

It can happen like this …

First, it's the insecurity of having no safe place to go inside oneself. Second, it's having no safe family; then, no safe society; and finally, adding the environment, no safe air, food, or water, which can lead them, as adults, to form a nearly insatiable need to feed that insecurity with "things." Usually toxic things, polluting things, killing things.

Yep.

Sad but true.

Jonah could grow up to be just like Justin Fellowes: cultivating an all-powerful reflection in the mirror that's the dying ocean.

Penelope is right.

There's barely enough oxygen in the water off the coast of southern California—or the rest of the United States coastline, not to mention countries like Nigeria—to feed a single krill.

I'm standing in The Falling MP Stables, leaning against a wall, watching Jonah as he leads Sam from his stall and over to the cross-ties. He clips both sides of Sam's harness, finds my grooming bucket on the side of the wide aisle, then reaches in for the hoof pick and gently begins cleaning Sam's hooves.

I've been reading about Justin in the news—the story has been online, in the newspapers, and on TV, including KLAT. His history doesn't sound unique: His father's a retired engineer; his mother's a teacher; there's one younger sibling, a girl; and the family still has a nice, comfortable home in a middle-class neighborhood.

Other than that info, what's been reported is that Majorca Point's Lieutenant Brady was forced to shoot Justin Fellowes in self-defense, and that Fellowes was pronounced dead on the scene by Detective Suzy Whitney. There's hardly been a mention of Joseph the butler's role in all this, nor has much been said about Penelope De Vos, only that she was at the Fellowes mansion in Pacific Palisades and suffered a minor injury that is being treated at Cedars-Sinai Medical Center in

Los Angeles. I'm hardly mentioned either, and there's been no specifi-
cation as to exactly what Justin Fellowes was doing when he was shot.

It seems that someone's keeping a lid on the media.

So, is it Detective Whitney or the De Vos family? I can't help but
wonder which one's got the power in this instance.

I'm waiting for Hugo to fill me in on these details, and—perhaps
because he knows too much—his assistant, Phaedra, called me yesterday morning to let me know he has been sent on assignment to
Ecuador to cover a possible coup. Apparently, all communications
are down, even the satellites that relay phone calls from the South
American country.

Hmmm.

I've tried to call him—and it rings and rings—but I've gotten no
computerized voice telling me of a system overload or breakdown
or whatever a damaged satellite might constitute. Again, I wonder if
the mighty hand of the De Vos family may be in this mix, and I'm
becoming worried about Hugo.

Jonah looks up at me, his gray eyes confused, and I wonder just
how long I've been immersed in my own world.

I make my way over to him, limping in Shelley's two-sizes-too-
big sneakers. My bare feet were scorched, cut by rocks, and are still
aching. Shelley and Dove each helped me to wash and put on antibi-
otic cream and bandages. I can't even get my boots on yet, and I have
to step from one bandaged foot to the other. The right foot is the worst.

Now I focus my attention on Jonah, hoping I haven't been unconsciously using him to hold up my own mirror while I congratulate
myself about aiding in the solution to Abigail Pryce's murder.

"Is everything okay, Jonah?" I ask. "You're doing a wonderful job
cleaning Sam's hooves."

He nods, agitated. "But *look*."

I go over and crouch behind Sam's bent right front leg and watch as Jonah holds the hoof against his left knee and carefully touches his child's finger to an area inside.

Sam immediately snorts.

Jonah touches it again.

Sam tosses his head up and down, the crossties rattling.

Jonah tells me, "It feels like there's a little swelling in there. Like it hurts. Like a cut might be there or something."

I touch my finger there as well.

Sam snorts, louder.

*I didn't notice Sam was uncomfortable.*

Jonah did.

Now this is where equine therapy, or any kind of therapy, can become most delicate and most fulfilling.

Because in my own ego-driven meanderings, I missed Sam's pain.

Now, I could either go into a litany of self-recrimination because I feel terrible that I was so unaware that I missed my beloved horse's injury.

Or …

I can put my own damn self aside and buoy Jonah's self-worth.

I quickly say, "My gosh, Jonah. You saw something I missed. Injuries in hooves can lead to very big problems for a horse. If you hadn't caught that, Sam could be in a lot of trouble. You're an awesome horse observer. You could be a healer. In fact, you can start healing Sam right now. Let's get a bucket of warm water, put in some Epsom salts, and we can—*you* can—soak Sam's hoof today."

Jonah's eyes are wide with awe and something else I've never seen in him before: confidence.

That's also where integrating the environment into a life situation can become … magical.

Because, maybe, I was *supposed* to be focusing on myself.

So Jonah could take over.

And maybe it was *Sam* who had fused with *me* the other day, instead of the other way around. Maybe he sensed I was in danger, running from Justin Fellowes's villa, down the hill over bramble, rock, and hot tar. Because it's unlikely he was cut in his stall or turnout.

Why not? I really *do* believe anything's possible.

Bad ... or ... *fabuloso.*

I limp to get the bucket for Jonah to fill with water.

—⁓—

After Jonah's session, we stand out in the dirt lot, the sun still beating down an extreme heat usually reserved for August, and Jonah turns back from a blank-faced Grandma Brown to ... hug me.

I say, "You could be a vet, Jonah. You have a gift."

He beams up at me, his forehead temporarily smooth, then runs to the waiting sedan.

I'm surprised to see Grandma Brown give me a hint of a smile with her usually expressionless lips.

I wave as they traverse down the winding road.

Then I get into my little red Ford because my feet hurt too much even to make the short walk back to my house.

I'm still recuperating.

I need to take a nap.

55

I'm lying down in the living room on my old couch with the thick brown organic stitching; I haven't bought a new mattress for my bed yet. I don't want to spend the cash right now. Which reminds me—I wonder how that new green company, Rialto World Energy, is doing? I haven't checked the stock market lately.

Too busy being a potential murder victim, I guess.

I sigh and stretch, feeling a little bit of my humor—or, as Hugo would say, my "salsa"— coming back.

*Bueno.* It's been awhile.

I muse on the stock …

Who would think Wall Street could be so relaxing?

Well, it sure beats homicidal maniacs.

Justin Fellowes is dead—yet something about this case is still bothering me. Maybe it's that there have been no reports of a confession from Penelope. She could be under police guard at Cedars-Sinai for all I know, and certainly no punishment could be harsher than what she's already done to herself.

So what is it?

The butler.

Joseph was the voice I heard that night outside my house—one of the men who threatened to kill me.

But who was the other?

Was it really Justin, as I thought?

But Justin had nothing to fear from me—not until Penelope drunkenly slipped up and mentioned the tape in her Bentley. He knew about the upgrades in my house—but was it because he'd been there? Or had he only heard about them ... perhaps from Joseph?

The whole afternoon seems like a blur now—what did Justin say?

I remember: *You have the third tape*, he'd said.

*At least, Anthony thinks you do. Which might be why he's been so chummy with you lately.*

Chummy?

Or the opposite?

I hear a knock on the door.

My heart abruptly lurches.

Is it Hugo?

I've been so worried about him.

He's never sent away on assignment—especially when he's got such a hot story, the Abigail Pryce murder, erupting at home.

My feet are still bandaged and elevated on the arm of the couch, and I carefully put them down on the floor and sit up. The throbbing is exquisitely *awful*, and I really don't want to walk unless I have to, so I call out, "Who is it?"

No answer.

I can't see past my kitchen counter to the front driveway, at least not without standing, so instead, I look over the back of the couch to the large slider that opens to the porch. I can see by the way the shadows fall across the dry, yellow-and-brown, brush-strewn slope behind my house that the sun is making its way to the ocean, but there's probably half an hour of light left—and that makes me feel more comfortable.

Safe.

I call out again, "Who's there?"

"Anthony, Emerald. It's Anthony."

I cringe.

And feel a beat of fear.

He's innocent, I remind myself. He had nothing to do with Abigail's death, or Christi Shah's. And everything that Justin said—how can anything a narcissist psychopath says be trusted anyway?

Anthony's innocent, and he's Charlie's brother.

I raise my arms above my head to God, Goddess, the Great Universe, praying for guidance.

But I already know what I need to do ...

I let my arms drop, and, for an instant, my eyes focus on my skin.

I can't imagine wanting to bleach it.

No matter how many times that girl on the playground called me "Two-tone Barbie." Or "freak" or "brownie" or "sandwich girl."

But then, I had parents who supported me—encouraged me.

What happened to Penelope? I think she suffers from full-blown body dysmorphia disorder. Her self-esteem may be irrevocably damaged.

I avoid Anthony for a few more seconds ...

And wonder about his wife.

Did she initially bleach her skin to suit a cultural philosophy? Or was it a spiritual mandate of cleanliness being next to godliness taken too far? Or was it an external show of cleansing the guilt she felt in regard to what her family's multinational corporation was doing to innocent people, and the environment, on a worldwide level?

It's all interconnected.

That's what I believe: Everything we do is reflected in nature and comes back to us, over and over again.

I decide I don't want to see Anthony.

Not right at this moment, anyway. And I'm a moment-to-moment girl. But how do I politely get rid of him?

I call out, "I'm sorry, Anthony, I can't make it to the door. My feet are injured. Please, can we talk another day? I'll call you when I'm feeling better."

I wait.

No response.

Okay. He's upset. Maybe he'll leave.

I listen for his car, even though the Porsche is electric and silent; the crunch of the tires on the dirt in the driveway will signal his departure. I hear a faint movement, a shift of dirt and air, and I lie back down, wincing as I raise my feet back up to the arm of the couch.

He's gone.

I'll call him later.

I allow my eyes to close.

I breathe, drifting off to sleep.

His voice is soft, gentle. "It's all right, Emerald, I understand."

My eyes fly open.

He's standing in the hallway.

How did he … ?

That sound … I thought it was tires. But he must have moved a concrete block and come in through the tarp that's blocking the second bedroom.

"Don't worry, Emerald," he says soothingly. "Everything's all right."

I'm dumbfounded—and *scared*.

Anthony's still standing in the doorjamb, dressed in a light-blue T-shirt, khaki shorts, and sandals. His mouth is still tender. His eyes are kind. He wouldn't do me any harm. Right? He's my friend.

"Forget that, Ez," I say to myself. "He broke into your house. That's not *friendly*."

I'm completely confused.

So what now?

If he means me harm—what should I do?

Make nice?

Or find a way to bonk him on the head?

I feel like a trapped animal.

What does a trapped animal do?

It chews off the foot that's caught in the trap.

Hmmm.

Not the best solution for me.

Unless?

I'm still prone and realize I must appear very vulnerable. Like a trapped ... coyote.

Maybe that thought can be beneficial.

Sure, I'm a trapped coyote: scared, but still wily.

"Hi, Anthony," I say as mildly as I'm able. "As you can see"—I motion my chin in the direction of my bandages—"my feet are injured. So please don't mind if I can't get up."

He nods solemnly.

"Did Fellowes do that to you?"

I nod back. "In a manner of speaking."

"I'm sorry," he says with compassion.

I'm having a very hard time figuring out what's going on.

"Thanks," I reply.

I wave my hand to one of the straight-backed bamboo chairs next to the wall.

"Have a seat," I offer.

He nods again and brings the chair closer, then sits down, facing me, his hands on his knees.

"Justin Fellowes," he says. "I was totally taken in by him. I thought he and I could do business ... I thought Abigail was safe with him ... "

His throat constricts, and he swallows several times, his face blanching.

I tell him softly, "I know you've had a hard time, Anthony. I'm so sorry. But why did you come in my house without my permission? Please, tell me. What's going on?"

His broad shoulders slump.

He puts his face in his hands.

His back shakes with sobs, but when he lifts his face to me, I see that his eyes are dry, and no tears will come.

He says in a hoarse whisper, "I can't … "

I whisper back, "It's me, Esmeralda. Come on. You can tell me."

Anthony's eyes become misty.

I'm getting closer to the core.

His core.

He begins to weep, a few sparse tears at first, then a well stream.

"We have to be sure this stays in the family," he says. "You have to help me. We have to help each other."

I feel a chill. As calmly as I can, I ask, "Anthony, what are you saying?"

"We have to destroy the tapes. All of them. Before they destroy us … "

I don't speak, not sure that my voice can remain calm any longer.

Anthony is still distraught. "Don't you know, Emerald? Don't you know? Justin told me that you have one of the tapes … "

So Justin hadn't lied, after all.

Except by omission.

Meaning: He'd never actually told me *what* Charlie had recorded on those tapes.

I remain mild, non-threatening. "I don't know what tape you're talking about, Anthony. I'm sorry."

He looks honestly confused. "But Justin said—"

"Justin said a lot of things," I tell him. "Charlie didn't leave me a tape. I wouldn't lie to you about that."

He's rubbing his face, as if trying to rub away his features, and when he replies, the moan of something long repressed rises up from his voice. "Your grandfather ... and ... my father. They did some bad things."

"What bad things?" I reply, my stomach lurching.

"They used your grandfather's truck. They were dumping poison off the cliff. The cliff where Charlie and Abby ... died."

"What?"

Now I'm sitting up.

Feet be damned.

"What are you talking about?"

He's wringing his hands, tears still streaming down his cheeks. "They'd pick it up from manufacturing plants, factories all over Los Angeles. In drums. Containers. It was a long time ago. Laws had just been put in place about the disposal of hazardous waste. There were a lot of companies that didn't want to pay for legal disposal. My father and your grandfather—they used to dump the containers in the middle of the night. They'd back the truck up to the edge of the cliff and throw them off. Into the ocean. They got paid lots of money. They did it together. It's a family secret. Charlie knew. She found out."

*¡Ay, Dios mío!*

I'm recalling, yet again, my *abuelo*'s anger at my dad taking water samples for PWE.

My dad had said there were a lot of chemicals in the water, some of them legal, some of them not.

I'm adamant. "I don't believe you. The EPA would be cleaning it up."

Anthony frowns. "What would they clean up? PCBs? Pesticides? PVCs? What kind of poison? You know as well as I do that it's all out there. How could they pinpoint what my father and your grandfather dumped?"

He's right—it's all out there.

But I insist: "I don't believe my grandfather had anything to do with it. You're lying, Anthony. Why?"

"No." He shakes his head, the sun-streaked curls bobbing just like Charlie's surfer curls. "I'm not lying."

And I'm remembering ...

We used to swim in that water off Charlie's cliff. We'd surf, boogie-board, snorkel. Charlie, Anthony, and me.

*Promise me, Emerald.*

*Don't swim in that cove anymore.*

"It's a lie," I repeat.

He stands, pulls a manila envelope out of his pocket.

I can see there are two shapes in it. One thin and square. One thicker and rectangular.

He pulls them out—a DVD and a cassette tape.

"This is some of the early footage from Abigail's documentary," he says, putting the DVD down. He holds up the cassette. "And this is the tape Charlie left for me. Gave it to me the day she died."

I stare at it, thinking of its duplicate, shattered by Abigail's and Penelope's hands.

"I listened to it only once," Anthony says. "Then I kept it locked up, in a safe, in a closet. I was never going to listen to it again. I thought it was best to let Charlie rest in peace. To let this whole thing rest. But when Fellowes started bribing me ... "

He trails off. A moment later, he continues. "I finally had enough. I wanted it to end, for all of it to end. I even thought about going to the police myself. But then he got Abby involved in that documentary. He turned her against all of us."

"Does that tape contain proof that my grandfather and your father were illegally dumping toxins in the ocean?"

Anthony frowns and ignores the question.

He tells me, "My mother wanted nice things. Expensive things. Designer clothes. Jewelry. New cars. My father made a decent living as a longshoreman, but she wanted more. Your grandfather just wanted to stay in the country. He wasn't sponsored, like your grandmother. So I think my dad might have … coerced him."

I sigh.

My *abuelo* was always afraid of being deported. He was illiterate, never made it past second grade in El Salvador, and he was afraid he wouldn't pass the citizenship test. He was afraid of many things. Which he made up for, sometimes, with anger.

I look at the cassette again. "Is it Charlie's voice?"

His grip on the tape tightens. "Yes," he replies.

I breathe.

"Can we listen to it?"

He looks surprised; then he says, "Yes."

"Are you here to harm me, Anthony?"

He appears shocked at the question, "No "

I look him in the eyes.

He says, "I thought you knew. That's why I'm here. You were Charlie's best friend. I really thought you knew about all this."

"Okay," I reply. "I think I have a tape recorder in my desk."

—⁓—

I get up and hobble to my bedroom, relieved that I'm not in my pajamas but in my standard riding clothes: loose jeans and a burgundy-colored T-shirt.

I go to the built-in desk that my dad made. Way back in a drawer is an old tape recorder. I pull it out.

Inside my left pocket is my phone. I take it out, turn the volume off, and quickly scroll down my contact list to a number I'd entered earlier.

I press send, keeping the phone open, so the person who answers on the other end can hear.

Wily, like the coyote.

But with the forethought of a squirrel, too.

Because I need an acorn.

Just in case.

I carefully slide the open phone back into my pocket and return to the living room.

The sun is almost down, and I can see the horizon start to glint red from the living room window. I catch a glimpse of the ocean—the beautiful, poisoned ocean, going from turquoise blue to a deep violet and gray hue.

The bright orb's changing light casts Anthony's face in pale orange.

I hand him the recorder, hoping the batteries work.

He slips in the tape and presses PLAY. A moment later, in her wistful voice, Charlie begins to speak. "I might as well let you know. I have cancer, Anthony. Mom wants me to keep it a secret. It's brain cancer. A rare kind. Mom's convinced it's from something in the ocean, but she won't say what. Something right off that cliff we swim at. She doesn't want me to swim there anymore. She keeps crying."

I hear Charlie pause and take a breath in her forlorn way. Then she goes on: "Don't worry, Anthony. I'm feeling pretty good right now. But the doctors say the tumor's inoperable. I … " She pauses again, her voice trailing, just like it always did. "I also wanted to let you know that I was at Emerald's house yesterday … and … I saw Mom's convertible in the parking lot at the cliff. I could see she was throwing something off the edge of the precipice. I heard her tell Dad last night that she'd tossed her pearl necklace—you know, the one she loves—off that same cliff, and that it was *his* fault. Dad got really mad. He told her to stay away from there. Told her they had enough problems without jail."

Anthony clicks the STOP button.

Tears blur my vision—I can hardly see him.

His voice is hoarse. "I wanted you to know the truth. About Charlie's illness."

My lips are shaking. There's so much emotion building inside me, wanting to be released, that I can barely control it. I feel as if I can't bear to spend another second in my body. Every pore of me wants to run away. Flee.

"Charlie," I whisper. "Oh, poor, sweet Charlie … "

Anthony clears his throat. He turns the recorder back on, and Charlie's voice resumes. "I haven't told anyone else, Anthony, and I want to keep it that way. I tried to tell Justin Fellowes that I was … unwell. I guess I told him because I wanted him … us … to be lasting. Even if it could never be true. I just wanted to feel something permanent, for a little while, since I know I'm dying. I wanted him to hold me. Love me. But instead he told me he doesn't have time for … for … what I've got." She pauses again and whispers, "So I don't want anyone else to know, not ever. I don't want anyone to remember me as sick."

I gasp.

Charlie says, in a voice more firm than I've ever heard it, "Do you understand, Anthony? Do you get what I'm saying?"

"No, Charlie!" I cry out.

Anthony hits the STOP button.

Now we're both sobbing.

Anthony says, "She goes on to talk about the dumping. She said my dad broke down and told her when she asked. And after I listened

to the tape, I confronted him. He was so distraught by losing Charlie
he confessed to me, too. I asked him about Mom, the pearls, and the
cliff. He told me about the hazardous waste and your grandfather. I
kept asking. He told me about the truck. The money. But if anyone else
were to find out—he, my mom … they'd be devastated. My dad said
he might even be arrested. I don't know. Your grandfather's dead. But
my parents are still alive. They're all I have."

I'm sitting, rubbing my eyes hard.

*Charlie.*

She never told me about the brain tumor. Never mentioned it.
Kept it secret—as if it were something I would judge. So she never
reached out. Never.

Who taught her to be so ashamed?

I work to quell my tears.

Taking big breaths.

Processing all of this.

Whether Charlie's cancer was triggered by chemicals in the
ocean, or genetics, or a combination of both, like an ancient priestess,
her mother had made the gesture of throwing her pearls off the cliff, as
if part of a ritual to appease the gods. Maybe she'd realized what was
really important—her daughter—but it was too late. And if her state of
mind in these last weeks has been any indication, she's spent the rest
of her life consumed by guilt, anxious, afraid everyone is out to get
her—"killing" her.

A horrible way to live.

Keeping it secret.

Keeping it toxic.

I look at Anthony, whose green eyes are still liquid, and I say,
"We have to tell someone. What if there are drums of poison just off
the coast? What if there are containers of pesticides, almost ready to
burst? We *have* to tell."

314

Anthony remains silent.

He puts the recorder on the floor.

Returns his hands to his knees.

Sits back in the chair.

I whisper, "It's for the best, Anthony. What if it did cause Charlie's cancer? What if other people have died because of it? There are carcinogens in those drums—that's why they're hazardous. We've got to expose it."

I glance at the DVD, still lying where Anthony placed it. This is what Abigail had planned to do. Expose it.

"We did nothing wrong," I continue. "And your parents? Maybe it will give them an opportunity to resolve their feelings. Give them a chance ... "

I pause, remembering Charlie's last words to me, in the school parking lot. She gave me a warm hug and whispered, "I've got to take my chances."

I wonder now: "Chances, Charlie? Where? In heaven?"

I shake my head and say to Anthony, "We've got to give everything—your mom and dad, ourselves, our *cove*, Anthony—we've got to give it a chance to heal. To regenerate. Give it the chance ... here and now. Please."

He nods, his mouth sad, his eyes down.

Then he stands, reaches into his pocket, and pulls out ...

A gun.

56

Anthony points the gun at me.

"Don't you understand, Emerald? I'm still moving forward with PWE. Now that Fellowes is out of the picture, DVI Green is all mine. But PWE can't know about the dumping. They can't know that it was my dad. I've got to look … clean … Emerald. I've got to have a green pedigree. That's *my* chance, Emerald. *I want my opportunity.*"

I shout, "No matter how non-toxic and non-intrusive your desalination pipes are, you can't stick them into toxic water and use it for drinking water!"

He shouts back, "The water can be chlorinated. It can be bleached!"

Then he's laughing—wildly, madly.

I feel as if I'm losing my mind.

I turn on my throbbing feet and try to run, but even fusing with the strength of Sam can't help me now.

I'm headed for the bedroom, but my feet will hardly carry me.

I hear one shot.

I'm not hit, but I trip avoiding a bullet I can't see, and I fall.

Am I coyote? Squirrel? Sam?

Or just me?

What can I do?

Another shot rings out—and also misses.

I'm on my hands and knees.

I can hear Anthony right behind me.

He's blubbering. "I don't want to do this, Emerald. I don't want to do this. I don't want—"

Then ...

It happens.

Once in a blue moon ...

No—make that a green moon.

The earth ... moves.

And this time, it's *fantástico!*

It's an earthquake—maybe a six-pointer.

A ... glorious ... *big* ... shaker.

The floor pitches with a loud crack.

I ... fuse ... with it.

Find my power in it.

This earthquake is rolling—like a wave.

I go with it—that natural, nauseating flow.

I'm tossed from one side of the room to the other.

I see Anthony fight the heaving motion, trying to grab onto the kitchen counter—but with that frantic attempt, the gun lurches out of his hand and slides down, down ... toward me.

I get it in my hands, point it at Anthony, and then, as quickly as the earth quaked, it settles.

For a moment, there's no motion, just silence, thick and raw, like a fresh, bleeding wound. There's got to be a new tear in the earth's crust somewhere. A big, gaping fault—maybe in my backyard.

Then, I hear a bird chirp. A coyote howl.

But my living room floor remains tilted—the foundation must

have slid.

Damn.

I've got no time to think about my slipping house, though, because Anthony's running toward me, down the hill that's my floor with both of his arms out, and gravity is holding me in place, pushed into a sitting position against the back wall of the living room, and I scream as loudly as I can, "Stop, Anthony! Stop, or I'll shoot!"

He keeps coming.

## 57

W ell, *that* was a doozy of a quake."
     I hear Detective Suzy Whitney's high-pitched, manic
chortle from the hallway. When she steps into the living
room, I see she's got a gun in her hands. She follows her exuberant
statement with, "Stop right there, Pryce!"

I'm still pointing Anthony's gun at him, too.

But he keeps running at me, and Whitney fires, shooting him in
his left calf.

He goes flying and just barely misses landing in my lap.

He raises his handsome face and looks up at me. He rasps, "I
couldn't really have hurt you, Emerald."

I just stare at him, horrified.

Lieutenant Brady comes grunting into the room from the same
place Detective Whitney must have entered: through the second
bedroom, past the tarp.

He pulls Anthony off the tilted floor and cuffs him.

Whitney, wearing a gorgeous indigo-blue suit and sheer stockings
with a bit of sparkle that show her legs running up to a point somewhere high above the horizon—a slight exaggeration, maybe, but I've

honestly *never* seen legs like that—starts reading Miranda, starting with, "Anthony Pryce, you are under arrest for the attempted murder of Esmeralda Green ..."

I cry out, "Anthony—"

He turns his face away from me.

"I want to go now," he mutters to Brady, and he begins to shuffle up the incline that my living room floor has become. He drags his wounded left leg, leaving a wide swath of blood behind him.

Brady trudges up toward the front door, too.

I cry out again. "Is money that important, Anthony? Is it more important than Charlie? Than Abigail?"

He doesn't answer, just keeps shuffling up the slope.

Whitney's voice follows him. "Your wife has confessed to second-degree murder," she says, and I turn to look at her. Anthony stops moving.

"She was about to be released from the hospital when she had some sort of breakdown," Whitney says. "We couldn't reach anyone at the Pryce home, and Penelope De Vos waived her right to whatever high-priced attorney she could have employed. Police were just taking her into custody when I got Dr. Green's call."

I have to force myself to remain in one place, on the floor, and calm.

A whole family—gone.

One dead, and now two in prison.

Whitney continues, "It's rather admirable, isn't it, Mr. Pryce, that your wife chose to unburden herself? We had Green's statement about her confession, but that never would've held up in court. She could easily have gotten away with it. Like you tried to get away with the slow murder of so many people whose water you're poisoning."

Anthony moans, as if a piece of glass has pierced his heart.

I must put my own hand over my mouth.

Anthony cries out again and collapses back to the tilted floor.

Brady lifts him up by one arm.

"It's a money thing," Detective Whitney says with a shrug. "They always want more than they've already got."

Our eyes meet.

I tell her, "Thank you."

She nods and, before she follows Brady and Anthony out the front door, says with a smile, "Thanks for calling."

I give her a weak thumbs-up.

She turns on her pumps and practically sashays out the door, putting some bite into closing it.

The sun is setting, flaring the room a crimson red and lavender with silvery yellow.

I stay where I am for a long time.

I stare at my tilted floor, wondering how much work and money will be required to fix it.

The earthquake saved my life.

But left me on shakier ground than before.

Soon, the house is dark.

"Charlie?" I whisper. "Are you there? Can you talk to me?"

I wait.

Maybe I'll wait forever.

# 58

It's a late afternoon in June, and I'm sitting atop Sam, who's nibbling on grass. We're at Charlie's cliff, or as near to it as we can get. I can see the parking lot where, almost twenty years ago, my best friend watched her mom leave her convertible to throw something off the edge of the precipice.

Her pearls.

Perhaps they'll find them.

You see, I called the EPA the day after Anthony tried to kill me and diligently relayed all the information he told me about the illegal dumping of hazardous waste by my *abuelo* and the senior Mr. Pryce off a cliff in Majorca Point in the county of Los Angeles, California.

They made me work to convince them.

I must have been transferred to a dozen bureaucrats, mostly because I had no hard evidence, but I kept repeating that in my personal and professional opinion, containers of toxic chemicals were most likely embedded in the ocean floor off the Majorca Point peninsula, and if they hadn't burst open already, they would.

Finally, after three months, the EPA sent somebody out to talk to me and to test the ocean water.

I met the man, Mr. Carver, down at Charlie's cliff, and described how I'd been told by Anthony Pryce that his father and my grand-father had picked up chemicals from LA factories a long time ago, then dumped the various containers over the edge in the middle of the night. I also let him know this covert activity had most likely gone on for years.

The man, with round glasses and a thin-lipped mouth, hadn't seemed very interested.

He'd driven a Prius, though, so I gave him credit for that. He also methodically took scans and samples of the dirt we were standing on. Then, he'd pluckily followed me down the very steep, worn trail leading to the cove, where he'd taken more scans and samples of the water.

I'd imagined my dad doing the same thing, so many years ago—except his equipment hadn't been so sophisticated; it was just a kit with petri dishes and vials. He used to lug it all in a big leather case down the formidable trail.

I stood there on the sand, absolutely entranced by the bureaucrat from the EPA. He probably thought I was odd, looking at him with such longing, envisioning my father collecting water in tubes and very carefully putting them in a case for PWE. I was around six years old, digging my toes in the sand, waiting for him to put his work away and come play with me. Later on, he received his Ph.D. in marine sciences and was one of the very first people to voyage with a small, so-called radical group of scientists to the island of plastic that's out in the Pacific Ocean, growing larger all the time. Though when my dad went, in the 1980s, it was still relatively small. They tried to warn everyone of it, but that's another story.

Anyway . . .

My dad, mom, and I would spend lots of time together at the cove beneath Charlie's cliff. We'd bring a large backpack and set everything onto the sand—blanket, umbrella, cooler—and then my mom would watch from the shade as my dad and I frolicked in the turquoise water. He taught me how to bodysurf at this cove. During the summer, we'd spend the whole day snacking on sandwiches, chips, and carrots—my mom always made sure we had carrots—while looking at magazines or reading books. We'd also build enormous sandcastles and talk of magical things, like blue whales with enchanted fairies dancing in their bellies and starfish that could travel up to the sky at night and twinkle, just for us.

Those were amazing days.

When I was older, Charlie and I would come here to swim, surf, and snorkel. There used to be an abundance of colorful fish, and sand crabs, too. We'd try to dig for the tiny gray crabs, but the sandpipers—those small but incredibly fast, long-beaked birds—would get to them first. I haven't seen a sand crab or a sandpiper in ten years, maybe more. But at that time, they were all over the beach. So we'd swim, then lay our beach towels down and talk about school, music, and boys, and be sure to douse our hair with lemon juice, trying to lighten our locks.

Anthony sometimes joined us. For the most part, he was the typical annoying brother, telling us we were boy crazy, or pretending to see sharks in the water while we were swimming. We'd scream and run out of the surf, but there was never any danger. He was also a talented surfer, and after a while at the cove, he'd let go of his morose attitude and joke, guffaw, and have a great time.

Yep.

It was a *buenísimo* time.

An innocent time.

It's also where Charlie decided to end her life.

And where Abigail lost her life.

And where I almost lost mine.

I shiver in the warm sun.

But, moving on …

I thought the man from the EPA probably thought I was a bit odd, staring at him for over an hour, barely moving, lost in my memories.

Then, after a while, I thought the entire EPA might have decided I'd fabricated the story about the dumping of hazardous waste, especially when I didn't hear a word from them for almost half a year.

But last month, in late May, as I was lying in bed, not yet ready to get up, the peacocks and their dawn chorus had been, remarkably, interrupted by an even louder force: a cavalcade of trucks down by Charlie's cliff.

I threw back the covers, my feet completely healed, and walked along my still-tilting living room floor to that place where I can see the cliff from the window that overlooks my porch—a porch that's sadly no longer there because it was too unstable to remain after the biggest earthquake to have hit the Majorca Point fault in recorded history.

I'm not alone—everybody's house is a mess.

But I'll get to that later.

Anyway, I saw three large trucks carrying cranes and other heavy machinery, along with a group of men and women in wetsuits and oxygen tanks.

I quickly pulled on my jeans and a T-shirt, along with my recycled cowboy boots, and hopped in my Ford.

Hugo's Hummer was parked behind my car—but I didn't wake him.

Hmmm.

I'll get to that later, too.

I maneuvered my car around his monster in the dirt driveway and headed down to the park.

There was Mr. Carver, arriving in his Prius.

He told me, just as if he'd seen me yesterday, "There's reason to believe we might find containers of toxins, and the EPA will be investigating."

Well, they're still investigating.

Their trucks remain parked on Charlie's cliff. They've got a couple of small boats anchored in the cove, a digger of some kind in the water, and an enormous crane. I really hope they're not destroying the kelp forests, but I did see them pull up a rusty white drum about four-feet high the other day.

When I saw the drum, I was gratified.

And shattered.

It's hard to forgive my *abuelo*.

I know he was afraid of deportation and probably intimidated by Mr. Pryce, and I'm sure the money was a consideration since he'd never had much growing up on a small farm in El Salvador.

Hugo actually told me more about my *abuelo*'s upbringing than my *abuelo* ever did. According to Hugo, whose own parents are also from El Salvador, it was not only the civil war that lasted there for many years during the latter part of the twentieth century but also the degradation of the land that caused many citizens to flee to *El Norte*. Hugo's own father was forced to leave because he'd confronted some kind of illegal mining taking place in the rainforests.

But when I asked Hugo to tell me more, he just shook his head.

My man: still imbued with mystery.

We were sitting on the brown-stitched couch, which Hugo thinks is hysterical-looking, by the way. I'd moved on to another topic: defending my sewing skills. But, honestly, we were both so relieved that the other was all right, we would have said anything about nothing just as long as we could *be* together.

But then, Hugo and I rarely talk about nothing.

Which is why I ... *like* ... him so much.

Later, I told him, "I finally put it together. What I was thinking about when I was being held at Justin Fellowes's house. Seeing the inlaid rhino tusk. Wondering why materialism has come to mean the same thing as beauty. I realized that if the idea of beauty is also connected to health, and subsequently cancer, we may all be jumping off a cliff. Really. How can we expect to survive if our health is connected to a beauty that seeks to find itself in the money derived from polluting ourselves? That's absolute madness."

Hugo put his arms around me, holding me close.

But I'm digressing. It's still very difficult to accept that my own *abuelo* harmed not only the ocean but also put his family in such a precarious situation. Truly. In the summer, we were *always* swimming in that cove. For all I know, the money he made dumping chemicals off the cliff could have paid for the house I now live in. That's a hard reality to accept, too.

Every day I try—and then I try harder.

I never want to forget the good in him.

The *upside*.

Or in Anthony, for that matter.

Or in the Pryce family.

Or even in Justin Fellowes—probably born a sensitive, smart kid, under way too much pressure to be perfect.

To be a ... saint.

And he was, for a while.

I researched how many kids' lives he'd saved: more than three hundred.

And, in the end, he also validated Charlie, I think. In his way, too late, he tried to cure her cancer.

Who knows?

Charlie may even have been the reason Justin decided to go into oncology and help children.

But he'd eventually fallen ... into his negative side.

I guess by the time Abigail died at the same place where her Aunt Charlie, whom she'd never gotten a chance to know, had lost her life, perhaps in part because Justin had been so callous at the disclosure of her cancer, Anthony simply followed what he'd always been taught: "You don't have time for anyone but yourself."

DVI hasn't been able to keep it quiet forever.

When Detective Whitney and Lieutenant Brady left my house that day with Anthony Pryce, they'd taken the cassette tape into evidence but hadn't noticed the DVD that Anthony had brought.

Maybe they thought they didn't need it—raw footage from Abigail recapping information they already had from the original source.

So I gave it to Hugo.

And there had eventually been a barrage of news, exclusive to KLAT: that Anthony Pryce and DVI had been covering up their environmental practices for years; that Penelope De Vos had been part of a bribery scheme against her own husband; that she had confessed to the second-degree murder of her daughter; that her lover had killed Christi Shah to frame her husband.

It was terrible—all of it.

A falling down of enormous proportions.

A landslide of horror and sadness.

But, again, I'm still trying to find the upside in it.

Like …

Look at the upside to come out of the exposure of the toxic dumping: There haven't been any suicides off of Charlie's cliff in months.

The reason?

All the EPA trucks and equipment set up in the area seem to discourage anyone who might be considering leaping.

So, in a way, my *abuelo* and Mr. Pryce may have helped save a few lives.

Is that a justification?

Or an ecopsychological integration? Weaving life and nature and circumstance together?

I'll take the latter view.

And look at the upside to a very destructive earthquake.

Besides saving me from Anthony's bullets ...

That six-point-two quake released not only a lot of pent-up stress and tension within the earth but also within our citizenry.

Once in a green moon, a disaster can become enlightenment.

Because Los Angeles has been a veritable eco-zone, the quake also seemed to release empathy en masse. Lately, it's as if all of southern California has come out to help find an explanation for the dolphins beaching themselves; some altruistic citizens have even set up camp in boats, and when they see any sign of a sea mammal in distress, they're quick to come to the gregarious creature's aid.

However, there's also a growing consensus amongst scientists, wildlife organizations, and laymen that what the dolphins need is food.

As Penelope tried to say: With the dwindling supply of oxygen in the ocean, there's not much for them to eat.

Of course, there's been a lot of vigorous debate about what to do. Some people advocate feeding the dolphins, while others are adamant that it will rob them of their independence.

But perhaps the most important factor in all this is: People are actually talking about it.

Before, nobody ever wanted to come out and say that a lot of sea life is starving to death.

So that awareness can only be good.

And the bees?

I don't know. Perhaps their navigation systems are confused by the emission of radiation by cell phones. It's also been theorized that a highly contagious bee virus is responsible for decimating their population. Either way, I've made the choice to use my phone only when necessary, and that's hard for a Google champion like me who occasionally gets stuck on the freeway.

As for the increasing array of bird species falling from the sky, I have no idea what could be causing that kind of troubling, massive tragedy, even though explanations in the media abound. They range from historical documentation showing numbers of birds that typically die off in such a manner, to speculations that it's yet another damaging effect of climate change, to a variety of religious groups declaring Armageddon.

For me, I will always pay attention to what nature reveals—I will take my chances trying to discern what's really going on.

I won't hide from it.

I won't deny it.

Which brings me to Charlie.

*I've got to take my chances*, she said.

In the last few months, I've done a lot of research on the seismic activity leading up to her suicide, and at that time, especially here in Majorca Point, it was pretty intense. I'll probably never know for sure, but it seems to me that having cancer and being told she didn't have long to live, although terrifying, may have been a little less challenging if the earth—whether she consciously felt it or not—hadn't been so volatile.

Who knows?

Maybe she would have taken her chances and fought the tumor, fought Justin, and fought for herself, just as she fought for me on the playground.

Yet confronting difficult realities, when it feels as if the earth is slipping out from under our feet, whether metaphorically or literally, can be tough.

For some people, it can seem impossible.

I reach down and give my golden boy a pat on the neck. "Thanks for being so patient," I say.

Sam gives a big, satisfied snort.

I breathe in the June afternoon, the sage and jasmine, and realize it's almost eighteen years to the day when Charlie left us.

"Charlie ..." I whisper.

I haven't heard her, or felt her, since the earthquake.

It's as if the shaking earth finally set her spirit free to go dance on the wind and in the heavens and the water of our souls.

"Charlie ..."

But she's gone.

59

I ride Sam back up to The Falling MP Stables, the sun beginning its descent into the Pacific. I watch, relaxed and blissful, as the orb flashes scarlet, orange, then deepest purple across the pale blue sky as I let my horse have his fill of grass before putting him in his stall for the night.

The wild grasses are now a brilliant green.

It rained about a week ago.

Not much, but it helped.

Sam's foot has healed, too.

I do believe Jonah's sense of empathy for Sam saved him from a possible permanent injury.

Jonah is now an aspiring vet; he's even doing better at school, and *he* wrote his mom a letter. That's what he'd wanted to tell me in that long-ago session. That he was going to write her—let her know his feelings. That she'd treated him badly. That he wanted her to apologize. She hasn't responded, but he's not afraid of the rejection anymore, which tells me his PTSD symptoms are subsiding.

Speaking of PTSD, Christi Shah's aunt, Sumitra Shah, called me a couple of months ago, and I've been treating her for PTSD and grief in the DVI Green building that Anthony designed in San Pedro. Attorneys for DVI have been liquidating their assets in the wake of the accusations against the company, and, in a fitting turn of events, the new green company that I like, Rialto World Energy, has purchased the building. Aware of the tragedy of Christi Shah's death, they allow Sumitra and me to use the conference room for our sessions, though we usually walk around the building where her niece used to spend her days, and Sumitra waters the plants and trees while she grieves the murder of her niece. We talk, and I help her polish leaves.

As I let Sam graze, I see Shelley and Dove just up the slope, sitting on their porch, enjoying the sunset.

I wave.

They wave back.

I smile.

Things are actually good—for this moment.

But I'm aware that life, being what it is—ever-changing these days—could signal at any second that I must return to adaptive mode and be ready for whatever may come, or go.

I look up at the sky; silver flares with the purple.

I wonder ...

Should I sell a little more of Rialto World Energy's stock tomorrow?

I bought it when Rialto went public last November, and it's turned out to be one of the best performers on Wall Street, thanks in part to the crash of DVI's reputation and hence their stock. But in the last few months I've started selling off a bit here and there—to buy a mattress made from organic, soy-based foam; to begin the process of rebuilding the foundation beneath my living room, which has taken precedence over the second bedroom. I actually think I may have to move out to complete the project. I also sold a few shares to pay for a tankless water heater, one that's made from recycled materials—I'm really excited about that.

Then there are the connecting pipes I'm supposed to purchase for PWE.

I'm not too happy with PWE.

Hugo did some research on Pacific Water and Energy's desalination aspirations—and it turns out, they really have none. They want to keep the same antiquated system in place—the one that vacuums the marine life into the cooling process and kills everything—because it will save them money. Just as DVI wanted to keep using their same old pipes—money.

Again—the health of the environment is a money issue.

I sigh...

If only Justin hadn't been swayed by greed, perhaps he and Anthony may have been able to make good on their original intentions with DVI Green—but at least the non-toxic method of desalination they helped to create still exists.

So, there's an upside in that, too.

—⧜—

I'm still holding the rope attached to Sam's harness while he munches happily, and I'm musing about the stock.

Curious about my next move.

Will I sell that stock, or let it ride?

I hear a crunch of dirt.

I turn around.

Speaking of rides ...

There's Hugo in his Hummer.

The ride of rides.

I mean the Hummer, not him.

Or ...

Wait.

Maybe I do mean …

It turns out that Hugo's monster Hummer gets better mileage than my Ford.

How so?

Well …

It goes like this …

A week after Anthony tried to kill me, Hugo returned, frantically arriving at my doorstep with flowers, vegetarian tamales, and love—lots of love.

He bathed my feet, bandaged them.

He fed me, sat next to me, listened as I cried about Charlie, listened as I cried about my *abuelo* dumping chemicals off the cliff. He held the tissue for my nose and held me while I slept.

Two days later, he needed to put in an appearance at KLAT. I hobbled out with him that morning to his Hummer, saying, "I'm sorry I've been so self-righteous about my car. I'm not perfect. I've got a lot of arrogance to make up for. I'm—"

He kissed me quiet.

Finally, he said, "Ez … *mi amor* … you did a great thing for me."

"What do you mean?" I looked up at him.

"My Hummer," he replied in a serious tone. "I converted it. It's got a new engine. Electric."

I gasped. "Why didn't you tell me before?"

"I wanted you to like me for who I am." He grinned. "Not my car."

We laughed.

Now he parks and walks over to Sam and me, a peppermint in his hand.

Sam gives a whinny and gobbles the candy up from his palm.
The sun sparks a sudden streak of lavender.
Hugo sweeps me into his arms, exuberant.
He whispers in my ear, "Now, will you call me Gabriel?"
I look into his tan eyes, glinting with gold.
I hold him closer, tighter, because I feel like I'm falling ...
Falling ...
"How about Gabe?" I reply, my voice quivering.
He kisses my neck.
My stomach's quaking—the geology of emotion.
It feels frightening.
It feels *fabulosa*.
*It feels so good to be alive.*

# Acknowledgments

I'd like to thank family and friends who've generously provided emotional, spiritual, and intellectual support. The first among them is Robert M. Fischer, my husband and forever love. I'd also like to thank Randy Bostic for her devotion to kindness; Jean and Cy Smythe, my mom and dad, for teaching compassion to horses and all animals; L. J. Diener for her brilliant "green" insights; Amy Edlund for her unfailing encouragement; Dr. Rosa Maria Villalpando for sharing her multifaceted experience of culture; Midge Raymond and John Yunker, my amazing editors and publishers—you have made my book shine! Finally, to my own best childhood friend, Jenny Crowley, who left us too early—peace.

# About the Author

Photo credit: Lori Dorn

Cher Fischer is an ecopsychologist who received her doctorate in clinical psychology in 2004. She was a professor of psychology at Ryokan College in Los Angeles and has worked with at-risk families and children as well as practiced health psychology in several hospitals.

She is the author, with Heather Waite, of *Moving from Fear to Courage: Transcendent Moments of Change in the Lives of Women* (Wildcat Canyon Press, 2001), which was a Los Angeles Times bestseller.

Born near a Superfund site in Spokane, Washington, and raised amid the lush nature of Minnesota, Fischer has long been involved in environmental issues and is passionate about the green movement in the United States. She is currently the head of the Green Team at her son's elementary school, which is implementing sustainable strategies in the classrooms and throughout the campus. *Falling Into Green* is her first novel.

Ashland Creek Press is a small, independent publisher of books with a world view. From travel narratives to eco-literature, our mission is to publish a range of books that foster an appreciation for worlds outside our own, for nature and the animal kingdom, and for the ways in which we all connect. To keep up-to-date on new and forthcoming works, subscribe to our free newsletter by visiting: www.AshlandCreekPress.com.

CPSIA information can be obtained at www.ICGtesting.com
Printed in the USA
BVOW060959260312

285857BV00006B/2/P